Kari & West

Club Decadent Book Four

K.C. Ford

eBook ISBN: 978-1-0691328-3-3

Paperback ISBN: 978-1-0691328-5-7

Cover Design: Katherine Ferguson

Edits: Katherine Ferguson

Formatted with Atticus

About

Enticed to return to the only other place he's ever called home by his one friend's impending engagement and his other friend's matchmaking, Weston Sharpe hopped on a flight from Glasgow to New York City. On the night of his friend's engagement, he meets a woman he can't get off his mind. She's gorgeous, defiant, and bratty - she wouldn't even tell him her name, leaving West desperately wanting more.

Kari Davidson has done a lot of living in her almost twenty-three years on this planet. Forced to grow up way too fast, modeling in Paris by fourteen, she learned quickly how everyone expected her to behave like an adult. By nineteen, she was caring for her sister because their mother had abandoned her on the neighbor's doorstep. She stumbled. She made the wrong choices, which almost cost her everything. Thanks to her job at Decadent, she now has stability for herself and her sister. And maybe she's ready to put herself out there again and find something real.

This is Book Four in the Club Decadent Series. Each book focuses on a specific pairing and can be read as a standalone. However, the series is best enjoyed in order. Please use the Look Inside feature and read the Author's Note to determine if this story is right for you. Meant for audiences 18+

Author's Note

This story is a MF high-heat, mild-angst, age-gap (15 years), bi4bi romance with a ton of Daddy Dom/Baby Girl vibes. There are unique family dynamics and Sunday brunch shenanigans. If that's all you need to know, skip ahead. If you need more details, please refer to the list of contents and tropes on the next page. Happy Reading!

This book is written in third person and dual POV. There is a large age gap (MMC is 37, FMC is 22-23). Tattooed and pierced MMC (very heavily tattooed and pierced). Ex-model FMC. Yearning and pining. Adult language and situations. Explicit sexual scenes between consenting adults, elements of BDSM and Kink (including: spanking, multiple orgasms, cum sharing, spit play, DP, pegging, and more). Consent – so much consent. Good girl praise mixed with a bit of degradation. There is some violence – the FMC is grabbed by her ex. The ex also meets his demise. Custody issues and abandonment issues. Pop culture references and a guaranteed HEA.

The Playlist

Music plays a big part in this author's and these characters lives. If you enjoy some great club bangers, love songs, songs to 'get it on' to, and dash of Canadian hits. This is the playlist for you. Enjoy!

Club Decadent Series Playlist by K.C. Ford

Contents

CHAPTER ONE

Kari

It didn't matter that Katherine Davis hadn't walked a runway in over two years. Kari's strut along the busy sidewalk drew a lot of attention.

She supposed it's possible that people stared because of her pissed-off expression; either way, more than one person looked her way as she approached the building at the end of the block.

She didn't have time for this detour. Anything longer than five minutes, and she'll be late picking her sister up from the sitter.

Kari told Spencer to throw away the things she'd left there when they broke up. She didn't need any of it. Yet somehow, the weasel convinced her to come get what she didn't even remember leaving behind.

Taking a deep breath, Kari centered herself. "You saw the real guy beneath the façade, and he's not your problem anymore. Let's get this over with."

Three months into their relationship, Kari ended things. Spencer shoved her against a wall one night when she was five minutes late for work.

On instinct and from learned experience, Kari kneed him in the balls, and he dropped to the floor, rocking and crying in a fetal position, effectively ending their brief relationship.

The next time she arrived for her shift, Kari asked him if he wanted to try touching her again. Spencer held his hands up in surrender, telling her he'd learned his lesson the first time, and Kari thought that was the end.

She was wrong.

Three weeks after she left Spencer cradling his balls, Kari regretted not blocking his number. She already knew she was going to be late picking up Izzy. For what? A pair of leggings and some makeup? "Fuck you, Spencer." Kari climbed the steps to his building and pressed the buzzer for 2B.

"Yo, who is it?"

She rolled her eyes and pressed the intercom to respond. "It's Kari. I'm here to get my stuff." She tapped her foot when he didn't answer and pressed the intercom again. "Hey, asshole, are you going to let me up, or what? I don't have time for this."

On the verge of turning around and leaving, Kari caught sight of Spencer through the front door. Did he bring her stuff? Nope. Nothing except his smug smile and empty hands, which pissed her off even more.

"What's going on?" she asked when Spencer opened the door and looked up and down the busy street.

"Come on." He urged, ushering her inside.

"Why didn't you bring my stuff down with you?"

"I wanted to talk."

"We have nothing more to say. You're lucky your balls are still intact."

"Come on, *Care-bear*. Don't be petty," Spencer said, reaching for her hand.

Kari jerked out of his reach. "Petty? I've told you not to call me *Care-bear* of all fucking things, and we've already established how I'll react if you touch me again. Hands off."

"Geez. Okay, okay."

When they reached his apartment, Spencer looked down the hall behind her. Kari turned to find nothing out of the ordinary and asked, "Why are you acting paranoid, Spence? Owe your dealer for an eight-ball or something?"

The cocaine habit he developed became another thing Kari berated herself for turning a blind eye to. She knew firsthand what addiction did to a person, yet she ignored the signs, desperate to have someone to depend on, all while knowing she could never rely on an addict.

She didn't have to search far for an example when her own mother, the original addict in her life, stole everything from her.

Spencer lured her in with a bit of charm and care at first. He let Kari lean on him while she struggled to find her way, and she missed the signs of the slimy snake beneath the surface. Once she grabbed her stuff and found another job, she'd never have to deal with him again.

"No, I don't owe anyone...," Spencer said, shaking his head. "Fuck it , never mind. Come in, and I'll get your stuff." He ushered her inside and locked all four locks on his door.

With each resounding click, a shiver skittered down Kari's spine, and she spun to face him. Her intuition told her to run. Spencer tugged on his short, dark hair. "I swear I've touched nothing for three days. Listen, I wanted-"

They both jumped when someone pounded on the door. Spencer stepped into her space with a frantic look on his face. He kept his voice low, less than a whisper. "Don't make a sound. Get in my closet and don't make a fucking sound."

Kari's gaze went to the door, the wood vibrating from the fist on the other side, making her heart skyrocket. Spencer pointed to the closet next to his unmade bed. Kari weighed her options, and she didn't have many. She won't risk a fight with an unknown assailant, and with her escape route blocked...

She stumbled a few steps when a rough voice shouted, "Spencer, I know you're in there. Open the fucking door. Now."

"Fuck." Spencer pulled at his hair, messing his careful style. He reached for a gun tucked into the back of his pants, making Kari gasp. He glanced over his shoulder and mouthed, 'Hide.'

Kari went to his closet and shoved it open. She crouched among Spencer's things, her breath coming in short, frantic pants.

Was her breathing always this loud?

She covered her mouth and clutched her phone, waiting for Spencer to unlock the door. The space between the slats allowed Kari to see what was going on, and she prayed the thin closet door would keep her hidden.

Spencer didn't even get the last lock undone when the person on the other side lost their patience and kicked the door open, sending Spencer backward with force. The gun he held skittered under his coffee table out of his reach.

A large man with shaggy brown hair stood in the doorway. He leered at Spencer. "A little birdy told me someone has sticky fingers. So where the fuck is the boss's money?"

Kari made sure her phone was on silent and opened a new text thread. She typed 911 and hit send with shaking fingers.

911: What's your emergency?

Kari: This is Kari Davidson. A man kicked in the door of my ex-boyfriend's apartment.

Kari: He has a gun

911: What's the address? We'll dispatch the police

Kari: 32 East 1st Street, Apt. 2B

Kari: Please hurry

911: Police are on their way

911: Try to stay calm. Are you somewhere safe?

Kari: Yes. In the closet

911: I'll update officers

The man stepped closer to Spencer. "I asked you a question. Where the fuck is the boss's money? I won't ask for a third time."

Spencer shuffled back and raised his hands. The man stood over him, the gun in his hand pointing at Spencer's chest. "Listen, Leo...I-I don't know what you're talking about. I didn't take any money."

"A little birdy told me otherwise," Leo taunted.

"Who-whoever said those things is lying, man."

Where are the cops? Kari strained to hear any sirens in the distance, hearing nothing beyond her racing heart and the confrontation in front of her.

Kari: I think he's going to shoot him. Please hurry

911: An ambulance is being dispatched to the scene. Can you tell me what's happening?

Spencer made a sudden lunge for the other man's gun, kicking him in the shin when he did, causing him to lose his footing.

"Motherfucker." The man dropped to the ground, taking Spencer with him, and they rolled behind the back of the couch, disappearing from Kari's sight. She heard some thuds. Fists meeting flesh. "I'm gonna fuckin' kill you," Leo shouted.

Oh, my God.

Kari's phone vibrated in her hand. *Shit. Right. The cops...where the fuck are the cops?*

911: Kari?

Kari: They're fighting on the floor.

Kari: I can't see them.

911: Where's the gun?

Kari: I don't know

The sound of a gun going off made Kari's ears ring. She gasped, not realizing how loud she was until the man who kicked Spencer's door in stuck his head above the back of the couch and glared at the closet.

Kari swore he'd stared right at her. She dropped her phone and covered her mouth with her hands when the man with the gun got to his feet.

If he finds her, he'll kill her.

Kari didn't want to die. Who'd be there for Izzy? Tears filled her eyes. Panic and despair froze her as the man took a menacing step toward her hiding spot.

Then she heard the unmistakable sound of a police siren outside the building. Leo heard it too and ran for it rather than risk more time checking what's in the closet.

Kari didn't move. She didn't breathe while her phone vibrated in her lap. It seemed like endless minutes passed, yet seconds later, police swarmed the apartment with their guns drawn.

It didn't take long for them to clear the bachelor-size suite. One officer checked the bathroom, while another scanned the kitchenette, and two more went to where Spencer lay behind the couch, radioing for the paramedics to bring the crash cart.

The last officer who entered wore a suit instead of a uniform and looked at least a decade older than the rest. Kari didn't take her eyes off him while he surveyed the situation. The paramedics came in behind him, hauling a stretcher and their equipment.

Is Spencer okay?

"Detective Wilkins," said the officer who cleared the bathroom, approaching the older man.

"What do you have for me?"

"One fatality. No sign of the suspect. Or the woman who contacted 911. We have officers canvassing for both."

Spencer's dead?

Kari whimpered, and the men turned toward the closet. The detective approached her hiding spot, while the other kept watch, his pistol raised.

"Lower your gun, Douglas. I've located the witness. Ms. Davidson? I'm Detective Wilkins. I'm going to open the closet door, alright?"

Kari whimpered again, trying to wrap her head around witnessing Spencer's murder.

The closet door slid open. "Hey...Kari, right? I've got a concerned 911 operator named Marie who wants to know if you're okay." The detective glanced over his shoulder. "Toss me a blanket, will you?"

The officer did as the detective asked, and Kari found herself surrounded by warmth, which calmed the shivers wracking her body. Detective Wilkins helped her to her feet, and her forgotten cell phone slipped to the floor. The detective bent to retrieve it, finding several unanswered texts.

"Is it okay if I let Marie know you're safe? She's like a mother hen and will fret until someone does."

"S-sure," Kari's teeth chattered when she tried to talk.

"There," he said, handing Kari her phone. "When we get to the station, if a kind woman with a heart of gold seeks you out, it'll be Marie."

His kind smile faltered. "Hey, you're in shock. We need to get you assessed."

"I'm...I'm not hurt." *Why did her entire body ache as if she'd gotten hit by a bus then?*

"And we're going to confirm your self-diagnosis at the hospital."

Hospital?

Kari didn't have insurance, and after her mother emptied her bank account, she didn't have the funds to pay for an emergency room visit either. "No hospital. I swear I'm fine."

"If the paramedic says you're fine, then no hospital."

"They'll say I'm fine," Kari said with a stubborn tilt to her chin. The detective stepped to her side, doing his best to block the gruesome scene behind the couch. Despite his efforts, Kari will never forget Spencer's lifeless body being loaded onto the stretcher.

Detective Wilkins walked her out of the apartment and to a second ambulance, waiting by the sidewalk. He pulled out his phone while the paramedic assessed her. "Ms. Davidson, this is my department-issued phone. I'll use this digital app to take notes while I ask you some questions. Okay?"

The paramedic shone a light into Kari's eyes. "Sure." Then she pushed the paramedic's hand away to look at the people loitering behind the police tape. *Is the guy who killed Spencer among them?* The true crime dramas she indulged in made her believe it's possible.

"I'll answer your questions, I swear." Her voice dropped to a whisper. "You haven't caught him yet, have you?"

The detective shook his head. "Not yet. Officers are searching the area."

"Is it possible for you to ask them somewhere more private?"

"Did the suspect see you?"

"I-I don't think so. The street was busy...and the guy pounded on Spencer's door after I got there...he might've when I arrived." Kari sucked in a deep breath and shrugged. "I don't know."

Her phone buzzed in her hand. Izzy's sitter's name is on the screen. "I have to take this." Kari caught the paramedic's name stitched to his reflective vest. "No need for the hospital, right, Bill?"

The guy gave her a brief glance and said, "Yeah, you're good."

Kari stopped listening after his yeah and pressed her phone to her ear. "Hey, Mel. I'm so sorry...something...uh...something happened, and I need you to look after Izzy a little longer. I'm okay...can you give me two hours? Thanks. Tell Izzy I love her, and I'll be there soon."

Kari disconnected the call and met Detective Wilkins's intense stare. "Clocks ticking, detective. Let's get this question-and-answer session underway."

CHAPTER TWO

Kari

Kari sat in a small room with a cup of lukewarm coffee clutched between her hands as Detective Wilkins asked her questions. "Why did you go to the apartment building on East 1st Street this evening?"

She refrained from rolling her eyes. "Like I said the first two times you asked. I went there because Spencer asked me to come and pick up some stuff I left behind after our relationship ended."

"How long did the two of you date?"

"Three months," Kari said with a shrug. "Give or take."

'Listen, I wanted to....'

What did Spencer want to tell her? Maybe he wanted to make a last-ditch effort to get her back. Hell, he might've shocked the shit out of her and apologized. It didn't matter now, because she would never know.

"Why did you end the relationship?"

Kari leaned forward and didn't blink when she met the detective's gaze. "Spencer put his hands on me and shoved me against a wall when I showed up late for work three weeks ago. I kicked him in the balls and ended things then and there."

She caught a glint of admiration flash in the detective's eyes before it disappeared. "Then why bother to get your stuff?"

Kari sat back. Her bravado was fading quickly. "Fuck if I know. I don't even remember what I left behind."

She's supposed to be sad, right? Angry? Scared? How's she supposed to react? One word kept rolling around her head: *numb.*

"The man who shot Mr. Cameron...did you know him?" Detective Wilkins shifted in his seat, his pen poised over a pad of paper, ready to jot down every word despite his phone sitting between them.

Kari did a mental flip through the past couple of months and didn't recall the scary motherfucker until he kicked in Spencer's door. "No, tonight's the first time I laid eyes on him. Spencer seemed anxious...even paranoid, when I got there. He brushed me off when I asked him about it. Then Leo showed up and-"

"Leo?"

"Um, yeah...Spencer called the guy who shot him, Leo."

"No last name?"

"I didn't hear one."

"What else did they say?"

"Um...Leo said something about Spencer stealing money from the boss."

"The boss?"

"Yeah, he said someone told him Spencer has sticky fingers. Then he asked Spencer for it back." Kari sipped the coffee and grimaced when the tepid, bitter brew hit her tongue. She set the cup aside.

"Spencer said they lied, and he didn't take any money. They struggled and fell behind the couch. I didn't see the gun go off. I heard it. It left my ears ringing."

"Is there anything else you can tell me?"

"I'm not sure. I guess I made a noise when the gun went off. The guy...Leo stared right at the closet. I know a door kept me hidden...." Kari gave the detective another shrug. "The sound of your sirens scared him off."

"Would you recognize this Leo if you saw his picture?"

Kari shuddered. An image of the menacing man filled her mind. "Yeah, I'd know him if I saw him."

Detective Wilkins opened an app on the tablet he brought with him. He typed in the name "Leo" and clicked "Search." "Our database allows you to search for a first name, and it's narrowed it down to fifteen hundred possibilities."

"Only fifteen hundred?" Kari asked, sarcasm dripping from each word.

"When it's put in the perspective of the eight and a half million people who live here? You're lucky it's not fifteen thousand." He turned the tablet around and placed it in front of her. "Click the arrow on the right to move to the next mugshot," he said, giving her a sympathetic smile. "I'm going to get a fresh cup of coffee. Can I get you one, too?"

"I'd prefer water, thanks."

"Alright. You look through those, and I'll be back with your drink."

Kari checked the time on her phone and winced. "I can't stay much longer."

"I know. You need to pick up Izzy, right? Is she your daughter?"

"She's my sister. I'm her...legal guardian," Kari said, and that glint of admiration flashed in his eyes again.

Wilkins nodded. "Take the next thirty minutes and go through what you can. If you don't come across the mugshot tonight, I'll make sure you get home, and we can pick this up tomorrow."

"Okay...thanks."

The detective nodded and slipped out the door.

Kari bent over the tablet, flipping through mugshots, wanting this night to be over. She needed to hug her sister and take a shower. Wash this never-ending nightmare from her skin. She wished she could scrub her mind clean of it, too.

How did she process witnessing someone's murder? Someone she knew? Kari shuddered again and flipped through another half dozen photos of men she never wanted to meet in person.

Then she came upon a face that'll haunt her nightmares for the foreseeable future.

His hair's shorter in the mugshot, but Kari will never forget the soulless eyes staring back at her. "Leo Freedman," she said, reading the name beneath the picture.

"It's him. The man who killed Spencer." Kari pushed away from the table as the soulless eyes staring back from the screen followed her movements, doing its best to torment her.

"Detective Wilkins," she yelled, pulling open the door. "Detective Wilkins?" Several people stuck their heads out of their offices in response to her anxious shout. Kari spied the one she wanted three doors down. "Detective, I've found him."

Wilkins approached, taking the tablet from her hand and ushering her back into the room. "Leo Freedman," he said after closing the door. He studied the image for a moment, then met Kari's gaze. "You're sure?"

"Yes, I'll never forget that face." Kari expected to have a lot of nightmares and PTSD because of his face. "It's him. His hair is longer and shaggier now." She wrung her hands together, anxiety making her stomach roll. "What happens now?"

"We'll issue an arrest warrant. If Leo Freedman's apprehended, there'll be a trial, and you'll need to testify."

Kari remained stuck on the first part. "What do you mean by if he's apprehended?"

Detective Wilkins set the tablet aside and met her gaze. "Ms. Davidson." He sighed, and his shoulders slumped with the weight of the things he carried. "Listen...Kari, this city has many places to hide, and while we do our best, our resources have limitations. Your identifying Leo gives us more to work with, and I promise to do everything I can to find him."

Kari believed the detective meant what he said. He'd do all he could, but he was right. Too many crimes go unsolved in this city. What did she need to do to protect herself and her sister? Did she need to move? Hide? "What do I do now?"

"Go home. You said it yourself; you never saw Leo Freedman until tonight. He doesn't know what you look like."

The detective pulled a business card from his pocket. "If anything changes, call me. Now, let me get this APB going, and I'll arrange for you to get home."

"I can grab a taxi or an Uber."

"No, I insist. You didn't ask for any of this. The least I can do is get you and your sister home safe."

Kari didn't have the energy to argue. "Okay, thanks."

"It won't be long," he said on his way out the door.

"Kari?"

Kari turned in her chair and met the warm brown eyes of the woman peeking her head around the door. "Yes?" When the woman entered the room Detective Wilkins had left her in, Kari straightened in her seat.

"My name is Marie Sanchez. I'm the 911 operator you spoke with. I'm so glad you're safe." She sat in the other chair and reached across the table with a comforting hand for Kari to take. "When Stanley...."

Marie's soft brown skin grew rosy with her blush. "Sorry, Detective Wilkins sent me this way when I inquired about you after my shift. Are you okay?"

Kari wilted beneath her comforting touch, and tears filled her eyes. "No...yes...gah, I don't even know at this point."

"Oh, honey...I understand." Marie came around the table. "Is it okay if I give you a hug?"

Kari sniffled and said, "Please." She stood towering over the woman.

"Damn, you are a tall one. Maybe we can do this with you sitting, and I can keep my face out of your breasts. No offense or anything. You're not my type, and I don't want to give the wrong impression," Marie said, giving Kari a wink.

Kari snorted with laughter and plunked back into her seat, allowing Marie to bend down and embrace her around the shoulders, offering comfort and a laugh when Kari needed it most.

"Is the detective more your type?" Kari asked when Marie let her go.

"Who, Stanley?" More warmth brightened until she glowed. "He's sweet. And I suppose it's mutual, but enough about me. Stanley mentioned you need a ride home."

"What? Oh, Marie, I can order an Uber. You don't need to go out of your way to drive me home."

"I'm not. Stan gave me your address. You live three blocks over from me. It's on the way. Come on."

Kari wasn't used to someone looking out for her. She'd basically been on her own since the age of fourteen and took care of herself. "Um, okay. If you're sure."

"I'm sure. Do you need to stop anywhere on the way? Cause I'm starving and craving a greasy slice of pie."

Kari followed Marie down a maze of hallways to the elevator and parking garage beneath. "I could go for some pizza. It's my sister's favorite and will go a long way in pulling her out of the pout she'll be in because I'm late picking her up."

"Nick's on 7th work for you?"

Kari's stomach rumbled. "Oh yeah, they make the best pies."

"Just you and your sister?" Mari asked, unlocking the door of her compact sedan.

"Yeah, um...a month after my sister turned two, our mother left her with the neighbor and never came back. Mrs. Palmer kept my number, and I dropped everything to get Izzy. I'll be forever grateful that she called me and not CPS. Being able to take care of my sister means everything to me."

"Mm...the way you must have pivoted your life to care for her. You're a strong woman, Kari."

Kari turned her head toward the window, staring at the people crowding the sidewalk. She didn't want to always be the strong one. The one who looked after everything. It'd be nice to have someone in her life who tried to ease her burdens and care for her for a change.

"I'd do anything for my sister." And right now, Kari needed to reevaluate her choices.

"This is my last week working in dispatch."

Kari turned back toward Marie at the abrupt change in subject. "No way. You don't look ready to retire."

The car's interior filled with Maria's laughter. "If you're telling me I look way too young to collect social security, I'll take the compliment, thanks. I'm leaving because the project of my heart has come to fruition. Lavender House opens in six weeks."

"What's Lavender House?"

"A home where women and their children can go to escape domestic violence and get back on their feet."

Kari looked at Marie's profile, and the light from the street danced across a silvery scar along her cheek. Marie glanced her way and met Kari's gaze. "I may know a thing or two about escaping an abusive relationship."

"I'm sorry, Marie."

"It's okay. A lot has happened since then. I'm in a much better place now."

They pulled into a spot up the street from Nick's Pizza, and Marie touched Kari's hand, stopping her from getting out of the car. "If you ever want to stop in, to talk or even volunteer, I'd love for you to come by," she said, handing Kari a business card.

Kari looked at it, then tucked the card into her pocket. "Can I think about it?"

"Of course, honey," Marie said, patting Kari's hand. "You have my number. If you decide to volunteer, you will be required to undergo a background check. I know a detective who can take care of the details."

Kari gave Marie a smile. "I'm looking for a new job. Let me get my schedule settled, and then we'll talk."

"Sounds good. Let's go get our pies. I'm eager to get into my PJs and put my feet up."

CHAPTER THREE

Kari

There was no way she could return to the Garden of Eden, and thankfully, Kari found a new place to work the following week. She'd come across people decked out in costumes and fet-wear and asked a person in line what was happening, and they gave her an excited rundown of Decadent's masquerade night.

Intrigued by everyone's sexy looks, Kari joined the line and asked to speak with the owner when she handed the bouncer her ID. He smirked and said, "Good luck with the boss."

Thirty minutes later, Kari walked back out with a smirk of her own and told the bouncer she'd catch him for her first shift on Monday.

Kari now has the best job with one of the best bosses she's ever worked for. Jasper Jones is stoic, serious, and reserved. Yet he treats his staff exceptionally well. Excellent pay and benefits, plus a membership to play on their nights off.

With the extra money, Kari hoped to move her and Izzy into a better apartment within the next six months. She'd breathe easier once they lived in a more secure building.

Her first three months working at Decadent flew by. Her schedule allowed for more flexibility to be there for her sister than ever before. She even volunteered at Lavender House twice a week during Izzy's school day. After everything she's endured since leaving her modeling career to take care of her sister, it's nice to have this kind of stability again.

Her social life is a whole different matter because she didn't have one.

Decadent became Kari's sanctuary. The club allowed her to dress with bold abandon, expressing her exhibitionism in a safe environment while soothing her voyeuristic needs. It opened her eyes to many new kinks and fantasies she'd like to try someday.

If she ever puts herself out there again.

Leo Freedman remained at large. His trail went cold after Spencer's murder. The latest update from Detective Wilkins is the same. There's no sign of Leo, and until there is, the detective can't arrest and charge him.

Kari didn't trust anyone enough to risk her body or her heart. Besides, there's a chest full of toys locked away in the back of her closet to take care of any immediate needs. She and celibacy have become besties in keeping her heart safe.

Tonight, however, Kari didn't need to dwell on her sex life or lack thereof. There's a more pressing matter to deal with, and she couldn't let it slide any longer. She marched up the stairs to where Jasper and Gray kept their offices. She needed to speak to her boss about her 'clothing allowance.'

Is she stomping up the stairs while using air quotes? You betcha.

When Kari asked Jasper about this after receiving extra money with her second check, he explained how he'd gotten endless compliments about the new hostess and her outfits. He wanted to ensure their guests' titillation from the moment they entered the club. He knew how expensive fet-wear was, and he told her the clothing allowance is nonnegotiable.

Kari accepted Jasper's reasoning because it helped. It helped a whole fucking lot. Fetish wear is expensive, even though she knew where to shop. The extra money left over each week more than covered what she paid the sitter to look after Izzy.

The thing is, though, Jasper upped the amount with every other paycheck, making her wonder if he knew how precarious her situation was.

Kari never wanted to be someone's charity case. She figured shit out on her own.

When she returned home to collect her abandoned sister from the frazzled neighbor, Kari made some other harsh discoveries. The main one? All the money she earned during her years of modeling vanished. Every. Single.

Cent. Her mother cleaned out her account and then dumped her sister on the neighbor and ran.

Fuck, she despised that woman and didn't mind the fact that Izzy didn't remember her.

In the first couple of months, Kari scrambled to find a job offering decent pay. It's how she ended up a dancer at the Garden of Eden. She took what she could get. There aren't many options for someone whose resume reads: GED, posing in front of a camera, and strutting a flawless catwalk.

Since she started at Decadent, things have improved significantly, but the two-thousand-dollar clothing allowance, up five hundred from her last check, solidified it. She and Jasper needed to talk.

Kari can't accept any more of his charity. She didn't want to get used to it and then have it taken away. Kari knocked on Jasper's door.

"Come in."

She opened the door and stuck her head inside. "Got a minute, boss man?"

The 'boss man' moniker came out of her mouth the night he hired her. He'd grumbled for her to call him Jasper, yet Kari knew the nickname amused him. She instinctively knew Jasper needed to smile more, and she enjoyed being able to give him a reason to do so.

Kari heard the whispers about Jasper's wife, leaving him with nothing more than a note. The way he kept such an emotional and physical distance from everyone else made Kari believe he still pined for her.

Jasper sat back in his chair and ushered her in. "What can I do for you, Kari?"

She dropped into the chair across from him and tossed the envelope containing her clothing allowance onto his desk. "This is too much."

Jasper steepled his fingers beneath his chin and gave her an unscrupulous look. "No, it's not."

"Yes. It. Is. You've increased the amount every paycheck. Are you bumping it to three grand next week?"

"I will if you need it to be. You bring value to this club, and I'm compensating you for it. I'd like to do more."

Kari didn't know what to say except ask, "Why?"

"I know about your situation. The background checks I do on everyone who works here are even more extensive than those done for members. I'm aware of your sister, Izzy, and the responsibility you've taken on. Also, I don't like the building you and your sister live in."

Jasper leaned forward. "You need someone to look out for you. For now, that person is me."

For some strange reason, this pissed her off, and the words tumbled from her mouth. "You're not my daddy." Kari rose from the chair, determined to stomp her feet and storm off in a huff.

Jasper pinned her with a hard stare. "No, I'm fucking not. Now, sit the fuck down. I'm not finished. We'll talk about whether you need a *daddy* later. You're not ready yet."

Kari sank back into her seat, deflating under his stern gaze. How can she be mad at Jasper for wanting to help? After all, she knew what he'd find when he did her background check.

As for the daddy issue? Best to leave those alone for now.

Jasper interlaced his fingers, his thumb tracing the ring finger of his left hand. He leaned on his forearms and held Kari's gaze. "I've got a confession, and in exchange for this confession, you can ask me three questions."

"Is the confession you want to make about me?"

Jasper's gaze grew calculating. "Is this your first question?"

"Fuck no. We're still at the negotiation stage, boss man."

Jasper made a noncommittal sound. *Is he impressed or annoyed?* Kari believed it to be a bit of both. "Yes, the confession has to do with you."

"Am I going to be pissed about it?"

"Probably."

Kari crossed her arms. "Are you gonna up my clothing allowance again?"

"If you agree to my proposition, I won't have to."

"There's a proposition involved now?"

Jasper rubbed a hand over his face in exasperation. "Fuck, you're a brat. Do we have a deal or not?"

"Three personal questions about you, which you'll answer in exchange for a confession and a proposition?"

Did poking the bear fill her with glee?

A little.

"Jesus Christ, Kari. You've already asked five questions. This is not a game of twenty. Do you agree to the terms or not?"

Kari won't pass up such an opportunity. She is curious about Jasper, and if this is her chance to garner some personal info about him, then she'll take it. Besides, how bad is his confession going to be?

"Alright, you've got yourself a deal. First question...." She tapped her bottom lip, contemplating whether to ease into it or hit Jasper with a hard one right out of the gate. She went with an easy one.

Since he knew about Izzy, Kari asked, "Do you have any siblings?"

Jasper's expression softened, filling with fondness. "Yes. I have a sister named Joanna."

Kari waved her hand in a go-on motion. "Oh no, boss man. I expect details. Give me more."

"Alright, if you insist. I became Joanna's guardian in her last year of high school when our parents died. She's twelve years younger, bossy, and feisty as fuck. Once you're in her orbit, her brightness will surround you, and you will have a friend for life."

"She sounds amazing, and I'm sorry you lost your parents."

"Thank you, and she is. The two of you can become great friends. If you're looking to expand your circle." Sadness flashed across Jasper's expression. "She and her husband, Jonathan, have gotten some heartbreaking news recently. I know Jo can use the distraction of a new friend. She and Jon host Sunday brunch each week. We'd love for you and Izzy to join us. Gray comes too because Joanna is an amazing cook. Jess...."

His words trailed off at the mention of his wife. Kari picked up the sentence trail, leading into her next question. "Jess...she's your wife?"

"I believe you're already aware she is. You've worked here long enough to have caught some of the gossip by now."

"Gray mentioned her once or twice."

"Ah, yes, he's the biggest gossip of all."

"Will you tell me about her?"

"Yes. Then, it's time for my confession and my proposition for you. I must admit I'm a little disappointed you threw a question away on information you already knew."

"Maybe I wanted to ease you into the big question because if anything is going to tell me about you, it'll be how you speak about your wife."

"Touché."

After Jasper told Kari about Jessica, the photograph hanging below his office window made much more sense. Beyond any doubt, Kari knew the portrait Jasper changed every couple of weeks was of him and his wife.

She wanted to know who'd taken the erotic photos. She didn't ask, though, since she'd already surpassed her allotted questions.

"Alright, I'm ready for your confession, though I must warn you there'll be no penance of Hail Marys for you."

Jasper's chuckle warmed her. It's the closest she's come to getting him to laugh. "Somehow, I'll survive." The hint of humor he displayed fled, and his expression turned serious, making Kari brace herself for whatever he planned to tell her.

"By the second week you worked for me, I noticed a pattern in the precautions you took when you left at the end of your shift," he said, catching her off guard.

Kari fidgeted in her seat. *Shit.* She didn't realize anyone noticed.

"There's not much I miss," he said, reading her mind in that uncanny way of his. "This is the part you're going to be pissed about. Either Gray or I have followed you home every night you worked since."

"You what? Gray's involved in this?"

Kari always checked behind her. She used her phone camera and reflections in storefront windows, and she never saw them. She also never saw Leo, thank fuck. But apprehension filled her. Maybe she missed him trailing her, too.

"You never saw us because we didn't want you to. I also know why you take such precautions. My guy at the 34th precinct, who runs the police checks for me, informed me I'd want to talk to Detective Wilkins when he ran yours."

Kari sat up; her breath caught in her throat. Jasper knew everything. "What are you guys? Secret agents or something?" Kari asked, desperate to deflect.

"Or something. Gray and I and a few others, like Joanna's spouse, Jon, and Everly, whom you know as Mistress Eve, belonged to the same elite military squad."

"No shit." Kari sat back, stunned yet not surprised by the revelation. "Who else?"

Jasper held up his hand, stopping her. "May I remind you? You've far surpassed your questions already."

"I'm trying to delay the impending scolding."

Jasper sighed and gave her an exasperated look. "It took a couple of weeks until your detective got back to me, and when he did, he filled in the missing pieces. I'm sorry for what happened to you." Jasper's gaze darkened. "No one is ever the same after witnessing someone's life being taken."

"I've looked over my shoulder ever since," Kari said, her voice nothing more than a whisper.

"I know you have, which leads me to my proposal. You live in a shitty building with no security."

"Gee, thanks. Tell me how you really feel. For the record, I'll be able to move into a better building in a few months. That place is all I can afford after my mother emptied my bank account," Kari said, defending everything she did under the circumstances she'd found herself in.

"I am not trying to diminish what you've accomplished, and you have, Kari. You've accomplished amazing things despite the odds being stacked against you. Be proud of the woman you've become. The way you've handled the responsibility of raising your sister is commendable. It's something I'm very familiar with. You and I are kindred spirits."

"Thanks...and thanks for answering my questions. I want you to know I'm not mad about what you did. I'm more shocked, I guess. No one's ever looked out for me like this. It's something a family member might do, like a big brother or something. I mean, I don't know what having a brother is like, though I imagine they'd be protective like you."

"Joanna tells me I'm an excellent big brother. If you want to know more, she'll pepper you with stories of my sordid youth at brunch." Jasper cleared his throat and pinned her with his gaze. "Let me know when you're done deflecting. We're not done discussing my proposal."

"I'm not deflecting," Kari stuttered.

"Look, you're used to bearing the burden alone. Sometimes, it's hard to recognize an offer of help when it's staring you in the face. What if you didn't have to wait a few months to move into a better place? What if you can move this week?"

"Um, amazing, yet kind of impossible since I haven't looked for a new place." The next few months are crucial for saving enough and working out a budget to expand her rental options.

"I own more property than the club."

While Jasper didn't flaunt his wealth, he wore the air of money with the confidence of someone who'd done it for quite some time, so it didn't surprise her.

"There's a building on Union Avenue. It has a doorman, so it's a safe environment. The school district is top-notch, with on-site 24-hour day-care. You won't have to worry about who will mind your sister if you're at work...or decide to take a bit of time for yourself. There's a two-bedroom apartment available. Say the word, and it's yours."

Kari stared at Jasper, dumbfounded. There's no way she can accept an offer like this. She can't imagine what kind of rent an apartment in a building like that costs. "I can-"

"Before saying something unnecessary like you can't afford the rent, let me stop you. I own the building and set the rent. I won't accept more than what you're paying right now."

"But-"

"No buts, Kari. Let me help you and Izzy. Say yes."

CHAPTER FOUR

West

West groaned when he stretched, feeling every one of his thirty-seven years. He picked up his phone and checked the time. *Shit*. Four-thirty in the fucking morning. He set his phone down and rubbed a hand over his face, knowing it's useless to go back to sleep.

The nightmare waited for him the moment he closed his eyes. They didn't occur often. When they did, he was up for the rest of the night with too much pent-up energy to burn.

It's Sunday, which means his gym didn't open until nine, and since he needed to be at the shop by ten, deciding to go for a run to shake off the dregs of the dream he couldn't even remember.

It might do him some good to clear his head, anyway. There was a lot he needed to decide, and he'd put it off long enough.

West pulled on a T-shirt and a pair of running shorts. The city still slumbered, and he wanted to get out there and bask in the peace before it all came bustling to life.

He laced his shoes by the door, then slipped his earbuds in and, with his playlist cued, he tucked his phone into the mesh pocket at his thigh and hit the pavement, easing into a steady pace.

The likes of Coldplay and Hozier carried him to the trails of Glasgow Green. West increased his speed along the familiar paths, letting his mind wander while his feet pounded the packed dirt trail. Despite focusing on his breathing or trying to sing along with his favorite songs, the things he needed to figure out filtered through.

Like the bits of conversation he had with Jasper six months ago, *'There's someone I want you to meet...'*

His words during their tumultuous drive the night they rescued Jasper's niece echoed in his mind. After all this time, is he ready to let his friend introduce him to someone?

Jasper Jones was second in command of their elite military squad. The group of eight has remained close, despite the physical distance between them. They each had a percentage in Decadent, the club Jasper opened several years ago, but West left New York shortly after Jess and Jasper's wedding, not going back for almost a decade.

It's been too long since he....

Hell, the last time West experienced a little fun, their friend, Xander, brought his spouses, Penny and Lex, to his shop for some ink, and he got to play voyeuristic listener, jerking off while they fucked in the back-room. Fun day of orgasms and tattooing. Except....

It left him feeling a little hollow. He didn't regret taking part in their fun. It's more like something's missing for him. Being given a glimpse into the connection Xander had with his partners and bearing witness to Jasper and Jess getting back together only amplified the emptiness in his heart, his life, and his bed. It's something he's ignored for way too long.

After West finished inking Penny with a tattoo like the one he'd already given Lex and Xander. Xander pulled him aside, telling West how the three of them planned a move to New York within the year, adding that Taylor intended to return when they did.

Meaning out of his squad, he'd be the only one left on this side of the pond. It's not the first time, and he has other friends. Even two of his cousins lived nearby. But....

He spent his childhood in Glasgow and lived in New York during his teens and twenties when he wasn't serving his country. Moving back here after his wife, Maggie, died seemed like the right thing to do, but staying away from the other city he called home didn't seem right anymore.

West yearned to return. He'd stayed away all this time for...reasons, staying single most of that time, too.

The sound of his breathing and blood whooshing through his ears broke through the decision, which pressed against the edge of his mind. West didn't want to be alone anymore.

With sweat soaking through his shirt and the sun rising, he rounded the last corner on his way back to his flat. He slowed to a calming walk, allowing his heart rate to return to normal. His phone vibrated against his thigh, and he smiled when he saw who was blowing up his messages.

> **Gray: Hey, asshole! When are you going to stop being a fucking stranger?**

> **Gray: I'm asking my girl to marry me. Then I'm going to give her my collar.**

> **Gray: I know how much you enjoy a show. <winking face with tongue emoji> So, how about you get your fucking ass Stateside?**

> **Gray: Miss you, brother.**

The decision seemed straightforward, and all signs pointed toward what he craved. It's time to return to the city that soothed his soul.

He typed a quick response.

> **West: I'm basking in the love from here, brother. <eye roll emoji>**

> **West: Keep it to yourself and send me the details. I'd love to meet your future wife.**

Another text from Gray came through, and West got the stupidest grin on his face.

Gray: She's...Addie is everything to me. I know you'll love her like everyone else does.

West: Amazing, brother. Can't wait.

He returned to his flat and grabbed a quick shower, then got on his laptop to book his flight. West read Gray's latest text. *Shit*, the proposal's four days away.

Nothing like his friend to leave the invitation to the last minute. It didn't give him much time to organize things with his shop manager. Or to reschedule any of his upcoming appointments.

Many of his clients flew to Glasgow just to have him tattoo them. They might not mind having him stateside either. He'll ask some of his connections if they have any space in their shops to rent.

He got to work on a list of everything he needed to do because he realized he didn't know when he'd come back.

CHAPTER FIVE

Kari

"Kari? Is everything alright?"

Kari gave herself a mental shake. It's time to put her past behind her. Neither Spencer nor the man who killed him can hurt her anymore. The cops found Leo Freedman floating in the East River six months ago and considered the case closed. It took her those six months to get used to not having to look over her shoulder every damn day.

A considerable part of her newfound security is because of the man standing in the doorway of his office, his face filled with concern. Jasper helped Kari out at one of the lowest points in her life. Thanks to him, she and Izzy now have friends who are more like family, a kindness she can never repay. With their support, she emerged from the shell she'd locked herself into.

"Kari?" Jasper said again, getting worried.

Kari did her best to give Jasper a reassuring smile. "Sorry, I got sucked into the past there for a minute." She waved her hand toward his desk. "I dropped the papers from the admin department for you to review tomorrow."

"Thanks, I appreciate your hard work, but like you said, I didn't need those papers until tomorrow." Jasper stepped inside and shut the door behind him, silencing the hum of the growing crowd below.

"Why are you hiding here and not waiting to get a signed copy of Addie's latest novel with Jess?"

Decadent's hosting its first book signing. Gray and Jasper set it up to coincide with one of the club's demonstration nights. The guests attending the signing can leave once it's done or choose to stay for a club tour and take part in demonstrations of Shibari and flogging.

"Shows what you know, boss man. I got my signed copy and all the NSFW swag I wanted when I helped Addie set up earlier." Unable to hide her smirk, she said, "Well...I suppose sexy character art is safe for consumption here. Plus, I dressed for the part."

"The naughty schoolgirl outfit?" Jasper asked with a wave of his hand, encompassing the short plaid skirt, the white button-down knotted above her navel, the shiny patent-leather, stacked Mary Janes, and the white ankle socks.

Kari's extra naughty touch with the innocent white boy cut panties framed the bottom of her ass cheeks, giving someone quite the view if she bent at the waist the slightest bit.

Those are things Jasper didn't need to know.

"Don't tell me you don't recognize the main character from Addie's first book? I swore Jess said the two of you acted out some of the spicier scenes," Kari said with a wiggle of her brows and a snort of laughter.

Jasper ignored her dig. "My wife is in line to get her own signed copy, and what did you call it? NSFW art? I'm heading down to meet her in a minute. I saw you come in here and wanted to check on you."

He studied her, and Kari did her best not to squirm under his penetrating gaze. "You sure you're okay?"

"I am." It's not something that happened overnight. Hell, she stayed celibate for over two years, only concluding while lost in her musings that she was ready to get back out there.

She wanted to meet someone. To forge a real and deep connection. Someone to explore her desires with. "I'm in a good place now, Jasper. I don't know how I can ever repay you for giving me a chance and looking out for me."

Jasper came closer and put his hand on her shoulder. The smile he gave her filled her with warmth and affection. "There's nothing to repay. You and Izzy are part of our family, and I'll always look out for you."

"Thanks, Jas. Y'all mean a lot to us, too."

"We want you to be happy, Kari."

Jasper slipped his hands into his pockets and stepped back, putting some space between them when he said, "With the danger being over, I figured you'd have ventured into the club on one of your nights off by now."

Having a conversation about dating and sex with Jasper is like him throwing down the concerned big brother card. It's nice, and also weird.

"I'm working up to it. No one's caught my interest." Kari sighed. "They say it'll happen when you least expect it. While I'm open to it, I won't force a connection, either."

"You deserve to be loved and cared for."

"And I deserve the right person to do that." Kari tipped her head back and stared at the ceiling, waving her hands in front of her face, trying to stave off the emotions about to burst like a dam.

"Alright, boss man, go find your wife and stop trying to ruin my makeup. Don't worry, I'll lock up. Just give me a minute."

Jasper gave her another reassuring smile on his way out. "Take all the time you need."

Despite her reassurance to Jasper, Kari didn't go back downstairs. When she locked his office, she stayed there, leaning against the railing, being a distant observer as Gray got down on one knee and proposed to Addie when she finished her book signing, almost ruining her makeup for a second time.

What was it like to want to spend the rest of your life with someone? To love someone and be loved by someone with such passion, she couldn't imagine a day without them. How did she even find such a person in a city of this magnitude?

Kari snorted. She's not even twenty-three, for crying out loud. Of course, there's more than enough time to find someone. She's had her share of flings and relationships while traveling the world, being left unsupervised to explore...to get taken advantage of by strangers, or worse, those closest to her, and it left her more than jaded.

She wiped a tear from the corner of her eye, blinking the rest away when a shift in the club's energy rippled through the air, and her gaze returned to the stage.

She gasped when Addie got on her knees, and Gray parted her lips with his cock.

The distance obscured the finer details, though Kari got the gist of the unfolding scene. A public claiming.

Yes, those are her friends, but being this far away allowed for a touch of eroticism and obscurity to their identities, and Kari ate it up.

She held an equal love of exhibitionism and voyeurism. She enjoyed exploring those desires from the sidelines. The extent of participation was the outfits she chose for each shift. Otherwise, Kari kept her head down and her desires under wraps. It's how she survived the last two years.

Now that she's safe, she'd like to try. Maybe approach a Dom on her night off....

Kari leaned further over the rail, getting lost in the couple on stage, when a throat cleared behind her, startling her into losing her balance.

She flailed her arms, trying to regain her footing, when a set of powerful hands gripped her arms, pulling her back from certain death against a solid wall of muscle. Her sexy version of a schoolgirl uniform offered little cover from the heat of his body.

"Damn, little girl. Are you looking for trouble?" Her rescuer growled next to her ear.

She didn't even get a look at him, and yet the gravel of his voice made Kari bite back a sudden and desperate urge to whimper, *'With you? Yes, Daddy.'* She dared a glance over her shoulder, shocked to find the sexiest man she'd ever laid eyes on.

Wavy blond hair teased a set of broad and powerful shoulders. Tattoos wrapped around his throat and disappeared beneath the collar of his shirt. Kari's eyelids drifted closed in a slow blink. When she opened them, the sexy man still held her in his arms, wearing a sexy smirk on his sexy face.

His gaze swept over her like a caress. And that smile...that wicked, sexy smile made Kari's tempered libido stand up and take notice. Then he amped up the sexy and bit his bottom lip.

Did she just whimper?

"Yeah, you did," he said with a chuckle.

Kari spun, and he let go of her, even taking a step back to be respectful of her space. She straightened to her full height, and with the additional inches of her stacked Mary Janes, she stood eye to crystal blue eye – *oh my fucking god, who has eyes this blue?*

Trapped in the consuming, icy blue depths of his gaze, Kari did her best to break free of the insane spell she found herself under and did the only thing she could think of: Kari got bratty.

"Who are you calling little? What are you, the big bad wolf?" Kari clasped her hands beneath her chin and batted her eyelashes. "Oh my, what big...eyes you have." *Like, the bluest, crystal clearest eyes she's ever seen.*

Kari slammed her apartment door, and she never slammed her door. She's respectful and quiet. She avoided annoying her neighbors. Tonight, she slammed her goddamn door.

The sound of his laughter echoed, dark and sinful, in her mind. The memory of its deep rumble skittering down her spine made goosebumps erupt all over her skin. Those gorgeous blue eyes raked over her from head to toe at her taunt, then back to collide with her gaze, giving her a heated look.

He crossed his tattooed arms; the ink extended from the top of his fingers until the black and grey designs disappeared beneath the edge of his shirt sleeve. Is he tattooed...everywhere? She had a powerful urge to strip him bare and find out.

Kari let out a frustrated sound. Desperate longing nagged her on the ride home, remembering how he hesitated to let her go once she'd caught her balance. How his calloused hands glided down the bare skin of her arms, dragging out the time he kept them connected.

Even now, the ghost of his touch lingered. The same desperation made Kari flip the locks while tearing off the sweatshirt and leggings she'd changed into before leaving Decadent.

With Izzy at childcare for the night, she didn't have to worry about being caught or heard. She needed...release and sprinted naked to her bedroom. Tits bouncing, thighs already slick with her arousal. Kari dropped to her knees in her closet and pulled the locked chest toward her.

Beachy blond hair, ice-blue eyes...tattoos, and fucking muscular. Kari's imagination went into overdrive. Images of him with those tattooed hands wrapped around her throat or gripping her ass, manipulating her limbs to bend them to his will. One leg hooked around his waist, the other pinned to the wall while he pumped his thick length in and out of her...

"Fuuuck."

Her fingers trembled with anticipation when she flipped the lid open. Kari stared at the familiar contents. Being celibate for over two years garnered her quite the assortment of clit suckers, dildos, vibrators, butt plugs, and nipple clamps...hell, she even bought herself a strap-on because it turned her on and made her feel powerful to have a dick swinging between her legs every once in a while.

She teased her nipples, trying to decide which toys to use. Her eyes landed on the lifelike dildo with the suction cup base. She grabbed it and stuck it to the floor.

There'll be no setting the mood tonight. No soft music, lit candles, or soft sheets. This is an absolute raw need, and Kari was desperate to satiate it.

She stroked the rubber phallus from base to crown, coating it with lube. "Mm...." She bet the sex god possessed an enormous cock, and she planned to enjoy sinking onto this monster to flashes of all those wicked tattoos and pale blue eyes. She grabbed one more item, her rose clit sucker, and straddled the rubber cock suctioned to the floor.

"Tell me your name, little girl...." Of course, calling her little girl again kept her silent and bratty as fuck. It didn't piss him off or irritate him, though. Nope. He gave her the sexiest grin, which caused her core to flutter and flood her white panties, the wet spot growing by the second.

Kari gripped the base of her dildo, parting her pussy lips with the crown, sliding it over her slit. She teased her clit, letting her juices mix with the slick lube.

She notched the head at her opening, and her gaze focused on herself in the full-length mirror hanging on her closet wall. Hair mussed; skin flushed; pupils blown wide with desire. Her hard nipples begged to be sucked while her thighs trembled with the effort to hold herself up.

Unable to fight the effort any longer, Kari lowered herself onto the cock. With her eyes locked on the mirror, she watched how it stretched her labia around the broad base. "Oh...."

Kari shuddered, and her eyelids grew heavy, imagining the man she wanted to call Daddy. The words tumbled from her lips when she rocked up and down on the dildo. "You're so big...*Daddy*...." Her pussy swallowed the rubber cock each time she lowered her ass to her heels.

When she couldn't edge herself a moment longer, Kari lined up the rose vibe with her clit. Revving herself up, she worked her way through the settings until she reached the one guaranteed to get her off – *you know the one...feels like a high-speed tongue flicking your clit with intense suction* – "Oh fuck, yes," she cried out when she reached it.

She cupped her breast, pinching her nipple, rolling it between her thumb and index finger. Her mind substituted them for large, calloused hands covered in tattoos, and her pussy clenched around the unforgiving phallus.

Close.

So fucking close.

Her imagination went into overdrive. The tattooed sex-god surrounded her, and it was his lap and his cock she bounced on. The echo of his deep, rumbling voice saying something she always wanted to hear. *"Come for me, baby girl. Come for Daddy."*

"Oh God. I'm coming, Daddy. I'm coming." Kari's orgasm ripped through her core, sending shock waves and shivers over her body. She rocked and moaned, soaking her dick substitute all the while wishing for it to be the sex god's perfect cock instead.

Kari pulled the rose from her sensitive clit, letting it tumble to the floor still vibrating. She pushed herself off the dildo with a groan and rolled onto her back, the cold floor a shock to her system as she gazed at her spent form in the mirror.

Is it possible for the man to be better than her imagination? She'd come face-to-face with crushing disappointment when other partners didn't pan out.

Oh, well. It's not like she'll find out what this guy's like, anyway. Before tonight, Kari had never seen him, and probably won't again.

CHAPTER SIX

West

West arrived right from the airport, the Uber dropping him off outside the nondescript-looking warehouse.

The driver gave him a sidelong glance and asked, "You sure you want me to drop you here?"

"Don't judge it by the outside, not when the inside is an out-of-body experience. You have yourself a good night now." West left the stunned driver to draw his own conclusions and used his security code to enter the club's staff entrance.

He took the back stairs, hoping to catch Jasper in his office, and then enjoy the climax of his friend's engagement.

West slung his carryall over his shoulder and kept his eyes on the stairs, counting each step to quell the sudden nerves this homecoming brought, until his gaze drew level with the landing and traveled the length of a pair of legs meant to be wrapped around his hips.

Creamy, flawless skin filled his vision, and images of the ink he might cover such a perfect canvas with filled his mind.

She bent further over the rail, lost in what was happening on the other side of the club. West's eyes snapped from the woman's delectable ass framed in a pair of not-so-innocent, ruffled white panties. He cleared his throat, trying not to startle her, and achieved the opposite.

Jesus.

Her foot slipped, and West reached out, catching her in time before she toppled further. He hissed when an electric current zipped from her skin to his. The woman's sharp intake of breath hinted she felt it too.

"Damn, little girl. You looking for trouble?"

Once steady on her feet, she turned her head and peered at West over her shoulder. *Fuck, she's gorgeous.* Warm brown eyes surrounded by thick, dark lashes. High cheekbones and full, pouty lips, painted in the deepest shade of crimson, clouded his vision.

She straightened to her full height and turned to face him. West loved women of all shapes and sizes, though tall women were his favorite kind.

"Who are you calling little? What are you, the big bad wolf?" she asked, clasping her hands beneath her chin and batting her eyelashes. "Oh my, what big...eyes you have."

Her brattiness shot straight to his dick.

She gave him her best haughty expression, and the smirk playing about her lips made him laugh. This little brat knew what she'd done to him. "How about you tell me your name, lass, and I'll let you know whether I am," he said, adding a growl for the full effect.

Her eyes widened, and West couldn't help but smile when those deep brown eyes slid over his body. Her tongue peeked from between her lips when her gaze reconnected with his. "I don't think so."

"No?" West gave her a smoldering look, even biting his bottom lip.

A rosy glow worked its way up her throat to her cheeks. Her lips parted, and her breath hitched. Then she caught herself, giving him an off-the-cuff remark when she turned back to look at the stage. "Besides, members aren't supposed to be up here."

"Then what are you doing up here?"

"I work here."

"Hm...the plot thickens." West sensed her hesitancy, and he decided not to press further. Since she works here, maybe he can ask Jasper who she is.

"Well, I won't keep you from your job, lass. Maybe I'll catch you sometime on your night off. I'd consider myself lucky if I did. Have a good night."

"I, um...." She hesitated, then said, "Yeah, enjoy the rest of your night."

West cut through the lobby, heading toward the private change room Jasper created for him and the rest of their squad, hoping to catch Gray and his fiancée, Addie. Then he can head to Jess and Jasper's and pass out.

His heart overflowed with happiness at the couple's news. They're expecting twin girls in a few months. Their love and what they did to find their way back to one another unlocked this readiness inside West to find someone for himself.

When he turned the corner, he found Addie and Gray coming from the other direction, oblivious to anyone else around them, allowing West to observe them unnoticed.

Addie's tall and curvy, with a shock of violet hair, complementing the rosy, satisfied glow of her cheeks. Her hips swayed with each step, and Gray tucked her into his side, his hand flexing at Addie's hip.

Gray pressed his lips to Addie's forehead while her fingers played with the leather collar at her throat. Raising her left hand. The solitaire diamond adorning her ring finger sparkled in the hall light. Gray's lips moved against her skin, his words reaching West a moment later. "I love you, baby."

They stopped walking, and Addie turned in his embrace to loop her arms around Gray's neck. "I love you, too." Addie tipped her chin, her lips connecting with Gray's, and their kiss turned into a heated display.

West didn't want to startle them. He also didn't want to be a voyeur, not when they hadn't established consent. He cleared his throat and dropped his bag to the floor. "Hey…sorry to interrupt. I wanted to congratulate the happy couple."

Gray lifted his head, and the smile he gave West is the stuff of dentists' dreams. "You made it." Addie seemed mesmerized by Gray's dimples, which West didn't blame her for, taking a moment to stare. She then turned to see who'd interrupted them, though she didn't look perturbed. She looked surprised.

"Jesus Christ. Are all of you gorgeous?"

Her off-the-cuff comment made West laugh, and he didn't know what to say. Gray tucked Addie into his side when they came to a stop in front of him. "Behave, babe. I promise I'll share some writing inspiration photos and stories with you later."

"You better." She winked and then stuck out her hand for West to shake. "Addison Carter, well, soon to be Addison Matthews…." Her words trailed off, and her brows drew together when she tilted her head toward Gray. "Hey, babe? Are you going to be upset if I stick with Carter?"

"Never." Gray fingered the leather collar that West knew he designed. "Why do I need you to change your name when I know you're already mine?" Gray's hand moved to cup Addie's jaw, and they both sported the look of two people ready to fuck. AKA, West's cue to leave.

"So…I'm going to call it a night. Pleasure to meet you, Addie. Congratulations to you both. I hear Joanna and Jonathan's is the place to be for

Sunday brunch. Jess informed me that my attendance is mandatory. Will you both be there?"

Gray put some space between himself and Addie. "Shit. Sorry, brother. I can't help myself when I'm around her."

"I don't blame you one bit."

Gray leaned in and gave him a backslapping hug. "Thanks. Yeah, Addie and I will be there on Sunday. It's become a bit of a competition." Addie elbowed Gray in the ribs. "I meant tradition. Your mind is going to blow when you get a load of all the food. You won't eat any better than at Jo and Jon's."

Addie offered him a hug, too, and West welcomed it. "Sorry. Gray's easy to get carried away over."

"You never have to apologize for loving one of my best friends."

Addie gave him a warm smile and squeezed his arm. "You're good for my creativity. Already have a brother's best friend's story idea brewing in the back of my mind. It'll be fun getting to know one another better."

West looked over at Gray in confusion.

"What can I say? Romance authors find their inspiration everywhere."

On the cab back to his friend's brownstone, West immersed himself in the sheer energy the city provided. He loved his life in Glasgow, the familiarity, and the precious memories of his mum and gran, but he couldn't deny how much he missed this city.

West keyed in the alarm code Jasper sent him, disabling the security system. He dropped his bag on the floor at the bottom of the steps. He opened the fridge to grab a bottle of water, checking his messages when his phone vibrated again.

> **Jasper: Since you didn't tell me about your visit, there's no food. Join Jess and me for breakfast tomorrow. I'll make sure the coffee's ready for you. We can place a grocery order for whatever you need.**

West closed the refrigerator. "No worries. Water is all I need."

> **Jasper: There are fresh towels in the closet beside the bathroom. See you in the morning.**

West needed a shower. He'd gone straight to Decadent from JFK to make it in time for Gray and Addie's engagement. Which brought the gorgeous woman he met tonight to the forefront of his mind.

Can he say they met if she refused to give him her name? It reminded him of her brattiness, which made his dick fucking hard.

He let out a groan, and he did his best to ignore his persistent dick. Jasper hinted that she was the woman he wanted to introduce West to. She's breathtakingly beautiful, and he also didn't miss the fact that she's at least a decade younger than he is.

He grabbed a towel from the stack in the closet, flicked on the bathroom light, and stared at himself in the mirror. He didn't want to over-analyze the noticeable age gap when he didn't even know the woman's name.

West stripped off his clothes, tossing each layer on the floor. His hand grazed his cock. "Fuuuck." He stepped into the shower, not letting it heat, and took a direct hit of the cold water, hoping to shock his cock into submission.

It didn't work.

As the water warmed, West reached for the body wash on the shower shelf. He lathered it in his hands, soaping his chest and under his arms when the scent reached his nostrils. He remembered the smell of soft lavender when he caught the woman in his arms.

His mind's eye replayed the visual, climbing those last half-dozen steps to reach Jasper's office. Stacked Mary Janes and white ankle socks followed by endless, toned legs with flawless, creamy skin.

A blank canvas to fill with his designs. To cover such perfect skin in a way to leave no doubt, she belonged to him. It was such a dangerous and possessive thought. The woman is not his anything. Much to his dismay, she remained a nameless enigma.

Those white panties cupping her perfect ass framed by her naughty-as-fuck plaid mini, though.... West gripped the base of his cock. Unable to resist the urge, he stroked upwards, his fingers tracing each bar of his Jacob's Ladder.

The water muffled his moan. Fuck, West wanted to shout her name when he came. He stroked his cock harder, and the perfect substitute fell from his lips, "Baby girl...."

West will never deny having a daddy kink, just not the age-play kind. He knew Jasper didn't hire anyone under twenty-five, making her about twelve years younger than him. He also knew Jasper took his ability to match people seriously; wanting West to meet her meant Jasper believed they'd be well-suited.

His balls drew tight, and his release tingled at the base of his spine when he remembered how she sassed him. Fuck, bratty subs are his kryptonite. *"Who are you, the big bad wolf?"*

He wanted to take her over his knee or bend her over some piece of furniture, turning her porcelain ass a fiery shade of red. West wanted to choke the brattiness out of her with his dick while he fucked her beautiful, bratty mouth.

"Fuuuck." His fingers circled his crown, his thumb sliding over his slit to collect the precum pooling at his tip. He spread it down his shaft, blending it with the lavender-scented soap.

He cupped his balls with his other hand. "Yeah, baby...I'm the big bad wolf who's going to devour every inch of you." West stroked faster, his grip tightening with the speed his orgasm raced down his spine. He didn't want to blow yet and tugged on his sac, edging away from an imminent release.

In his vision of her, she turned to face him, confronting him with her bratty little attitude. West caught sight of the way she'd knotted her white button blouse above her navel. The strip of skin she left exposed...he imagined tracing it with his tongue. With images of his hands and mouth on her, holding back his orgasm became impossible.

He stroked himself. Harder. Faster. His fingers rolled over each piercing along the underside of his cock. The image of a little pink tongue following the path his fingers took made West's orgasm barrel up his shaft until ropes of cum landed on the black and white subway tiles. "Fuck yes, baby girl."

The adrenaline of his release faded, and West tipped his head back beneath the spray, washing the remaining suds and cum from his body. It's when the jetlag hit him like a brick. He turned the water off and dried himself off.

He strolled naked back to the main room, where he left his bag and threw on a pair of grey sweats. Bone-tired, he crawled beneath the cool sheets. The moment his head hit the pillow, however, his brain went into overdrive.

Like what Jess and Jasper might say to him when he joined them for coffee. Will Jasper bring up the mystery woman? He rubbed a hand over his face. Despite his active mind, his body will not let him go without sleep any longer. He drifted off, knowing that if he placed a bet, he'd put money on his friends not saying anything.

Funny thing, when he joined them for coffee, they proved him right.

CHAPTER SEVEN

Kari

"Hey. Who won the contest this week?" Kari closed the door and came up the stairs to the kitchen with Izzy trailing behind her, eager to find out which of her friends out-baked the other.

The Sunday brunch tradition at Jon and Joanna's developed into a competition for who prepared the most goodies for the ladies to take to Lavender House. It started a few months ago, and now every Sunday the ladies pack up the extra food and bring it to everyone staying there.

She came to a sudden halt at the top of the stairs.

Kari didn't find Joanna cooing at her daughter, Sara-Jane, or Jess keeping Jasper from sampling all the food, or even Addie and Gray with mimosas in their hands. Nope.

The sole occupant of the kitchen? The same man she can't get out of her head. Like, she masturbated to the memory of him.

More than once.

Oh, God. Is it written all over her face?

Kari met his electric blue eyes, and the words flew from her mouth. "What the fuck are you doing here?" Her pulse beat harder; her breath came faster. She needed to charge all her favorite toys this week; she'd used them so often.

All because of him.

He wore his hair down like he did the night at the club until, still not saying anything, he gathered the golden blond strands between his fingers and secured them in a topknot with an elastic from his wrist, displaying a fresh undercut beneath.

It made the guy even sexier.

"Yeah, what the fuck?"

Don't make it worse, don't make it worse, don't make it worse.

Kari made it worse. "Shit." She looked down and met her sister's mischievous gaze. "Don't do it, Izz. Please don't do it."

Izzy gazed back at her with a devilish glint. "Shit." Kari's face went up in flames.

"You have a kid?" The tattooed sex god asked, making Kari spin to face him. He kept his tone low, giving nothing away, and said, "She seems fun."

"I am fun," Izzy said with a hand on her hip, making him laugh.

Why did it have to be the sexiest laugh she's ever heard?

Kari stole another quick glance, then dropped to her knees to deal with her sister and her smart mouth. He wore a light blue button-down that complemented his eyes. With the sleeves rolled to his elbows, Kari tried to memorize the sex god's tattoos covering his hands and forearms.

Ugh, stupid sex god. Those tattoos, though. Again, she wondered if he had them everywhere.

He left the top two buttons of his shirt undone, and his ink went from below his chin, around his neck, and beneath his collar. Figuring out which part of him didn't have tattoos might be easier.

Years of modeling for designers and photographers wanting to highlight her flawless features meant she'd never gotten another besides a semicolon behind her ear. She'd love to get more. Is this guy a tattoo artist? Maybe he can design something for her....

An image of him inking the word MINE in elegant script filtered through her mind. *Oh, em gee. What the actual fuck?*

"She's my sister." Ugh. Why did her words have to sound all high and breathy?

"She's also my mom," Izzy supplied.

Kari dropped her head into her hands with a groan. "Not helping, Izz. The kindergarten moms hate me already."

"Nah, they're jealous because you're tall and pretty."

"Really not helping, Izz."

"Not helping what?" Jasper asked, strolling into the kitchen with everyone else following behind him. Like they planned this. "Oh, good. You two have met."

"Not in an official capacity," Kari grumbled, getting to her feet.

"Let me correct such an erroneous error. Weston Sharpe, say hello to Kari Davidson and her sister, Izzy. Kari and Izz, meet my friend, West." Jasper lifted Izzy into his arms to get his special greeting from her.

"Hi."

"Hi."

"Did you save us food, Jas?" Izzy asked, disrupting their super awkward meet-cute.

This is not a meet-cute.

"Of course we did, Izz. Want me to help you get a plate?"

Izzy squirmed out of Jasper's arms. "I can get it. Auntie Jo, where's Janie? I want to help sit," Izzy said to Jasper's sister, Joanna, when she stepped out from behind him.

Jo gave Izzy an indulgent smile. "She got excited while waiting for you and tuckered herself out. I'll need your help when the ladies drop everything off at Lavender House, though. You can pick a story out to read to Sara-Jane."

"Yes...," Izzy squealed. "I already know the one I'm gonna pick."

Throughout the exchange, until Joanna took Izzy by the hand and out of the room, West didn't take his eyes off Kari, tracking her every gesture.

Is anyone seeing the tension growing between them?

"I don't know about the rest of you," Jess said, looking around. "My growing babies and I can use some more food." While Addie and Gray smirked and coughed behind the drinks they held. Kari swore she heard, 'Fuck it out,' amongst all their coughing.

Oh, so they noticed.

Kari had the strangest urge to wind herself around West like a cat in heat despite being surrounded by people. And, you know...the fact that they've exchanged like six words. *What's wrong with her?* She needed some distance and some clarity.

Kari caught her friend's attention, stopping them from making their escape. "Hey, can we head to Lavender House now since it's Connie's birthday?"

Connie and her mother are two of the newest residents, and Kari wanted to give the little girl something special. Besides providing a roof over their heads, they helped with resources, pro bono lawyers, or, as Jessica did, working as a private nurse.

"Oh, right," Jess said through a mouthful of quiche. "I forgot. This pregnancy brain thing is no joke. Ladies, assemble the delivery SUV."

"Jessica." The way Jasper said her name landed somewhere between a purr and a growl, stopping her in her tracks.

"Yes, Sir?"

"Jon, let's check if Sara-Jane's awake. I don't need to see my brother going all Dom on my sister." Joanna shuddered, tugging her husband out of the room. Kari heard her muttering, "Nobody needs to know those details about their sibling and best friend."

Jasper carried on, ignoring the sounds of fake vomiting his sister made when she passed him. "Jess, do I need to remind you that you're not to lift a thing?"

"What's Lavender House?" West asked.

Jasper glanced between West and Kari, giving her a subtle nod to explain, then returned his attention to Jess. "Let's finish this discussion in the other room, wife," he said with all the subtlety of an elephant in a china shop.

"Well, I kind of want to find out how all..." Jess waved her hand, gesturing toward them. Kari gave her an 'Are you kidding me, right now?' death stare. "This plays out."

"Let's go, Jess." Jasper placed a protective hand at the small of her back, guiding her out of the room. "You're incorrigible. I swear the impending birth of our twins is making you brattier by the day. Don't forget I'm keeping track."

"Duh. Why do you think I'm doing it?"

"Sweetheart," he growled, and Jess giggled. Their voices and the rest of their conversation drifted away when they entered another room further down the hall.

"I'm glad they figured things out."

"We all are," West said from beside her, making Kari jump because she didn't realize he'd come closer.

"Sorry." He moved a step back.

"No worries. I, uh...scare easily."

"No worries," he said with a smirk. "I'll do my best not to do it again."

"Thanks."

"Will you tell me about Lavender House, or do I have to interrupt the happy couple down the hall to get an answer?" West asked, making a half-assed attempt to follow Jess and Jasper.

"Wait. Unless you want to walk in on them fucking."

This made him chuckle. "It's not the first time."

Kari's eyes widened. *Does he...like to watch?*

"Among other things." When she gasped, he said, "That may be a conversation best left for another day."

Kari's cheeks flushed, and her words came out at a speed reflecting her flustered state. "Yeah...um, Lavender House is where I volunteer. The girls and I bring food there every Sunday. It's become a bit of a tradition since Addie likes to use baking to relieve her writer's block, and Jess stress-baked for two days when she came to her first brunch after coming home, and well, now they do it every week."

West looked around Joanna's kitchen, at the counter laden with an assortment of brunch foods and baked goods. "Which is the stuff you made?"

"Oh, baking isn't my thing, um...," Kari looked for the dish she'd placed on the crowded island, spying it beside Addie's melt-in-your-mouth chocolate chip cookies. "I make a mean rocky road brownie."

Kari's breath caught when West picked up a square and, holding her gaze, popped the marshmallow, walnut, and chocolate treat into his mouth.

"Fucking delicious," he said with a moan. An honest-to-God sex moan came from the sex god, adding to his sex-godliness. Then he licked the chocolate from his fingers and washed his hands. "Let me help the guys load the SUV, then I'll drive you where you need to go."

"You can't." The look on West's face made Kari stumble. "I mean, you can help load Gray's SUV; you can't come with us. There are no men allowed. No matter how upstanding you are."

West stepped closer, and she didn't hate how he encroached on her space. It did, however, mean that his question caught her off guard. "Kari, what kind of place is this?"

She put the lid on the dish after setting aside a few brownies to avoid meeting his inquisitive stare. "It's a home for battered women and their children. I know the woman who runs the place. I started volunteering there after I got my job at Decadent." Kari shrugged, trying to play it off like no big deal.

Even if it's a big deal to her.

"Kari...have you...has someone...?" Rage on her behalf contorted his voice, prompting her to spin and face him, which brought them closer.

"No, I'm fine. There's...." Izzy skipped back into the kitchen, and Kari's words trailed off, unsure of what she planned to say, anyway.

Izzy wore strawberry jam on her chin and butter on her fingers. "I get to go this time, too. Right, Kari? I'll help with Janie later. I want to give Connie her present," she said, licking her fingers.

West gave her space, and Kari scooped Izzy into her arms, preventing her from using her sleeve like a napkin. "Not while wearing your breakfast, you're not. Let's get you cleaned up, kiddo." Kari let Izzy sit on her thigh while she balanced her in front of the sink, helping her wash her hands and wipe her face.

She looked over her shoulder at West, finding his gaze intent on them, and cleared her throat. "Maybe we can also save that story for another time."

West nodded.

"What story?" Izzy shouted.

"A grown-up story, Izz."

"Like the ones on your Kindle? I don't like them. They don't have any pictures."

Kari snorted and glanced back at West, finding him trying not to laugh. "Thank goodness there are no pictures." She turned to her sister and said, "Hey, Izz? Can you go to the washroom while we load the car?"

"Yes…," she yelled, running out of the room. "Guys, it's time to load the car."

"Izzy, no running. Damn, she keeps me on my toes."

"She's pretty cool, though." West held the basket they used to take the food in while Kari packed it. Then everyone filtered back into the kitchen after Izzy's shouts sounded the alarm.

"Thanks. We're in a good place now, and I'd never change having Izzy in my life for anything."

"So, you're her…?"

"Guardian. Raised her through those terrible twos until now."

"I'm sorry. Did your parents pass away?"

"Unfortunately, no. I suppose it's another one of those stories meant for another day."

"Ah, well, I think it's commendable. I hope you're proud; it takes a lot of courage. Not everyone's lucky enough to have someone like you in their lives."

The smile West gave her made Kari's stomach flutter. He took the basket, and her gaze followed him out the door behind Jasper, carrying the rest out to Gray's vehicle.

CHAPTER EIGHT

West

The front door closed, cutting off the girl's laughter. West sighed, thankful for the respite from the overwhelming urge to throw Kari over his shoulder caveman-style and squire her away. He's never had such a visceral reaction to anyone like this.

He, Jasper, Jon, and Gray sat around the dining table. West looked at his friends...his literal brothers-in-arms. Their varying expressions, from the curious look on Jonathan's face to outright superior satisfaction on Jasper's, meant the discussion they're about to have is going to suck for him.

"Jesus Christ, Jasper." West rubbed a hand over his face. Seeing Kari again without a stitch of makeup made it clear there was a greater age difference between them than he'd first believed. The question is, how big? "How old is she?"

"Almost twenty-three."

"Almost twenty-fucking-three?"

"Yeah, her birthday's next month."

Gray and Jon gave him a grunt. Otherwise, they remained silent, letting him and Jasper duke it out. Fuck, West's surprised they didn't pop some popcorn for the show.

"You want to work your matchmaking magic between me and Kari, who's fifteen years younger? How does she even work at the club? Don't you have rules about not hiring anyone under twenty-five?"

Jasper smirked. "Kari has a way of making herself an exception to the rules." His expression turned fond, and West saw Jasper's affection for Kari written all over his face, which led him to insert his foot into his mouth in the most epic way.

"Have you fucked her?"

"Oh, shit," Jonathan muttered, trying and failing to disguise the comment with a cough.

The moment the words left West's mouth, he wanted to take them back. By Jasper's dark look, he should. He also wanted to know the answer, needing to appease this unexpected...jealousy.

"Because it's you, and you're fucked in the head over her already. I'll give you the answer to the stupidest fucking question you've ever asked me because you already know the answer. Jessica is my everything. Kari is like another sister. I helped her out when no one else did. I'll let you kick your own ass for asking such a stupid question once you get to know her."

West already regretted it.

"I look out for Kari, too," Gray said, pointing a finger at West. "Let me stop you from inserting your other foot into your mouth and ask if I've slept with her. I'll save you the trouble and tell you no, I haven't. Brats with daddy issues are your thing, not mine."

"Gee, thanks, asshole." Irrational emotions warred inside West. Guilt for not being there for Kari because Jasper and Gray helped her in his stead. *Fuck*. He wanted to hurt them and thank them at the same time.

What the fuck is wrong with him?

West never reacted to such extremes about someone he's attracted to. He's had more open relationships than monogamous ones. He's not a jealous man. Not until now. Not until...this woman.

Why now? Why her?

Jasper interrupted his inner spiral. "I know what you're going through right now...something similar to what I did when I found Jess again. I didn't let it discourage me. It made me fight for her and for us even more."

"Fuck, I'm glad you and Jess worked everything out."

"You and me both, brother."

"Alright, what's the 4-1-1?"

"There's not much for me to say. Those are Kari's stories to tell you, not mine."

"Fair enough. I haven't forgotten that Jess's stories were for her to tell, so I get it," West said with a pointed stare of his own.

"You got me there." Jasper shrugged, and then a smile lit up his face. "And look how it worked out for me. You told me you're ready to take a chance. Kari is worth the chance."

"I know."

"Told you," Jon said to Gray, then they high-fived, and money exchanged hands.

"Fuckers." West ignored the two stooges and focused on Jasper. "Tell me everything you can, then."

"You've met her sister, Izzy, and I'm sure you've surmised Kari is her guardian. I'm sure you've also figured out Kari's done this on her own. She's resilient, kind, and a giving friend. She may be young, but she's lived the life of someone twice her age."

Jasper shared a look with Gray, who nodded after their silent exchange. "I'll tell you why she ended up on Decadent's doorstep demanding to speak to the owner, all sass and fire, like the brat she is."

All four grunted in agreement.

"It's one reason Gray and I looked out for her like we did."

Jasper steepled his fingers, and West knew he'd get some sound advice. Whether he wanted it or not. "West, everyone at this table is more than equipped to retrieve any necessary information. I'm suggesting that you get it from the source this time. It'll change your life if you do."

West may have contemplated *researching* after their tête-à-tête at the club, needing to learn everything about Kari. Jasper's gaze shuttered. "Ask her, West. She needs someone she can confide in and depend on."

"Life changing, huh?" West asked, still skeptical.

"The best kind."

"Listen to him, man," Gray chimed in. "Addie is everything to me, and we met because of Jasper."

"It's true," Jonathan said in the quiet way he has. "Joanna is the other half of my soul. It's no joke when Jas tells people he'd like to introduce them."

"Yeah, even when it's my baby sister," Jasper said to his brother-in-law, bumping his shoulder. He sipped his coffee, then leaned his elbows on the table.

"Understand, I weighed the pros and cons of introducing you and Kari for quite some time, and I know that you're what the other needs. I saw how you looked at her the night of Gray and Addie's engagement."

West scoffed, not ready to face what everyone else considered obvious. "Oh, yeah? How?"

Jasper studied him, his intense stare enough to make a nun shift with guilt. It's fucking unnerving when words hit like a punch to the gut. "You looked at her like she's already yours." He reached over and gripped West's forearm, his words harsh and to the point. "Kari isn't Maggie."

He needed to hear those words from Jasper. During their rescue mission, he confided that things between him and Maggie had fractured in the last couple of years of their relationship. The guilt after her death almost consumed him.

"I know, you know this."

West gave him a sharp nod. "Tell me. I promise I'll ask Kari for the rest."

Jasper took a deep breath and ripped off the bandage. "Kari witnessed her ex-boyfriend's murder."

"Fuck." West's voice grew loud, and Jasper raised his hand to stop him.

"Like everyone who works for me, I did a thorough background check, and my contact at the station told me to get a hold of a detective. It took the guy a few weeks to get back to me. Until then, I didn't know the full extent of what had happened. Once I did, the precautions Kari took when she left work made a lot more sense. From then on, Gray and I kept an eye on her."

"The night it all went down, Kari hid in a closet, and the killer didn't find her. With the guy in the system, she identified him, and even though the cops did their best, his trail went cold. Until six months ago, when they found the guy floating in the East River and the case resolved itself."

"You don't believe it is?"

"There's no evidence to suggest otherwise."

"What do your instincts say?" They depended on Jasper's instincts more than once during their missions back in the day.

Jasper shrugged. "I don't believe Kari's in any further danger."

West's worry eased.

"Stay for a while. Get to know Kari. I promise you won't regret it."

"You know me, Mum would've called you a *randie*, always trying to put people together." West's laughter dissolved into a sigh. "I'm interested. So fucking interested. If Kari doesn't care about the age difference, then I won't either."

Like a synchronized swim team, their heads swiveled toward the door when they heard it open.

"We're back," Jess called. She entered the dining room first, one hand on her rounded stomach and the other supporting her lower back. Jasper leaped to his feet, ushering his wife into the chair beside him.

"Are you okay, sweetheart?"

"I'm fine. It seems Twin One and Twin Two are holding a wrestling match today, and the ring is my kidneys."

Jasper wrapped his hands around his wife's protruding belly and kissed her forehead. "Let me reason with them." And damn, if West didn't get a little swoony when Jas leaned forward and let his deep voice rumble against Jess's stomach. "Girls," he admonished. "Give your mom a break. It's time for a nap."

Jasper kept his hands on Jess's stomach, and the rippling waves of two babies sharing a small space calmed. "There."

"It worked? They stopped kicking?" West asked with amazement.

Jess and Jasper hit a serious snag in their marriage a few years ago. She left him with nothing more than a note, and when Jess sought West out to do the tattoo sleeves adorning her arms now, she confessed the real reason she walked out on Jasper, hoping her confession would help her mental block. Guilt does like to fuck with a person.

When West helped Jasper rescue his niece from Ukraine, he and Jess reunited. Something about absence makes the heart grow fonder and the sperm more potent with their twins due at the end of summer.

Jess gave West an indulgent smile. "They sure did. Ugh, I can't believe I'm jealous because they're already daddy's girls, but it's like damn witchcraft when he gets them to settle with his voice alone. I'm powerless not to be amazed by it."

West got snagged by the *daddy* comment when Kari entered the room with Addie, Izzy, and Joanna trailing behind her. *Fuck,* she's stunning in a pair of leggings and a burgundy sweater, her dark hair loose about her shoulders, framing her features in such a way as to steal his breath.

"Did you boys enjoy your bonding time?" Kari asked, taking the chair next to Jess and across from him.

When Jon and Grey muttered, "You bet." And, "We sure did." Joanna and Addie gave them odd looks while West ignored them, keeping his gaze fixed on Kari.

When he caught her eye, Izzy tugged Kari's sleeve, gaining her attention. "What's up, Izz?"

Izzy peered up at Kari with the greyest eyes he's ever seen. The kid's halo of blonde curls made her appear angelic, though West knew a little devil lurked beneath her adorable veneer.

"I'm SOOO...hungry," she said with the perfected dramatic flair of a five-year-old. "Did they save me food?"

"I don't know, Izz. Did you remind the boys to save you some?"

This must be a game they play with Izzy. "Yesss..." she shouted while Jasper, Gray, and Jon searched around and under the cleared table.

"Hm...I was kind of starving today."

Izzy squealed. "There's no way you ate..." Izzy looked at her hands, raising each finger, doing her best to make her point, holding up all ten. "...this many cinnamon buns, Uncle Jas."

"You got me, Izz." Jasper pulled a plate with a cinnamon bun the size of Izzy's head from behind his back and set it in front of her wide-eyed face.

Kari made a noise, drawing West's attention, laughing when he caught her sending eye-daggers Jasper's way. "Karma is on its way, boss man, taking the form of the twin daughters your wife's carrying."

West's laughter joined everyone else's as Jasper paled.

CHAPTER NINE

West

Izzy's head drooped onto Kari's shoulder. "Is it time to go, Izz?"

Izzy yawned. "Yeah."

"Let's get your coat and shoes on, and we'll head out."

"Can I escort you home?" West asked, eager for a little more time with them.

Kari offered him a sassy yet tired smile after zipping Izzy into her coat. She leaned in. "We aren't at the 'knowing where I live' stage yet. However, I look forward to next week's brunch."

"Me too, Wes. You're cool, and I like your pictures," Izzy said, pointing to his ink.

"Tattoos, Izz." Kari corrected.

West got down on her level and looked at Kari's younger sister, whose resemblance was unmistakable despite their different hair and eye color. "You have such beautiful hair, lass. It makes me want to ruffle it, but my mum taught me to always get permission first. Can I ruffle your curls, sweet Izz?"

Izzy gave him a scrutinizing look for a five-year-old, then nodded. "Yes, be careful, okay?"

West couldn't imagine being anything but, and with Kari's eyes on him, he reached out and fluffed the soft curls framing her face. "I promise to always be careful with you, Izz." His gaze shifted upward, meeting Kari's. West hoped she saw the sincerity in his eyes because it included her, too.

"We'd better get going," she said after they stared at one another for a few more seconds.

West bent his head and smirked at the breathy tone Kari used. It thrilled him to know he affected her as much as she affected him. He tamped it down when everyone else said their goodbyes. Addie and Gray had already left, taking the ninety-minute drive to get to their farm in Connecticut.

"Alright, lass." West didn't have a problem working for it. He held the door open for them, watching them head up the drive and down the sidewalk out of sight. When he closed the door, he turned and faced the knowing looks from his friends.

West passed on the offered ride back to the brownstone with Jasper and Jess, choosing to walk to work out his excess energy.

It wasn't enough, and when he got back to the apartment, he changed into his running gear and headed toward the Promenade. He ran along the waterfront with Lady Liberty in the background, happy to be in the city he once called home. Perhaps he'd call it home again.

The next morning, West joined Jess and Jasper for coffee. Despite the grocery delivery arriving at his door at the same time as theirs, it's quickly becoming their morning ritual. And when Jasper lowered his steaming mug to mention that Kari worked the early shift at the club the following night, and that maybe he'd like to drop by, West made plans to go, hopeful Kari might join him once she finished her shift.

West arrived at Decadent and used his code to enter the private lounge. He didn't expect anyone else to be there, and finding Everly Hayes sitting on a club chair, polishing one of her knee-high Doc Martins, caught him off guard for a second. It's been too long since they'd seen each other, and West missed their camaraderie.

"Don't you have obedient puppies who polish those boots for you with their tongues?"

Everly was the lone female on their military team, one of the most decorated and dedicated soldiers he's ever known. She and West were the team's snipers, which meant they spent a lot of time together and got to know each other well.

"Hey...Sharpie." A rare smile crossed Everly's stunning features when she used the nickname given to him years ago. She dropped her boot to the floor and stood. They embraced each other in a backslapping hug. "I heard a rumor you returned. Is it for good?"

"Still undecided." The moment West said the words, a vision of Kari filled his mind, and they left a bitter taste in his mouth. Returning to Glasgow didn't appeal to him anymore. Yet he's nowhere near ready to admit it to himself, let alone anyone else.

Everly dropped back into her chair and picked up the boot she'd polished to a military shine, pulling it on and lacing it up.

"Seriously, don't you have a stable of willing subbies to do your bidding?"

Everly peered up at him with a glare, then got to her feet. The thick soles of her boots brought her eyes level with his.

"I have a naughty pup who needs to be punished, and since he loves to lick my leather, I'm going to offer him the opportunity to hump my boot dirty in front of everyone for the reward of licking it clean."

"Devious, Mistress Eve."

"Only the best for my pup," she said with a wink. "I'll leave the space for you to do your thing."

West didn't mean for her to rush off. "You don't have to leave on my account, Eve."

She adjusted the collar of her jacket in the full-length mirror, then threw him a smirk over her shoulder. "I'm not. My pup's waiting for me. Catch you later. Oh, and West?"

"Yeah?"

"Kari's special. Don't fuck it up."

West's eyes widened with surprise. "You too?"

"Night, Sharpie." With those parting words, Everly closed the door.

West headed toward the front, hoping to catch Kari at reception. When he reached the lobby, he came to a staggering stop, even leaning against the wall to remain upright.

And West believed he dressed with provocation in mind.

He had nothing on Kari.

She wore a red full-body latex catsuit and tied her hair in a high ponytail, the extended length reaching her ass. A black leather corset cinched her tiny waist, making it appear smaller, and the stiletto-heeled thigh-high leather boots completed her sexy-as-fuck outfit.

He's fucked.

Wholly and utterly fucked for this woman. Once he got his dick mostly under control, West rounded the corner and stepped up to Kari's desk.

She raised her gaze from the tablet, and her jaw dropped. *Yes...take it all in, little girl.* On top of the tattoos covering eighty percent of his body, he also possessed several piercings, and Kari's getting an eyeful of a couple right now.

He dressed to entice, and by the look on Kari's face, he succeeded.

West wore leather pants tucked into his combat boots. He commissioned one of Gray's handcrafted leather harnesses, and every part of him on display captivated Kari's attention.

West wanted more than her eyes on him. He wanted her hands on him.

"*Sweet Jesus.* Covered in tattoos and pierced."

She may have mumbled, but West heard her loud and clear. He leaned in and said, "These aren't my only piercings."

She gaped at him for thirty seconds until her professionalism kicked in. "Uh...good evening, Mr. Sharpe. Will you be needing a private room this evening?"

"I didn't realize we're on such formal terms, Ms. Davidson. Will you be joining me if I reserve a private room?"

Kari dared to roll her eyes, and West pictured her over his knee, turning her ass the same shade as her red latex bodysuit. "I try to treat all guests professionally upon their arrival. I don't play during working hours."

A surge of possessiveness hit West, and he almost demanded to know who she played with during her non-working hours. He shoved the urge down. Kari has every right to do what she wants and with whom she wants. "Well, I'm more than a guest, and Mr. Sharpe is not what I want to be called. Unless...."

"Unless what?" Kari asked, moving closer, taking the bait.

"Unless you want to enjoy a game of the *Professor and his Naughty Student*, I'm more than happy to get another look at you in your naughty schoolgirl outfit while you call me Mr. Sharpe and ask what you can do to get a better grade."

Kari's cheeks heated, and she shook her head in exasperation.

West leaned over the counter, separating them. "Alright, what do you want to call me?"

She countered with a bratty, "What do you want to be called?"

West stroked the inside of her wrist, and she leaned over until they met in the middle. Her lips parted, and West heard her make the softest little moan. His hand moved from her wrist to her jaw, and he cupped her face. "We both know what I want to be called. It's why you want to say it, don't you, little girl?"

The moment his lips ghosted over hers, Kari rocked his world and flipped it on its axis. "I prefer baby girl, Daddy."

A lightning bolt of desire shot straight to his cock. Their breaths mingled, fanning each other's lips. "You're fucking beautiful, baby girl."

Kari's eyes darkened with desire.

"West. I didn't expect you this evening," Jasper said, appearing at the counter beside them.

Kari jumped, and West didn't like the space she put between them. "I just finished checking him in."

"Is that what you were doing?" Jasper asked, then turned to West. "And here I thought you tried to sneak in without saying hello."

"You know damn well when I arrived. I used the staff entrance," West growled, still stuck on the fact that he's no longer touching Kari. "Are you cock-blocking me right now?" West asked out of the side of his mouth.

"No, I'm giving you a helping hand. Kari," Jasper said, turning his attention toward her. "West needs to get reacquainted with Decadent. He hasn't attended our club for a very long time. I'd like you to give him a tour and show him what's new. When you finish, take the rest of the night off, maybe have some fun, and make use of...the facilities."

"B-but, boss man," Kari sputtered.

"No buts. Simone will take over the desk, and you've more than earned a bit of downtime. Go show this guy what he's missing out on."

"I...um okay."

Good girl. West wanted but dared not say.

"Hey, Kari," Simone said when she arrived to take over. West didn't miss how the other woman's eyes trailed over him, and then she gave his girl a playful nudge with her shoulder. *Yeah, she's his.* His subconscious already claimed her, waiting for the rest of him to catch up.

"Damn, girl, enjoy the rest of your night," Simone said, turning to check in the guests behind him.

"Yes, what Simone said. I'm going home to find my wife and have some fun of my own. Have a good night, you two."

When Jasper walked away, Kari looked over at him and offered a hesitant smile. "Shall we?"

West gestured for her to lead the way. "After you."

Kari inclined her head, moving past him. West never knew he'd be such a simp for someone until he met this woman. Fuck, he'd follow her anywhere and everywhere.

CHAPTER TEN

Kari

*O*hMyGodOhMyGodOhMyGod...

Kari's pulse raced. She called Weston Sharpe, *Daddy*, and she fucking loved it. Judging by the smoldering look West gave her, he really liked it, too.

West followed her toward the door held open by Tony, the club's head of security. Then he stepped into their path and stopped them from entering.

Kari smirked when Tony's dark gaze landed on West. "You doing okay, Kari?" His stern demeanor hid the giant teddy bear beneath.

"Yeah, Tony, I'm good." She patted the big man's chest with affection, and a rumbling growl came from the man behind her.

"I expect her to be treated with respect...sir." Tony glared over Kari's shoulder.

"I agree. Kari deserves the utmost respect. Which is what she will receive from me."

Oh, wow....

West pressed closer, his body heat seeping beneath the latex she wore, and she leaned back against him. Tony stared him down a moment longer, nodded, and moved out of their way.

"Everyone here looks out for you. Are all your friends and family like that?"

Kari shrugged. "Before finding a job at Decadent? No, people never looked out for me...not like the way they do here. Jasper runs a tight ship, and those who work for him are good people who take care of each other. As for family, it's Izzy and me. Why?"

"Nothing, it's just...."

"Just what?"

"I'm dealing with some internal conflict because I want to be the one who looks out for you."

Kari tried to use laughter to brush off the literal romance novel material spilling from his lips. "You can always join my squad. It takes a village to keep my shit together."

She moved to walk past him, and West stopped her with a hand on her elbow. He tilted his chin and captured her gaze. Kari got lost staring into his silvery-blue eyes.

"No. It means people care about you and want what's best for you." He rubbed his thumb over the latex covering her forearm, and Kari cursed the layer separating them, wanting his touch on her bare skin.

Every inch of her bare skin.

"I'm still getting used to everyone caring." The effect his touch had on her showed in the breathy way her words came out of her mouth.

"Well, get used to one more, baby girl."

Is it getting hotter in here?

Kari needed to get her breathing under control while her heart and brain fought over how fast is too fast to fall for someone. What better way to accomplish it than by flaunting her catwalk skills? Well, there are better ways, but she used what she had.

Kari gave West a sultry smile, then spun away. The short hallway leading into the club gave her the perfect setting. After years of strutting down a runway, she walked in front of West with confidence, and she relished the way his gaze roved over every inch of her.

"Are you trying to make me break my promise to Tony? Because you're making me want to disrespect you real fucking good right now."

Kari giggled, adding a little jiggle to her hips when she landed each step and heard West groan behind her. She caught the tip of her index finger between her teeth and peered over her shoulder. "You gonna tell me about the other piercings you have? There's none on your face or ears."

The low thump of the bass grew louder when they emerged by the bar on the upper floor. The club upheld a strict two-drink limit if you wanted to play. "Drink?" And Kari wanted to play.

"Yeah, I'll have one." A thrill shot through her. One drink meant West wanted to play, too.

When they reached the bar, she shivered with anticipation. He placed his hands on the sleek wood on either side of her, keeping a barrier between her and everyone else. They ordered. Kari chose a glass of champagne while West chose a neat Macallan. With their drinks in hand, she turned in his arms and met his interested gaze.

Kari sipped from her glass, letting the bubbles burst against her tongue. She eyed his wicked-looking nipple piercings secured between the rings of his leather harness and wanted to lean in and flick them with her tongue. Bet he'd taste fantastic.

Down girl.

Kari leaned back on her elbows, and West's hands slid closer until he stroked her arms with his thumbs. The simple touch aroused her even more.

"Hm...." Her gaze skated down his exposed, toned abs. "No belly button piercing either." Carrying on with the conversational interrogation, "Gotta be a cock piercing...Prince Albert?"

He let out a low, guttural grunt. "Nope."

"You do that a lot."

"What?"

"Grunt."

"It's because you're a wee bit of a brat, lass."

"And you...like my brattiness?"

"Aye. I more than like it, if we're being honest."

"Honest is good." Kari grew more emboldened. She straightened, bringing their bodies closer. When West didn't stop her, she trailed her free hand over his chest, grazing his tight nipples with her fingertips. She moved her hand down between them and wrapped her fingers around his erection.

West's very hard, very long, very thick cock fit her hand perfectly.

Fuck.

"Fuck."

She thought it; he said it.

"What do you think you're doing, baby girl?"

"You know, I'm not sure. I've never been this forward with someone. And I didn't get your consent. I'm sorry." Kari tried to let go. West stopped her, placing his hand over hers. He pressed her palm harder against him.

"You're right, you didn't, but you have my permission, lass. Don't stop. I don't shy away from public displays." West applied pressure with his middle finger along hers, and with his lips next to her ear, he asked, "Have you ever heard of a Jacob's Ladder?"

Kari remembered one of her model friends talking about being with a guy with one, and her eyes widened because with the pressure of his hand against hers, she felt the bars piercing the underside of his cock. "Um...I believe I know what it is."

His breath fanned her cheek. "If you're a good girl, I'll let you get close and personal with my cock. Let you count every rung." West squeezed her hand, making her squeeze his dick, and he rocked against her.

This man is all kinds of temptation.

She's never engaged in public sex, and now she fought the urge to beg West to strip her bare and lay her out on top of the bar despite it being a club no-no and a health and safety violation.

West moved her hand to his hip. "Easy, lass. We've got plenty of time." He shifted and leaned against the bar, staying close. "What about this tour you're supposed to give me? I'll admit, I'm well-versed in the lifestyle and know my particular kinks, as well as the equipment required to partake in them. So why don't you show me something you'd like?"

"Hm...alright." Kari tapped her lips with the fingers she had pressed against his clothed cock – *his huge, fucking cock...how many rungs did his ladder have? Three? Four? Ugh, focus, Kari.* Instead, she stalled.

"Um...why don't you tell me some of your kinks? What if I like the opposite of what you like?"

"Darlin', I doubt we'd be standing here like this if they didn't align." He teased her hairline with the tip of his nose. When his lips reached her ear, he said, "Show me...I bet I'm right."

"What are we betting?" Kari looked around, deciding what to reveal to this man.

"You give me your number if I'm right."

On the other side of the upper floor, where the private kink-themed rooms were located, Kari recognized the two couples she'd checked in earlier, heading into a room with a viewing gallery for a more intimate voyeuristic experience.

She'd picked up on their chemistry, finding all four attractive, and when the light turned green above the viewing room's door, wanting voyeurs to their sexual play, she knew what she wanted to *show* West.

"Deal." Kari finished her drink, and West did the same. They set their empty glasses on the bar, and she held out her hand. "Come with me."

West entwined their fingers, and Kari led him to the narrow walkway the staff used to avoid the crowd. The security guard stationed there let them by when he realized it was Kari.

Zane stood at the station on the other side. The DM on duty tonight monitored the private rooms, and those who came and went from them.

"Hey, Z," Kari said, snagging Zane's attention.

"Evening, Kari. You're not at guest services tonight?" His observant dark eyes did not miss their clasped hands or how close West stood beside her.

"I'm giving a tour to Mr. Sharpe and taking him into the viewing room. I also have the rest of the night off. Have a good night." Kari moved to step past Zane, though the warning tone and the way he said her name made her freeze in place, causing West to tighten his grip on her hand.

"Kari.... You know the viewing rooms are for more than just viewing. If you intend to take part, I'll need to check in with you like every other guest who enters these rooms."

"You're right. Sorry, Z."

"Are you a willing participant?"

Her cheeks heated. "Yes, I'm a willing participant."

"As am I," West said, not waiting for Zane to ask.

"I bet you are," he said with a lingering glance. "Alright, you two, have fun. I'm sure there will be others joining you." He gestured to the door with the green light. "You can head on in."

West leaned in close as they headed toward the door. "Baby girl...I guarantee I'll get your phone number when we leave this room. I love to show off, almost as much as I love to watch. The question is...which one's your favorite to do?"

"You mean the answer isn't obvious?" West's chuckle sounded wicked in her ear, sending a shiver down her spine.

"Damn. A bratty lass is hands down my number one favorite thing."

"Alright, we'll see if you get my number by how this all plays out. Satisfaction is key, Mr. Sharpe."

She felt the rumble of his laughter against her back. "Keep it up, baby girl; punishing a brat is my second favorite thing."

Kari decided now was a good time to ease up on her brattiness when they stepped into the viewing room. She and West moved to the far corner, where a couch ran the length of the back wall. Footlights encircled the space, keeping it in shadows, with the focus on those on the other side of the glass.

West pulled her back to his front, his warm breath teasing the sensitive skin behind her ear. His body molded to hers, and his hard length pressed against her ass.

The door opened, and more people entered, sending curious glances their way. Then they, too, focused on the foursome beyond the glass.

West's grip on her hips tightened. "This looks promising." It didn't matter how many others surrounded them. Kari lost focus, and when her eyelids drifted closed, and her head tipped back, she didn't care about the show happening in front of her anymore because Weston Sharpe surrounded her.

The man has muscles for days, and he's huge *ev-er-y-where*. Kari arched and circled her hips, eliciting a groan from his lips.

West's hand moved to the zipper at the base of her spine. His fingers played with the tab. "Is this okay?" Kari nodded, and he nipped her ear, the arousing sting going straight to her core. "I need your words, baby girl. You say the word, and we stop. Okay?"

It's been far too long since she allowed another person to give her pleasure, and she wanted this man to be the one to give it, more than she'd like to admit. Yet she admitted it all the same. "Yes...I want this. I want you."

West tugged the zipper down, his fingers tracing the skin he exposed, pausing when he found her bare and slick between her thighs. She shivered when he dragged his chin along her throat until his lips pressed to her ear. "No panties? You play dirty, baby girl."

Kari reached back and looped her arm around his neck. She turned her head, letting her lips graze his cheek. "I can't help it. You've made me want to misbehave."

"And that makes me like you even more. Now, pay attention to the show. Daddy's going to make you come."

Kari lifted her head and opened her eyes, shifting her focus to what was happening between the foursome on the other side of the glass.

They'd tied the brunette woman to the bed. Both men knelt between her legs, feasting on her pussy, pleasuring her while the blonde woman dropped her lace panties and seated herself on the brunette's face.

West kept one arm banded around her waist while his other hand dipped between her legs. Kari's limbs shook when the calloused pad of his fingertip brushed against her clit.

"Fuck, you're wet for me, baby girl. You're going to come all over my hand, aren't you?"

"Yes."

The scene in the other room intensified. The men stood between the brunette's spread thighs, kissing with such passion, licking her orgasm from one another's lips. Then they lined up. The first fucked into the brunette's pussy, and the second man worked his cock into his ass. The blonde rode the brunette in a relentless pursuit of her own release.

As hot as the foursome was, she was more interested in the man bringing her closer to her own orgasm. Kari turned her head and bit West's jaw and whispered the word "More" against his skin. She didn't care about what happened around them or in the other room. She wanted him. "Please, Daddy."

Kari rolled her hips, and West pressed two fingers inside her. He twisted his hand, rubbing against her G-spot while his thumb circled her clit.

"Yes...."

Moans echoed around them. The others in the audience found their pleasure as the foursome on the other side of the glass found theirs.

"Listen to them getting off, baby girl. I want your cries of pleasure drowning theirs. Come for me."

West's fingers pumped in and out of her faster, his thumb a steady pressure on her clit. "I...I'm coming...I-" Kari's body seized, and her pussy clenched and pulsed around his fingers while she cried out in ecstasy.

"Fuck yes." West kissed her neck, sucking and nipping at her skin. He didn't stop, and her first orgasm rolled into a second, catching her off guard as she shouted his name. "Such a good girl."

Kari collapsed against him, and through dazed eyes, watched West suck her release from his fingers. "Looks like you know how to play dirty, too."

"Fuck, you taste sweet. Did I win the bet? Do I get your number, baby girl?"

West made her come in front of a room full of strangers, and his focus remained on her and getting her digits. "Yeah, I think you've earned my number," she said, brushing her lips against his.

West adjusted the latex and pulled her zipper back into place, then guided her around the others toward the door. "My phone's locked in my dressing room, and I need someone to help me out of this catsuit. You game?"

"Lead the way, baby."

CHAPTER ELEVEN

West

West wanted Kari with a kind of desperation he's never experienced for another person.

He followed her, devouring the sight of her in all that red latex while her taste lingered on his tongue. They reached the elevator, and no sooner did they step inside than West had her pinned to the back wall. "Fuck, I want to do more than taste you. Will you let me, baby girl?"

The elevator pinged, and the doors slid open. Kari slipped from beneath his arm, giving him a coy look. "My dressing room is this way."

West prowled after her.

Kari stopped at the door at the end of the hall. "I've got a private dressing room because of my extensive wardrobe. Sometimes I'll change mid-shift unless I've chosen to wear something like this, which, once I'm in, I'm in for the night. Well, until someone helps me out of it, anyway."

West didn't want anyone else helping her get in or out of her outfits. "Who's helping you in and out of your outfits, baby girl?" He didn't recall ever sounding this...*growly* either.

Ever.

When did he become such a possessive alpha-hole?

Kari rolled her eyes. "Ugh, the women I work with give me a hand with a zipper, buckle, or clasp when I need it. You know you're quite territorial for someone who hasn't even gotten my number yet."

What can he say when she's right? Which turned him on even more.

West closed the door behind them, and Kari's scent surrounded him. Floral and soft, he found it calming....

It also made his cock rock-fucking-hard.

He looked around the small space. The wall to his left housed built-in shelves filled with accessories, and in the far corner were two racks of outfits. A counter covered in makeup and hair products sat to his right with a lit mirror mounted above it.

Kari cleared her throat. "The...uh...door automatically locks in case you wanted to know ."

"It didn't cross my mind because if anyone tried to open that door without permission, they'd be dealing with me."

West caught the hitch in her breath and the way her nipples puckered beneath the latex. *Perhaps his irrational possessiveness is turning her on just as much.*

Kari's hands moved to her hips, striking a pose, and jarring him from his thoughts. "You gonna help a girl out or what?"

West lowered to his knees. "Anything for you, baby girl. Hold on to my shoulder." Kari did. He lifted her left foot to rest on his thigh and lowered the zipper.

He slipped the boot off her foot, exposing her sexy, red-painted toenails. His thumb pressed against her delicate arch, massaging her instep to loosen the muscles held captive in her high heels all evening. She moaned. West set her left foot down, then he gave her right foot the same tender treatment. He held her gaze and lowered to kiss the top of each foot. She gasped. "No one's ever...."

When Kari reached for the front of her leather waist corset, West stopped her. "You asked for my help, so let me."

His fingers skimmed the top of the corset, right below her breasts. He gripped both sides and worked each eyelet hook free until it dropped to the floor with a thud.

Kari lifted her chin, giving him access to the zipper at the base of her throat. He tugged it down, exposing a slice of pale, smooth skin.

West reached between her legs and pulled the zipper the rest of the way. Kari peeled off the latex, like shedding a second skin, leaving her bare body on breathtaking display for him.

Desperate to drop to his knees and bury his tongue inside her, Kari beat him to it. She placed her hands on his thighs and met his gaze. "May I?"

West stared into her dark brown eyes and cupped her chin. "This isn't a tit-for-tat exchange, baby girl. Making you come is all the satisfaction I need."

"It isn't...I mean, I want...ugh." Kari's bottom lip jutted out in a sexy pout. "I want to know how you have your cock pierced, and you promised I could get up close and personal with it. I want to explore and taste you."

West teased her bottom lip with his thumb. "How can I refuse?" He tipped her chin with his index finger and held her gaze. "You're going to do what Daddy tells you, aren't you, baby girl?"

"Yes," she moaned.

"Yes, what?"

Her blown-out pupils made her warm brown eyes look like dark, endless pools. She tipped her head back further and said, "Yes, Daddy."

West didn't think he'd ever stop wanting her to call him that.

"Good girl. Undo the button on my pants. Show me how well you follow directions."

Kari's fingers glided up his thighs. His muscles rippled and flexed beneath her touch. She paused the journey of her hands when her fingers framed the thick bulge of his cock, currently trying to bust through his zipper.

She held his gaze. "Yes, Daddy." She slid her hands over his length, caressing him...testing the boundaries of his orders until she flicked the button open.

"Brat," he admonished. "The zipper next. Careful," he cautioned. "My cock is eager." When she lowered the zipper, his pants bunched around his thighs, and his erection strained against his black boxer briefs.

Kari stared at him and waited.

"Such a good girl. You've earned your reward. Take my cock out."

She took her sweet time, tracing the outline of his dick, his piercings visible beneath the stretched cotton. She tugged the waistband of his briefs down, exposing him at last.

His dick twitched as Kari's gaze traveled down his length, counting the five metal frenum piercings on the underside of his cock. With the one below his crown, the one in the middle, and the one at his base being thicker gauges than the other two.

"Like what you see?"

She licked her lips, not hiding her hunger for him, then lifted her gaze to meet his. "Yes."

West rocked his hips, shifting closer. "You can touch," he said, stifling a moan when she did, sliding her fingers over each rung of his ladder.

Kari's little pink tongue darted across her bottom lip, leaving it glistening with her saliva. "Bet they feel amazing."

"I'm told they do," he said, and Kari's eyes narrowed.

However, she didn't demand who said such things...no, in retaliation, Kari leaned forward with her naughty, pink tongue extended and ran it from the first rung at his base, licking over each one until she lapped at the one below his crown.

Then the little minx sucked the head of his cock between her lips, lapping up the precum from his slit.

Her moan vibrated down the length of his shaft.

West shuddered, holding onto his control by a thread. He pinched Kari's jaw and pulled free of her mouth. "Did I say you could taste?"

"No, Daddy." Her voice was only a whisper.

"Naughty girl. Daddy's going to tell you a story. I want you to close your eyes and picture it."

Her eyelids fluttered closed.

"Those larger gauges are strategic. When I take you, bent over on all fours, the one below my crown will drag across your G-spot each time I slide into you. When I'm pounding your pussy deep, the one in the middle is gonna take over, pressing on your sweet spot, taking you right to the edge."

Kari shuddered and rocked her hips, seeking pressure on her clit; air won't satisfy.

"Now, the thickest one at my base...it's for me. When I sink inside you nice and deep, and it slides past your pussy lips, plugging my cum inside you, holding it there until I decide to let it spill from your opening."

"Oh, fuck yes, West. I want it. I want it so badly. Please...."

"I can tell, baby girl. There's a copy of my latest test results on my phone. They're negative, but I can't show you until I grab my stuff. Right now, I'd love nothing more than to fill your belly with my cum, but I won't until you've seen my tests. Tonight, Daddy is going to come on your tits."

"I haven't been with anyone for over two years. My results are negative, too."

"Thank you for telling me, baby girl. For your reward, you get to explore Daddy's cock with your mouth a little longer."

West let go of her jaw, and his hand moved to the back of Kari's head. His hold remained gentle yet firm when he lowered her mouth to his dick. He stopped, holding his cock a breath away from her parted lips. "Look at me." The moment she did, he said, "Tap my leg twice if you need me to stop."

"Yes, Daddy." Her lips caressed his tip.

"Bratty girls get their asses turned a fiery shade of red, baby girl."

"Sorry, Daddy," she said, doing the same damn thing.

West gripped the base of Kari's ponytail tighter. "Open." Her lips parted, and West guided the first couple of inches into her mouth. "Swirl your tongue around me. Yes...explore my cock. Discover what Daddy likes."

Fuck, it's everything. Everything Kari did, he liked.

"Now, close your lips around me and suck. Take all you can."

West wanted to keep his eyes on Kari while she swallowed his cock, yet the moment her lips sealed around his crown and she hollowed her cheeks to suck him deep, it became too much.

His head dropped back, and his eyes closed. He let out a deep groan of ecstasy when his crown dipped into the opening of her throat.

He fought his encroaching release, returning his gaze to Kari's, needing to connect on every level...needing to watch her take him deep. "Fuuuck," he said when she gagged and swallowed around him. "Fuck, that feels good, baby girl. Can you take more of me?"

"MmHm."

"Daddy's going to fuck your face. How do you stop me if it gets to be too much?" West pulled her off his cock, letting her answer.

"I tap your leg twice. Like this," Kari said, demonstrating two brisk taps against his thigh.

West didn't hesitate, shoving his cock back into her mouth, holding it there while he praised her and issued another command. "Such a good, obedient girl for Daddy. Play with your pussy until you come. Let me feel you moaning around my cock when you do."

Kari's hands dipped between her spread thighs. He let her suckle the head of his dick while she circled her clit and shoved three fingers into her cunt.

"Yes, lass. Fuck your tight little cunt. Imagine my cock filling you like no one else ever has." West worked his cock in and out of her mouth, sliding deeper. He used both hands to hold her head in place.

Kari gurgled, hummed, and gagged around him, saliva dripping onto her perky little tits. The hard points of her nipples became shiny with spit. Any minute now, he was going to add his cum to the mix.

Fuck.

Her moans grew to a fevered pitch, and West's orgasm barreled down his spine while his balls drew tight to his body. The moment Kari screamed around him with her orgasm, he sank into her throat one more time until her nose pressed against the trimmed hair at his groin.

"Swallow around me, baby girl. Milk me right to the edge. Yes...you're coming like a dream for Daddy."

Kari gripped his thigh when West cut off her air. His orgasm worked its way up his cock. He pulled free from the wet heat of her mouth, stroking his length once, and his cum rocketed from his tip, splashing against Kari's chin, throat, and tits while she gasped for the breath he'd denied her, still riding the wave of her orgasm.

"Look at you covered in my cum. Fucking beautiful," West said, memorizing the mascara-laced tears tracking down her cheeks, her swollen lips, and the copious amount of cum covering her throat and breasts.

"Thank you, Daddy." Then, Kari made his dick twitch back to life, pulling the three fingers still jammed in her cunt and soaked with her juices free, massaging their combined release into her breasts.

Kari whimpered, and West snatched her hand by the wrist, staring at her shiny fingertips, slick with their combined release. "Fuck. If you don't stop teasing me, baby girl, I'm going to bend you over this counter and fuck you. I'm not fucking in your dressing room, our first time."

Kari whimpered again, and West kissed her lips, coaxing her toward the counter, turning on the water in the little sink. He washed their hands, then grabbed a clean cloth and cleaned her throat and breasts.

He righted his pants and then helped Kari wash her face and remove her makeup. She pulled her natural hair from the tight bun when she removed her hairpiece. West rubbed his hands up and down her arms, loosening her tight muscles. "Are you okay?"

"I'm more than okay...." This time, she left Daddy unsaid, and it fucking bothered him. "This entire night's one of the hottest sexual experiences I've ever...well, experienced."

West met her gaze in the mirror and held it. "We are going to have more than tonight. Now, let me help you get dressed, baby girl."

West picked up the sweatshirt and leggings from the back of the chair. "Is this what you planned to wear home?"

At her nod, he said, "Raise your arms for me, lass." He dressed her piece by piece, concealing her nakedness beneath the soft material. Kari sat in the chair, and West kneeled to pull on her socks and slide her favorite pair of Chucks onto her feet.

He stayed on his knees and held out his hand. "Give me your phone, lass. I want your number."

Kari bit her bottom lip. Then she reached into her purse, unlocked her phone, and gave it to him with a new contact page open.

West added his number, saving himself in her phone as *Daddy West*, which made him fucking hard all over again. "I sent myself a text so I have your number, too."

"Why? Don't you trust me to send you one myself?" Kari asked, her sass returning.

West brushed her hair behind her ear and stared into her eyes. "Trust has nothing to do with it. My patience has limits, and I promised you a set of test results."

Kari's cheeks heated, and she gave him a cautious smile. With her face bare of makeup, she looked all of her twenty-two and three-quarters years. He let the idea of their age gap settle between them, waited for the uneasiness to show itself, and when nothing happened, he sighed with relief.

The more he got to know this woman, the more he realized the age difference didn't matter.

West pressed a kiss to her forehead. "Can I walk you out? I'd much rather escort you home, but I know you're not ready to have me in your space yet."

She traced the leather straps of his harness with the tip of her finger, staring at it to avoid meeting his gaze. "It's not like I don't want you in my space, it's...I'm not sure I'll want you to leave if you do...which sounds kind of crazy, and I also have Izzy to consider...."

West tipped her chin, not letting Kari avoid his gaze any longer. "I understand, baby girl. The feelings buzzing between us are intense, and it's okay for us to pump the brakes and slow things down a little."

"Thank you...for understanding."

"How are you getting home?" The idea of her walking the streets this late at night to the train station is something he can't abide.

Kari held up her phone and pulled up a car service app. "Don't worry...Daddy. I have a standing order for a ride home on the nights I work. Jasper insists on it."

"From now on, I do too." Elated, she'd called him Daddy again.

Kari smirked. "They always wait for me outside the staff entrance, and they'll be there by the time I'm out the door."

"Good. I'll walk with you. My stuff's in the private lounge near there, anyway."

Kari gathered her belongings, and he picked up her discarded catsuit and corset, draping them over the chair.

She shut off the lights and shut her dressing room door. West placed a hand on the small of her back and escorted her to the staff entrance, where a car did indeed wait for her. He kissed her lips and told her to text him when she arrived home to let him know she'd made it safely, then watched the vehicle until it drove out of sight.

When he returned to the private lounge, West grabbed his stuff and got changed. He picked up his phone and checked the text on his screen. He swiped open his phone and saved Kari's number under *Baby Girl* in his contacts, then opened the text thread and typed.

> **West: Hey, baby girl...I had a great time tonight, and I meant what I said.**

> **West: Negative STD Test <attachment>**

> **West: I always keep my promises.**

CHAPTER TWELVE

Kari

Kari's phone buzzed, making her smile. West didn't waste any time. She liked a man who's...eager. She opened her phone and muffled a gasp, reading West's texts. "He didn't." The driver eyed her in the rearview mirror. "He saved himself as Daddy West."

"You okay back there?"

"Yuppers," she said, already typing a response.

> **Kari: Daddy West? A little presumptuous, don't you think?**

Not thirty seconds later, her phone buzzed.

> **Daddy West: How so? You're saved as Baby Girl in mine...**

Kari almost dropped her phone. *Baby girl*. When West says it...texts it, he's saying so much more than just an endearment. Did she want what being his *baby girl* entailed? As far as first dates went...*wait, was it a date? Hookup or meetup?* She bit her bottom lip and wiggled in her seat just a smidge.

They flirted and teased. West got her off. Kari got him off...as far as first times with a new partner went, it was pretty damn fantastic.

Thank goodness the car pulled up in front of her building. She thanked the driver and hopped out, sending West another message as she entered the lobby and headed for the elevator.

> Kari: The car dropped me off. I'm home safe and sound...

> Kari: ...Daddy

Kari's phone pinged the moment she stepped inside her apartment, making her smile. One filled with promise. Something she hadn't experienced in a long time settled inside her.

Hope.

> Daddy West: Thank you for telling me, baby girl.

> Daddy West: I had a great time tonight. You give one hell of a tour <winking face emoji>

> Kari: I had a great time, too. You're the first person I've given any kind of tour to <smiling face with halo emoji>

> Kari: I have something for you, too

Kari walked into her bedroom and rummaged through her dresser drawer, finding the negative test results she received at her physical three months ago. She snapped a photo and sent it to West.

Kari: <image sent>

Daddy West: Thank you for trusting me, baby. The next time we hang out, we're having a serious chat about me taking you bare.

Daddy West: Picturing my cum filling you...fuck, I'm hard again thinking about it

"Holy fuck. Why is that so hot?"

Kari fanned herself while she sat on the edge of her bed. The memory of being on her knees for this man, gazing up at him, stroking his pierced cock...sliding the head past her lips.

The way he took care of her after, cleaning her up, dressing her, then walking her to the car to make sure she was safe.

"He makes me want things...all kinds of things."

The happily ever after kinds of things...

Daddy West: Hey, if my dirty talk is ever too much for you, let me know, and I'll dial it back

Daddy West: I want you turned on, not creeped out <worried face emoji>

"Creeped out?"

> **Kari: Definitely not creeped out...**

> **Kari: Please don't stop. I didn't know text messages could make me wet, yet here we are. <woman shrugging emoji>**

> **Daddy West: Baby girl...the things I can't wait to do to you... <smirking devil face emoji>**

Kari's mind filled with possibilities, and she needed to slow this conversation down. Otherwise, neither of them will get any sleep.

> **Kari: While I REALLY want to know what those things are...it's late, and I should get to bed.**

> **Kari: Can we chat more about those things tomorrow? <smiling face with hearts emoji>**

Kari's phone suddenly rang, and her elation over West calling to say goodnight faded when she saw the number for Izzy's daycare. There's only one reason they'd call her at this time of night.

"Hello?"

"Kari, hello. It's Glenda."

"Hi, Glenda. What's going on?"

"It looks like Izzy isn't feeling well. She has a fever of 100 degrees and a red rash on her neck and chest, which she keeps scratching. We believe she has chickenpox."

"Chickenpox? How's that possible? Don't her vaccinations keep her from getting it?"

"Well...it's a viral infection, and it's still possible to contract. Symptoms are mild when they happen. Izzy's symptoms, however, are not. Are her vaccinations up to date?"

Are they?

Kari assumed her mother...she stopped herself right there. Assuming the woman who gave birth to her and Izzy did any of the responsible parenting things she's supposed to do is a naïve assumption to make. And now, because of her ignorance, her sister is sick. "I don't know; maybe? I...." Her words trailed off, and her shoulders slumped with defeat.

Glenda knew a bit about Kari and Izzy's background, and understanding softened her tone. "It's okay. Check with her pediatrician in the morning. Izzy's asking for you. Are you able to come pick her up?"

"I'm home from work and can be down in a few minutes," she said, pacing back toward the front hall.

"Excellent. Oh, and Kari?"

"Yes?"

"You've had the virus or got vaccinated, correct? It's dangerous to get chickenpox as an adult."

Kari remembered being sick and itchy at some point when she was a kid. "Yeah, I've had them. Have Izzy ready in fifteen minutes, and I'll be down to get her." Kari disconnected the call and set her phone on the entryway table, missing West's text.

Daddy West: Can't wait <smiling emoji>

Daddy West: Night, baby girl

With just enough time to shower and throw on some clean sweats, Kari headed to the second floor to collect her sister. When she arrived, Kari saw Izzy's glassy eyes and felt the heat radiating from her little body. "Oh, Izz...."

"Give her an oatmeal bath, cover the spots with calamine lotion, and keep Izzy hydrated. She'll be fine in a couple of days," Glenda said with reassurance.

"Thanks for everything, Glenda." Kari picked Izzy up and cradled her in her arms.

Her sister dropped her head onto Kari's shoulder. "I'm hot, Momma," Izzy murmured on their slow walk back to the elevator.

Kari knew Izzy didn't feel well when she slipped and called her momma. "I know, Izz. I'll get you some cold juice when we get back to our apartment."

"Apple juice?"

"Yeah, you can have some apple juice, sweetie."

Kari's mind raced with everything she'd need to do, like letting Jasper know she won't be in for the next couple of nights. They can't go to brunch either. Jess is pregnant, and Sara-Jane is too young to be vaccinated yet.

They rode the elevator back to their floor, Izzy tucked in her arms, though she squirmed to ease the itching. "I'm itchy, Momma," she whined when their apartment door shut behind them.

"I bet. Let me get you some juice, and then we'll get your itching under control."

"My itching's outta control?"

"Yeah, Izz. I promise to help in a minute." She set Izzy down on the couch to monitor her and dug in the fridge for juice. Kari planned to grab groceries during the school day tomorrow, but she won't be able to now. She'll get some things delivered instead.

When she gave Izzy her juice, she asked, "Can I have my blanket?"

"Sure, baby, let me go get it." On her way to Izzy's room, Kari snagged her phone, which notified her that the battery was less than five percent. "Shit, it's almost dead." There's enough juice to send Jasper a message, though.

> **Kari: Boss man, Izzy's sick. I won't be able to come in for my next couple of shifts. Sorry to leave you short. She can't go to childcare.**

Unsurprisingly, Jasper's answer came immediately.

> **Boss man: No worries. Sorry, Izz isn't feeling well. Let me know if you need anything.**

> **Kari: Will do. Thanks.**

Less than two percent battery. "Yeah, yeah. I get it; you need to be charged."

"Kaaarrriii, I'm so...hot and itchy," Izzy cried.

"Let me get the lotion, Izz." The phone can wait. Her sister can't. "Please let there be some calamine lotion in the first-aid kit." She kept it under the sink in her bathroom and jogged in there to get it.

"Oh, thank fuck." She grabbed the half-empty bottle along with some cotton swabs. "This will have to do until I can get more tomorrow."

"Kaaarrriii."

"Coming, Izz."

CHAPTER THIRTEEN

West

Baby Girl: While I REALLY want to know what those things are...it's late, and I should get to bed.

Baby Girl: Can we chat more about those things tomorrow? <smiling face with hearts emoji>

West: Can't wait <smiling emoji>

West: Night, baby girl

He checked his phone and reread those messages several times throughout the day while he toured the area, viewing several properties with the realtor he'd hired. If he wanted to make his move permanent, he'd need a prime location to set up shop, and it was early evening by the time he returned to the brownstone.

He wanted to share his news, and the first person he wanted to tell was Kari.

The third location the realtor showed him today would be an ideal location for his shop.

> **West: Evening, lass. I hope your day's going well. Jasper's not here, and you must be at work by now. Have a good shift <smiley face emoji>**

> **West: I'd love to escort you and Izzy to Sunday brunch. Let me know.**

West reread the last group of messages he'd sent. *Jesus...*he didn't mean to sound so...*clingy*. Or is it more cringy? It's both. Two days have gone by since he heard from Kari, and he's getting a little worried. He even brushed off Jasper and Jess's offer of a ride to Jon and Joanna's, hoping she'd text or call.

She didn't.

He sprinted up the steps of Joanna and Jon's and knocked. West opened the side door leading up to the kitchen and took the steps two at a time. He found Jasper mid-bite, and Joanna scolding him for taking the cookies meant for Lavender House.

"It's one cookie, Jo. There are still three dozen for everyone else," Jasper said around a mouthful.

Joanna spotted him first. "Hey, West, glad you made it."

"Is Kari here? I think she's avoiding me."

Jasper and Joanna gave him weird looks.

"What? Why are you guys looking at me like I'm an idiot? Are she and Izzy in the dining room?"

"Kari's not in the dining room or avoiding you. Izzy's sick. She got chickenpox from a kid in her class."

"Kari sent me a message late Thursday night," Jasper said. "She apologized for needing to call out of work for the next two nights. Izzy can't go to daycare and risk infecting more kids."

Thursday night's the last time he heard from Kari, too. "Did anyone check on her?" West asked, pulling out his phone in case she responded. He grew even more concerned when they shook their heads.

"I sent her a message yesterday. With Jess's pregnancy, I can't risk being exposed." Jasper's brow furrowed with concern. "She never got back to me."

"I called her an hour ago to find out if she wanted us to drop some food off at her place. I got her voicemail." Joanna checked her phone on the counter. "There aren't any missed calls or texts. I figured she'd let me know by now."

West wanted to come out of his skin, unable to stand the uncertainty for another minute. "Give me Kari's address. I'm going over there to make sure she and Izzy are okay."

Jasper sent a location ping to his phone. "She lives in the apartment building I own on Union Street. I'll call the front desk and give them your name. Otherwise, they won't let you up."

"Appreciate it, brother."

"Here," Joanna said, grabbing a couple of containers and filling them with food. "Kari must be exhausted, looking after Izzy and keeping her from scratching her skin off. I'm sure she's fine."

"I hope so." West took the food and Jasper's offer to drop him off. He grabbed his keys, and West followed him to his car.

CHAPTER FOURTEEN

Kari

K ari staggered toward her front entrance, not sure if she was imagining someone pounding on her door or not. "Coming," she said, not wanting to shout and wake Izzy. She didn't want more knocking to wake her sister, either.

Fuck, her head hurt. And she's hot. Why is she hot? She's in a tank top and sleep shorts, for crying out loud. An outfit she didn't even remember changing into.

This isn't good.

Kari caught herself with a hand on the doorframe, dizziness threatening to topple her over. When did she last eat or drink anything? She honestly couldn't remember.

Izzy's itchy and cranky, and Kari's running on little sleep. She Googled the best ways to soothe a kid with chickenpox, noting that the worst part was the sores in her mouth. Popsicles helped. Kari had run out of them last night and needed to get some more, but she didn't have the energy to open a delivery app and place an order.

Being a single parent is really fucking hard sometimes. She just needed some rest and someone to look after her for five minutes.

The steady knock resumed after an all too brief respite. At least it wasn't a hallucination. Maybe it's Joanna or Addie. Her hand froze over the deadbolt as she stared through the peephole at Weston Sharpe.

"Kari?"

His familiar deep voice sounded through the door, and Kari realized this was no fever dream. West's at her apartment.

Damn, he looks good.

It's too bad; it felt like she got hit by a truck. Kari blinked, staring at him through her peephole. He leaned against the doorframe and looked down.

"Kari, your shadow is peeking beneath the door. Open up for me, baby. I'm here to make sure you and Izzy are okay."

Kari tried to open the door. *Why's it taking so much effort?* When she flung it wide, the momentum carried her with it. The room spun, and so did she. Then everything went black.

CHAPTER FIFTEEN

West

"Holy fuck, Kari!" West caught her mid-faint and scooped her into his arms. He closed the door with his foot and pulled her to his chest. Heat radiated from her. "Jesus, you're burning up."

"Mm...what?" she mumbled, rousing. "Don't wake, Izzy. She's...sick."

"Pretty sure you're sick too, baby girl. I won't wake Izzy. Which way to your bedroom?"

She pointed left, and West found the door at the end of the hall open. "I'm hot." Kari reached for her neck, scratching at a couple of red spots there. "And itchy."

West grabbed her hand. "Shit, you've got the chicken pox, too."

"Nooo...chickenpox party. Gotta look after Izz...something else Mom lied about," Kari rambled while he set her on the bed.

West took in her flushed cheeks and dry lips. "When's the last time you drank something?"

"I...what day is it?"

"Fuck. You've got to be dehydrated. Stay there. I'm going to get you some water. Pedialyte or Gatorade might be better, though."

"Not going anywhere."

"Try not to scratch either."

"Ugh...I'm itchy. I used the last of the calamine lotion on Izzy."

"I'll be right back." West found Kari's dead phone on the side table in the entryway. "No wonder she didn't respond to anyone's messages." He found a charger, and the moment the battery got a bit of juice, her screen lit up with unread texts.

West grabbed his phone, opened a grocery delivery app, and prepared an order. He headed into Kari's kitchen, filled a glass with ice, and surveyed the contents of her fridge and cupboards, adding a few more things, like Benadryl, stuff for an oatmeal bath, and a few things for Izzy.

Speaking of...Kari will want to know if her sister is okay. He headed across the living room to the bedroom opposite Kari's, and peeked inside the open door, finding a calamine lotion-spotted Izzy asleep starfish style in her little kid-sized bed.

West tiptoed into her room and brushed her soft cheek, finding her warm, though not feverish like her sister. He pulled the blankets Izzy had kicked aside back over her and crept back out. He snagged the glass of water, and when he returned to Kari's bedroom, he rushed to her side.

"Kari, what are you doing?"

She moaned and writhed on the sheets. West sort of found it hot...the pervert in him most definitely did...except she's going to hurt herself.

"I swear...this doesn't count as scratching...I'm...rubbing my skin..." She rolled over and squirmed on her stomach.

West swallowed because his dick wanted in on all her rocking and rolling. And now is *definitely* not the time. "Kari, you have to stop. It's going to get worse."

The delivery of supplies, including the stuff needed for a soothing bath, is about an hour away. If she kept itching, she wouldn't be able to stop.

"Please...it feels too good."

"Stop, baby girl." West came up with a solution he hoped worked. "I'm going to swaddle you to help calm you down and get you over the urge to scratch." Kari whimpered while he wrapped her in the blankets she lay on.

West smoothed her hair back from her face, wincing at how feverish she'd become. The sooner he got her still. The sooner he'd get some water into her.

He wrapped her legs, bringing her blankets around them. Then West tucked her arms to her sides and wrapped the blanket around her torso, calming her movements.

He gathered Kari in his arms and got on the bed behind her, leaning against the headboard. With her lying against his chest, he nestled her burrito'd body between his spread thighs.

"I placed a grocery order. It'll be here in less than an hour. When it arrives, I'll get you bathed and slathered in calamine lotion. For now, you need to focus on not scratching your skin off."

He reached for the glass and held the metal straw to her lips. "Drink, lass. It'll help, I promise." The anxiety gripping him since Kari fainted, eased when she swallowed the cool liquid.

"Easy now. Don't drink too fast. I'll make you and Izzy some soup when she wakes, okay?"

Kari shifted and let go of the straw. "Izzy. I...need to check on her and make sure she's okay."

He held Kari a little tighter in case she tried to get up. "Already done. I looked in on her when I got your water. Izzy's sound asleep. She's a touch warm, but not feverish."

Kari relaxed in his arms, but then he heard her sniffle. "I've never seen her this sick. I didn't know what to do at first."

West's heart broke for her. "No...baby girl. You did such a good job. Izzy will be fine." His lips grazed her temple, and he tried his best to soothe her. "Daddy's here to make sure you're okay. I'm going to look after you both. Let me take care of you."

"Thank you," Kari said. "You know, it's kind of sexy when you refer to yourself as Daddy."

West nuzzled his lips along her hairline, dragging her soft, flowery scent into his lungs. He pressed his palm to her forehead. "Kind of, huh? Is this you talking or the fever?"

"Pretty sure it's me, regardless of the fever. At first, I convinced myself that what we did was nothing more than role-play."

"And I'm sure I've clarified that this isn't role-play for me."

"You did, and don't glaze over the fact I said at first."

"You're right, sorry."

West heard her breath catch. "Thank you." Kari wiggled in his arms. "I enjoyed calling you Daddy. It's checking a box I didn't know needed checking until I met you."

"This might not be the best time to discuss things, not with you being sick. You need to be clearheaded when we have this conversation." He hesitated, then said, "I'd like to discuss drawing up a contract between us."

Kari fell silent, and he thought she might've fallen asleep when she said, "I understand the need for discussions about likes and dislikes...things someone is willing to try or things they will not. I have no problem having those discussions."

"Don't hold back on me now, baby girl. Give me what comes after the 'but' you've left hanging in the air."

"I'm not sure if I want to have the parameters of my relationship laid out in point form on paper."

West rubbed his palms over the blankets to soothe her without scratching her. "It's much more than that. It's what to expect from one another, like how I want to take care of you, protect and cherish you."

Kari squirmed against him, and West did his best not to conjure more lecherous ideas when she said, "I can't look at you when I'm all wrapped up like this."

"Hold on." West eased out from behind her, set her empty glass back on the nightstand, and doubled up the pillows to lean Kari back against. Then he straddled her legs and bent over, caging her in with his palms gripping the headboard on either side of her. "Better?" he asked, meeting her hazy eyes.

"Yeah, it is." She licked her lips and stared into his soul. "I don't need those things on paper. Give me the actions...like showing up here and demanding to take care of us. I've never gotten that...and I want it. I won't disregard your need for the written. Let me consider it. In the meantime, we can talk about anything and everything. I'm an open book."

"I appreciate your honesty, lass. If we have open communication, consent, and a safeword. I can work with that."

"We need a safeword?"

West held her chin between his fingers. "Baby girl. It's non-negotiable." He tucked the soft strands of her dark hair behind her ear.

"I promise to always check in with you and talk to you. If things ever get too intense in the heat of the moment, you need a word that stops everything. What if words like 'no' or 'stop' are part of our play? It's important to have a word and a physical signal to stop everything. Whatever you choose, I'll use it, too. We can use a double tap or a peace sign for a nonverbal cue."

"Okay. I'll come up with a word."

West grew uneasy. "I didn't mean for us to go into these kinds of details tonight. You're sick, and I don't want you to regret talking about this now."

"Something about the best-laid plans, right?"

"Yeah, something like that."

"Hey, at least it made me forget about the scratching." Kari let out an adorable groan. "Ugh, at least it did. The bottoms of my feet are itchy."

"We need something to take your mind off it. I'll have you in an oatmeal bath in about thirty minutes. Promise."

"The blanket burrito is helping. The sensation to scratch is still maddening."

West shifted beside her and tucked her into his side. "Why don't we watch something?" *Something to make them laugh after their conversation.* He picked up the remote from her nightstand and turned on the TV perched on top of the tall dresser in the corner.

He pressed the voice search option and said, "Friends, The One With The Chickenpox."

Kari turned her head, and West felt her stare. "You want me to forget about the urge to scratch my skin off with an episode of a sitcom about it?"

"What? It's hilarious. Plus, the laughter will make you forget. Maybe the irony will, too."

"Alright. Chickenpox. It'll be our word."

"Chickenpox is our safeword?" West asked, rolling the word around in his head.

"Everything stops with chickenpox," Kari sing-songed. Silence fell between them for a beat, then they burst out laughing.

West wiped the moisture from the corner of his eye. "True, and not something I'll forget." His phone chimed with a notification. "Supplies are here. I'll grab them, then I'll get you settled into a soothing bath."

He kissed her lips, and when he pulled back, Kari smiled at him with such openness that his heart got a little more involved.

Maybe a lot more involved.

"Thanks for reading a bedtime story to Izzy tonight. I knew she'd sucker you into two."

West's laughter echoed in the confined space of Kari's bathroom, where he'd carried her after Izzy fell asleep. "I enjoyed it. She's a great kid, Kari. You're doing a wonderful job raising her."

He gripped the hem of her top. "I'm going to take this off, okay?"

"Okay."

West pulled off the black tank top and lounge pants Kari put on after her bath and set them on the other side of the sink, leaving her in a black cotton bra and panties. He placed a folded towel on the counter and lifted her onto it, all while willing his dick to stay down when she parted her thighs to bring him closer.

He swallowed a groan and bit his lip, captivated by the way he fit perfectly between them. There's no shame in his desire for her. It's not like he planned to act on it. She's sick, and he's here to take care of her. But her fever did not cause the heat pinkening her cheeks when her gaze dipped below the waist of his grey sweats.

Damn...she's got him bricked up.

West cleared his throat. "Not the time, baby girl." Kari gave him a little pout when he picked up the bottle of calamine lotion and soaked a cotton swab. Her pout turned into a sigh of relief when he lifted her right foot and dabbed the two spots on her arch, finding another by her ankle.

"Mm, thank you. Those three spots are already better, I swear."

"You're welcome." West dabbed at the spots until her right leg contained a pattern of little pink dots. He didn't want to miss any, catching the one

143

at the back of her knee after his first pass. "There. One leg's done." He reached for her left foot when her question made him pause.

"Did you ever get married or have kids?" When he said nothing, Kari stumbled over her words, trying to walk back the question. "I mean, you've got this nurturing way about you; it made me wonder...you don't have to answer or anything."

It's not an unexpected question, given their age difference. West dabbed the calamine lotion up her left leg, holding her gaze while he did. "No, lass, sorry. You just caught me off guard. I'll answer anything you want, and it's both yes and no. Yes, I got married. No, Maggie and I didn't have children."

"Did you and Maggie have a Dom/sub dynamic? Did she call you daddy?"

West's chuckle bubbled past his lips despite the seriousness of their conversation. He shook his head. "No, she didn't. I can't even picture her saying it. She and I...it's complicated..."

"Oh."

He knew he needed to tell her everything if he wanted something real with this girl. "We kept our relationship...open, and I didn't discover my inclination to want to be someone's daddy until Jasper opened Decadent."

Kari bit her lip, and West didn't like the way she silenced herself, so he tugged her bottom lip free. "Out with it, baby girl."

"Is an open relationship something you want with me?"

West stared at her for a moment. He let the idea of someone else fucking Kari percolate, and it took less than a second to know with this woman that's a hard fucking limit.

He cupped Kari's cheek, his thumb caressing the delicate bone. "Fuck, no. The idea of someone taking what's...." He shook his head.

"I like to play. To be a voyeur, and at other times, an exhibitionist. I won't share you, baby girl. I know we're just getting to know one another, but I can tell you right now, it's a hard limit for me."

"Hard limit," she said, her brow furrowed, trying out the words. "Good, because I'm not sharing my daddy, either."

Kari peered at him from beneath her lashes, and West wanted to bury his cock deep inside her. He won't, not yet. Fuck, he wanted to, though.

The urge almost overwhelmed him when Kari said, "We're really doing this? All the getting to know each other stuff?"

"Baby girl...." The words came out in a low rumble, which seemed down-right feral even for him, and he wrestled with whether to say the words on the tip of his tongue and opted for honesty above all else.

"You don't invest these kinds of details in a fling. We've already crammed six important 'getting to know each other dates' into the past ten hours anyway."

Kari dragged her teeth over her bottom lip. "You consider being stuck with me and the pox," – careful not to use their safeword – "six important, getting to know you type dates?"

"Yeah. I do." West kissed her lips, keeping it gentle despite Kari teasing the seam of his lips with her tongue.

She pressed a hand against his chest, feeling the steady rhythm of his heart beneath her palm. "Where's Maggie now?"

West took a deep breath, ripping off the band-aid of a dark period of his life. "She died in a hit-and-run accident over a decade ago during my final deployment."

Kari's eyes became glassy with tears, and she sucked in a sharp breath. "I'm so sorry."

"Thank you. I carried the guilt with me for a long time. Maggie's death will remain senseless and tragic." West swallowed hard, dabbing the cotton swab over the arm she held up.

Kari's voice quieted, and West strained to hear her. "Do...do you think you'd still be together and have kids if she didn't...?"

"If she hadn't died?" He studied her long, elegant fingers, dabbing a spot between her index and middle. West's never shared what he's about to say with anyone, not even Jasper or Gray.

"Maggie took our open relationship to another level, dating while I'd gone off on missions. I used to go on a lot of missions, and she didn't enjoy being alone. She needed more than I provided. I found out later that she was walking home from her boyfriend's place when it happened. So, to answer your question, no, we would never have had kids. She was in love with the guy and, unbeknownst to me, planned to file for divorce when I returned home."

When he met Kari's gaze, she looked at him with sympathy. She cupped his face, and he leaned into her touch. "God West, I'm sorry. I don't know how you dealt with everything."

"Besides a therapist, you're the first person I've told. Not even Jasper knows. I let everyone believe my heartbreak kept me away all these years when my guilt actually did because I still have a chance to find happiness. Maggie never will."

"Um...how did you find out?"

"Well, Maggie's boyfriend showed up at my apartment a month after her funeral. I was in the middle of packing to return to Glasgow when he turned up on my doorstep. The guy, Steve, blurted out that he was Maggie's boyfriend, then burst into tears, grieving for Maggie like I did. Even more so. I asked him in for a beer. We sat among my moving boxes and talked for the rest of the night."

After finishing her left arm, West soaked another cotton ball and dabbed at the six spots across Kari's upper chest and collarbone. The more he talked and covered her in lotion, the more he realized she wasn't the only one finding some relief.

When he reached the spot on her cheek, Kari grabbed his hand and traced her thumb over the last tattoo he'd given himself. It's a semicolon on the fleshy part between his thumb and forefinger. Then she met his gaze with a question in her eyes.

West shrugged. "I'm on the other side of things. We all have a past, lass. Some are a bit more tragic than others."

Kari tipped her head forward and tilted it to the right. "Look behind my ear."

"Did I miss one of your spots?"

"No, you didn't. Remember the night we met, and you asked if there were any tattoos hidden beneath my naughty schoolgirl uniform?"

"Kind of hard to forget, lass. I also remember you didn't give me an answer."

"Yeah, well...I have one. Look."

West shifted her hair back and folded the shell of her ear forward, exposing the delicate skin behind it, and the little semicolon tattooed there.

He found breathing a little tricky as another of their interconnected puzzle pieces slipped into place. "Looks like you may know something about overcoming tragedy."

Kari looked at him with haunted eyes. "Yeah, I do."

CHAPTER SIXTEEN

West

He fell asleep on top of the blankets with Kari beneath, but during the night, he got under them with her, holding her tight while she slept, and the sound of her whimper woke him. West sucked in a breath when she cried out, "No." And he realized she was having a bad dream.

West flicked on the bedside lamp. "Kari, baby, wake up." The heat radiating from her felt like a furnace. She struggled, her limbs getting tangled in the sheets.

"Baby girl." West gave Kari's shoulder a gentle shake. "You're having a nightmare; you need to wake up."

"Wes?" She shuddered and opened her eyes to focus on him.

His smile was one of relief, and he kissed her forehead. "Right here. Are you okay?"

"Yeah." Kari shivered, and he reached behind him, pulling his shirt over his head to dry the sweat from her cooling skin. She gripped his wrist, shoved her face into his shirt, and took a deep breath. "Gawd, you smell good," she said, giving him a lazy, desire-filled look when she pulled the material away.

With her other hand, she teased his pierced nipples. West tossed his shirt aside and pulled her close, tucking them both back under the blankets, stilling her wandering fingers.

"Hey...none of that right now. Do you remember what you dreamed about?"

Kari sniffled and wedged a little closer, nestling her face beneath his chin. Fuck, she felt so good wrapped in his arms.

"Yes, I remember."

When she didn't elaborate further, he asked, "Do you want to talk about it?"

"I don't want to, but it's probably better if I do."

"Was it about your ex? The one you saw murdered?"

Kari lifted her head to meet his gaze. "How did you know?"

West brushed her hair back from her face. "Jasper told me enough to explain how you came to work at Decadent. He told me the rest needed to come from you." He pressed a kiss to her forehead, thankful her fever had broken.

"In my nightmare, Leo, the guy who killed Spencer, always finds my hiding place. No matter what really happened, he finds me in my dreams, and when he does, I never survive."

"No one should go through what you did. I'm so thankful that bastard didn't find you. You stayed hidden and came home safe. You're so brave, baby girl."

"It's hard to believe I am. It's the guilt, the kind to hit me out of nowhere. I haven't had a nightmare in months, and I guess I'd convinced myself I'd gotten over it."

"I'm not sure survivor's guilt ever goes away. We become better at coping with it."

"It's not survivor's guilt." Kari held his gaze, her top teeth dragging across her bottom lip, trying and failing to hold the words back. "It's a relief. I'm relieved Spencer can't hurt me or any other woman who might've fallen for his charm, and I'm relieved they found his killer floating in the river. The guilt I feel is over the relief I feel."

West held her face between his hands. "Your ex, he...hurt you?"

"Spencer grabbed me and shoved me against a wall. It happened once, and I ended things with a powerhouse kick to his balls."

"Fuck yes, baby girl. He should never have laid a hand on you."

West kept his appearance calm, while inside, he raged at the injustice of time travel not existing, preventing him from going back and killing the fucker himself for daring to put his hands on her.

He kissed her, then pressed his forehead to hers. "Thank you for telling me. I know this is hard to accept. Please try. There's nothing for you to feel guilty about. Your ex is the one who got tangled up with the wrong people. The decisions he made put him on that path."

"I know...I spent enough hours in therapy to understand that Spencer's actions aren't my doing. It's...."

"The guilt. I know, baby." West pulled her close, tucking Kari's head beneath his chin again. "You need your rest. Is it okay if I stay under the covers and hold you close like this while you go back to sleep?"

"Yes, please." She yawned against his throat, her lips brushing his pulse point when she did.

"Sleep, baby. Daddy will keep the nightmares away." Her breathing slowed, and she relaxed in his arms. West kept his promise, staying awake until the sun cracked the horizon.

"Kaaaaarrrrriiii!"

"Oof." West's eyes flew wide open when Izzy landed on him with the expertise of a WWE Piledriver. "Uh...morning, Izz."

"Wes? What are you doing in Kari's bed?"

"Isabella Rose Davidson. What have we talked about regarding the personal space of our bedrooms?" Kari asked, sitting up beside him. He hid his smile when Izzy's eyes grew wide at the use of her full name.

"Um...is the rule, our bedroom is our private space, and we're supposed to knock first?"

"Did you knock, Izz?"

"No." She crossed her arms and glared. "Neither did Wes, and he's in your room."

"You're right, Izzy. I didn't knock. It's a mistake I'm going to correct. Can you pass me my T-shirt on the floor there?" She looked at the dark blue pile of crumpled cotton he pointed to, nodded, and handed it to him.

He pulled the shirt on, tugging the hem over the waistband of his sweats, and climbed out of bed.

"What are you doing?" Kari asked out of the side of her mouth.

West smoothed Kari's hair back and kissed her forehead. "I'm correcting my mistake. Come on, Izz. We have a door to knock on and permission to seek." Together, they marched through the door and pulled it closed.

Izzy looked up at him and asked, "Now what?"

"We knock." West gave her an encouraging smile. "Go ahead, Izz. Knock on the door for both of us." She closed her hand into a little fist and banged on the door three times. "Good job." West offered his hand for a high-five to keep her from hitting the door anymore and hurting herself.

"Who is it?" Kari asked.

"Kari, it's Izzy and Wes. Let us in." Izzy glanced up at West, and he quirked his brow. "Oh, yeah. Please." She finished with a shout.

"You can come in."

Izzy got to the handle first and flung the door wide. She ran in and launched herself into the center of Kari's bed. Luckily, Kari moved to sit up against the headboard, out of the way of Izzy's exuberant bed gymnastics.

"Excellent landing, Izz." When it looked like Izzy wanted to do another launch, Kari stopped her. "You get one launch. No more."

"Maybe Wes didn't catch all of it." Hopeful for another running leap at her sister's bed.

"I saw the whole thing. A most excellent launch and landing, fare Izz." Giving his best Keanu from Bill and Ted, making Kari laugh.

This seemed to appease the energetic five-year-old. "My best one yet."

"Looks like you're doing better," Kari said with a tired smile.

"I am. Can I go to school today?"

"Remember, we have a virtual call with your pediatrician, and if they give the okay, you can go to school tomorrow. But...if Dr. Sloan agrees, you can go to daycare for a few hours to play with some of your other friends this afternoon."

"Yesss."

Despite Kari's best efforts to hide it, West saw how Izzy's returned energy drained hers. "You know, Izz, I need some help to make breakfast. Will you be my breakfast-making assistant?"

"Oh, yeah." Izzy climbed off the bed and ran out of the room. "I know where all my favorites are. Let me show you."

"I'll be right there." West leaned over, placing his palms on either side of Kari's hips. "Rest while I feed the Energizer Bunny." He kissed her forehead, and she reached up, cupping the side of his throat, guiding his lips to hers.

"Thank you. Thank you for being here. For looking after Izzy and me. I know we've kind of jumped into the deep end with how fast things are going, and I want you to know it means a lot."

Unable to resist, West kissed her again. "Baby girl, I'm really comfortable jumping into the deep end with you."

With Kari relaxing in her bath, West took on drop-off duty, escorting Izzy to her childcare on the second floor. She got the all-clear from her pediatrician and can return to school tomorrow.

An afternoon of playing with friends is the break Kari needs to recover. And thanks to the call she made, he can now take Izzy to and from daycare. Honored that Kari trusted him with this.

"Come on, Wes," Izzy called, skipping ahead of him toward the elevator, excited to hang out with her friends.

"I'm coming, Izz. You're fast, though. How will I keep up?"

She hummed a tune when they left the apartment, and with the hall's acoustics, she sang, "KARI, IT'S YOUR BIRFDAY. HAP-PY BIRF-DAY, KARI...."

"When's Kari's birthday?"

"THIS WEEKEND," she bellowed with a healthy dose of jazz hands at the finale of her performance.

"Thanks for telling me, but please remember to be mindful of your neighbors."

"Right, sorry." Izzy gave him a calculating look, then scooted around the corner, and he picked up his pace in a race to the elevator.

"Wait, Izz." West bolted around the corner, worried she'd hop on the elevator without him. The doors opened right when he arrived. A woman stood off to the side, looking between them.

"Oh, sorry, ma'am. We're going down and can wait for the next one," he said, taking Izzy's hand to make sure she didn't step on.

The woman's eyes widened, and she pressed the button, keeping the doors open. "It's okay, this elevator is going down," she said, her voice raspy like she'd smoked most of her life. She didn't look like a hardcore smoker, yet he didn't miss the telltale signs of Botox and fillers when he and Izzy stepped into the elevator.

West leaned in to press the button for the second floor, and he met the woman's gaze. Her eyes were a striking shade of grey...much like Izzy's. The woman pressed G for the garage.

Wouldn't she have already pressed it if she were going down?

He stepped back and positioned himself between the woman and Izzy, getting a weird vibe from her, which made him hyper-aware of how she stared at them.

"Beautiful day, isn't it?"

"Yes, ma'am." His blunt, yet polite answer didn't dissuade her from further conversation like he hoped.

The woman leaned to the left, trying to catch Izzy's gaze. "Is your dad taking you to the park?"

West squeezed Izzy's shoulder, tucking her further behind him. He didn't believe Izz to be shy, yet she followed his cues to stay silent. "No, ma'am."

She opened her mouth to say something else when the elevator dinged, indicating they'd reached the second floor, and relief filled him. "Enjoy your day, ma'am."

West held Izzy's hand, the woman's gaze boring into their backs until the door slid closed.

"Wes, Wes," Izzy said in a dramatic whisper, tugging on the hem of his shirt.

"What's up?"

"I did not like that lady."

West looked back at the elevator. The lights above it showed it stopped on the first floor. *Didn't she select the parking garage?* "How come, Izz?"

"She gave me the heebie-jeebies," she said, scrunching up her face. "I didn't like it."

From the moment the two of them stepped into the elevator, something about the woman rubbed West the wrong way, and now the unfiltered instincts of a child cemented it for him.

"You listen to those instincts, Izz. They won't ever steer you wrong. Let's drop you off with Glenda, and you can play with your friends."

"I won't get anybody sick?"

"Nope, just fun with your friends, and later, you, Kari, and I can have dinner together."

"Can we have pizza?" Izzy asked, jumping up and down.

While West figured it'd be an easy sell, he wanted to clear it with Kari first. "If it's okay with Kari."

"Yes." Her little fist shot into the air. "Kari loves pizza."

CHAPTER SEVENTEEN

Kari

I s this what true contentment is like?

Kari paused at her bedroom door, unsure how to handle any of this. She wanted to...keep West. To fall asleep in his arms every night. She wanted him to live here with her and Izzy, sharing their lives. Even in her head, the notion sounded crazy and way too soon, yet it felt...right.

She pinched the skin on the inside of her arm. "Ouch." Alright, this isn't a dream, but damn it felt like one. One that might disappear in an instant.

When he'd taken her hand earlier and led her to her closet in her bedroom, he asked, "What are you in the mood to wear?" Kari almost responded with "Whatever you want me to, Daddy," but she knew now was not the time. She went to grab something for herself, and West tugged on her hand, bringing her back to his side. "No...tell me what you want to wear."

"Oh, I have these red silk pajamas. I figured they might feel nice against my skin. I can get them."

"Not this time, baby girl. Let me take care of you." West guided her into the bathroom, leaving her by the counter while he filled the tub and adjusted the water temperature to her liking.

He picked up her favorite bath oil, brought the open bottle to his nose, and breathed in the lavender scent. "Mm...smells like you." West met her gaze, his light blue eyes now stormy with desire. "You want a little or a lot, baby girl?"

Now, there's a loaded question. Kari glanced at the bottle of oil in his hand. "Maybe...somewhere in the middle?"

West smirked. "Aye, lass. Somewhere in the middle it is." He drizzled oil from one end of the tub to the other.

Kari reached for the hem of her shirt, and West moved toward her with lightning speed. "Did I tell you to get undressed?" His voice was soft yet stern.

"No," she said, a blush heating her cheeks. "Sir."

West gripped her chin, not allowing her to look away when he made his intentions clear. "I want to undress you, Kari."

"Oh-okay, sorry."

He paused, his fingers gripping the waistband of her lounge pants. "There's nothing to be sorry for." He tugged her pants down, lowering to his knees when he did. His lips grazed the curve of her stomach. "I want to show you it's okay to let go around me."

Compelled to be honest with this man, she said, "I'm afraid...afraid the moment I do, it will all slip away." Her fingers tangled in his hair, and her body got ahead of her brain, guiding his mouth closer to where she wanted him most.

West's lips caressed the sensitive skin below her navel, and she shivered despite the warmth of the room. "I will do everything to earn your trust, baby girl. I'll never abuse it."

He pressed his face to the juncture of her thighs, his hot breath searing her panties, and Kari tightened her grip on his hair. Her body was waiting for her mind to catch up and surrender to the man kneeling at her feet.

"Don't hurt us, okay? Izzy's feelings are even more important than mine," she said, looking down at him.

West dragged his nose along the edge of her panties until his lips grazed her hipbone, and he looked into her eyes once again. "Never. It's the last thing I'd ever want to do."

"Thank you."

West tossed her pants and underwear in the hamper, then stood, cupping her face in his palms. He pressed a gentle kiss to her lips, and Kari felt the words neither of them was ready to say. When he put enough space between them to take her top off, his gaze raked over her. "Fuck, you're beautiful."

She glanced down, taking in the scabbed and fading red marks on her body. She'd eaten little over the past few days and knew she'd lost precious weight from her lean frame. "I don't know about–"

West stopped her disparaging words with his fingertips pressed to her lips. "You are. Your compassion and the way you care for your sister and the friendships you've curated show every day how beautiful you are."

Kari pressed her lips together and blinked away the sudden onslaught of tears. "Thank you."

West lifted her hand to his lips, kissing her palm. "Always. Let me help you into your bath before you catch a chill." He held her hand as she eased into the fragrant water. When she settled, he pulled her tub tray across the middle.

He set her eReader up in the center, adding a bottle of water and a bottle of Gatorade on one side, and a dish of strawberries on the other. Then, he leaned over her and kissed her forehead. "Enjoy your bath, baby girl."

West disappeared from her bathroom, but reappeared a minute later, setting the folded pajamas beside her fluffiest towel.

"Izzy's waiting for me. She insisted on picking out her outfit. I've gotta admit, the kid's got style. I have your keys. Take your time, and I'll be back soon."

"Kay, thanks." She picked up her page-turning remote once West closed the bathroom door, getting lost in the Sapphic vampire romance. Kari didn't realize how much time had passed until the cooling water made her shiver.

She got out of the tub, dried, and dressed, desperate to get warm again. When she entered her bedroom, she paused and stared at the bed. West changed the sheets, leaving her fuzzy cardigan and matching socks draped over the end like he knew she'd be cold.

Kari appreciated the gesture and put them on, getting warmer by the second. Having someone anticipate her needs is one thing; getting used to it is another. She took a deep breath and then padded down the hall toward the living room on silent, sock-covered feet.

West sat on the sofa, and the smell of fresh laundry permeated the air. The folded pile in the basket at his feet and the black cotton thong he'd helped her out of earlier were in his hands.

Dude's just out here folding her underwear like it's no big deal. Domesticity looks good on him.

"Thank you for changing the sheets and doing the laundry. You didn't have to."

West had changed his clothes, wearing the grey sweats he slept in last night with a black t-shirt that molded to his chest and shoulders. He left his feet bare and his hair loose, looking relaxed and at home.

Looking like he belonged there.

He set her thong on top of the pile like he handled her underwear every day.

God, she wanted him to handle her underwear every day.

"I don't mind. Now, you don't have to worry about it."

It's nice not to worry for a change.

West got close and cupped her cheek, looking her over. "You look rested. How are you holding up?"

Kari leaned into his touch. "Good...all thanks to you. You've taken such good care of us."

He kissed her, humming against her lips. "Speaking of Izzy, she told me...well, more like she sang an exuberant song about the fact it's your birthday when I dropped her off at childcare."

"Oh, yeah...I, uh, turn twenty-three on Friday. You know, closing the age gap between us by this much." She held up her thumb and index finger, the tiniest bit apart.

"I know the age difference should be a factor, but it's not. Getting to know you has made it easy to forget. You're mature, you've seen the world, and you've taken on such responsibility, handling everything set in your path. Those fifteen years between us? The more I get to know you, the less they matter."

"As long as the people involved are consenting adults, I give little thought to someone's age. It's how we vibe, you know?" Kari's cheeks heated.

Fuck it.

She's on a roll and might as well keep on rolling. "The night of Addie and Gray's engagement, after I got home...well...it makes sense now."

West's brow furrowed, trying to piece it together. "What does?"

"The way I didn't even make it to my bed, masturbating on the floor of my closet. I suctioned a dildo to the floor and fucked myself with it. The vibe I pressed to my clit made me come so hard I almost blacked out. All while thinking of you."

"Shit. For real? After you sassed me that night and refused to tell me your name, I got back to the apartment and took myself in hand, coming with you on my mind. It's crazy...I want to fuck you. Bend you over the nearest surface and sink my cock into your tight little pussy. Yet...I want to get to know you more."

Kari's pussy fluttered, well aware *she* was being discussed. "Wow, knowledge over pussy...alright, you want to get to know the not-sick version of me? Can we play twenty questions?" Kari batted her eyelashes, testing the waters with him.

West smirked, giving her the briefest acknowledgment; otherwise, he didn't rise to the bait. "You can ask me anything, lass."

"Oh, I know," she said, settling into the corner of the couch with the water West handed her. He sat beside her within touching distance, just not touching - yet. "Explain the Scottish-American accent."

West met her gaze and quirked his brow. "'Tis a wee bit of a tale, lass. And a sad one," he said, leaning into his accent extra thick.

"I suppose if you've walked this earth long enough, we all have a sad tale or two."

"I suppose...."

She nudged his shoulder, then laid her cheek against it. "I'm serious about wanting to know you." Kari traced her finger along one of the many tattoos on his forearm. "I want everything you're willing to share with me. Even the sad parts."

West pressed a kiss on the top of her head. "Alright, you asked for it. My mum and dad ran like oil and water, according to my Gran, fiery to the point they threatened to consume one another. Quite the image for a six-year-old to digest, but Gran always said it like it is. Ornery, you know? Though she loved me in her own way."

"My folks split months before my birth. My dad returned to the States, and my mum remained in Glasgow, raising me. Me, mum, and Gran. Three peas in a pod. I've got wonderful memories of being raised by two strong-willed women who loved me very much. Gran passed away when I turned twelve, and when Mum got sick the following year, my dad flew over and cared for her until she passed."

"Oh, West, I'm sorry," Kari said, squeezing his arm. To have experienced so much loss...Kari's eyes filled with tears for him.

His hand covered hers. "Thanks. Not a day goes by that I don't think of them. Those six months with all three of us together became cherished, precious memories. Whatever differences my parents had disappeared when my dad showed up on our doorstep. Mum called him after her diagnosis, and he arrived on the next flight."

"Did your dad have a part in raising you?"

"Not until that point. Dad stayed away at Mum's insistence. Truth be told, I was fucking pissed when he showed up on our doorstep. Mum sat me down, explaining the terminal diagnosis she'd received. I sobbed like a wee babe in her arms. She asked me to give my dad a chance and to forgive her for keeping us apart. What's a boy to do? I granted my mum's dying request."

Kari's heart broke for West when he brushed away a tear from the corner of his eye, and the tears she tried to hold back landed on her cheeks. She grabbed a tissue from the box on the coffee table and handed one to West, too.

"Fuck, I'm glad I did. We spent those months as a proper family, and I got to know my dad. He went above and beyond to get to know me, too. After Mum's funeral, we stayed in Glasgow for another month, tying up loose ends and settling her estate. Then he brought me to his home in Jersey."

"No way. You lived in Jersey?"

"Yup. I got into a lot of fights in those first few months until I did everything to lose my Scottish brogue. Now, I have a weird mix of the two. Things settled down after one too many visits to the principal's office. I even played American football during my senior year."

"Is your dad still around?"

"Yeah, he and my stepmom retired to Miami several years ago. I'll visit them at Christmas."

"I'm glad. Family is important." Kari relaxed while West massaged her palm. "Mm." She shifted against him, getting more comfortable.

"There's something I'm curious about," he said after a minute.

Kari tilted her head to meet his gaze. "Oh? What are you curious about, Mr. Sharpe?"

"Well, I've seen some of your ad campaigns-"

She sat up and faced him. "Oh, em gee, did you Google me?" Her eyes widened in surprise when a telltale blush gave him away. "I'm surprised you found me. I used an alias when I modeled."

"When you didn't show up for Sunday brunch, Joanna told me to search for the name Katherine Davis, and I did on the drive to your apartment."

"Yeah...my agent believed Kari Davidson to be too mundane, and the name Katherine Davis screamed top model. So, Katherine Davis, I became."

"You've done some stunning photoshoots. Why did you give it up?"

"How did you put it? Ah, yes. It's a wee bit of a sad tale."

"You don't have to tell me if you don't want to, lass."

"No. I want to tell you. Let me preface by saying I won't blame you if you believe someone ought to have called child protective services. I experienced the life of an adult, too young to know any better."

"By the time I turned twelve, I'd already reached five-nine. One day at the mall with some friends, an agent approached me and gave me their card. I didn't plan to do anything with it until my mother found it in my pocket while doing the laundry. She insisted I pursue it and pushed me into it."

Kari shrugged. "I didn't mind doing print ads at thirteen. Then, my agent landed me a spot at fashion week in Paris when I turned fourteen. My mother's eyes glowed with dollar signs, and she shoved me out the door, eager for me to go."

"She didn't go with you?"

"Nope. An issue with my mother getting her passport."

"On your own in Paris at fourteen? Oh, baby girl," West said, wrapping his arm around her.

"It's not all bad. It's not all good either. I learned that despite being a child, I had to behave like an adult."

"Did someone take advantage of you?" Steel laced West's voice when he asked.

"If you want to know if someone raped me, the answer is no. If you want to know if I found myself in situations where it could've happened, the answer is yes." Every one of West's muscles tensed. "It didn't, though. I maneuvered my way out of those situations...for the most part."

"I can't believe your mother didn't go with you."

"Mm.... Who knew a criminal record for possession would make traveling out of the country...difficult? It's one of the many things I didn't know. What teenage girl needs to ask her mom if she has a criminal record?"

"Oh, lass." West pressed another kiss to the top of her head, and Kari fell for him a little more when he did.

"It's okay," she said.

"It's not okay, baby girl. Things are different now. I'm here, and I want to care for you."

Nope, definitely falling more than a little.

"I figured it out and managed pretty well. I got more jobs and came home less. Then, my mom told me I'd be a big sister. Izzy's father had already bailed. I tried to come home more often, and I'm glad I did. It's how the neighbor knew to contact me when my mother never returned. She dropped Izzy off for three hours, then three days passed without a word."

"Jesus. Poor Izzy."

Kari shuddered at the memory. "She was two, and I'm thankful she doesn't seem to remember the trauma. By the time I'd gotten there, Izzy was inconsolable. I apologized to Mrs. Bianchi and begged her not to call child services. That I'd take care of everything. It got worse, though."

This time, she tried to hide her tears from West, but he heard her sniff and tipped her chin up to meet his gaze. "Fuck, baby girl. I wish I could go back and fix it all for you."

An irrational thought gripped her. "We might not be together now if that were possible." A tear escaped, sliding down her cheek, and West caught it with his thumb.

"Baby...."

"No. Let me tell you the rest. The landlord showed up the next morning with an eviction notice. He said my mother hadn't paid the rent for two months. I told him I'd take care of it. I modeled for years; money isn't an issue. When I went to the bank to grab the rent, the teller informed me my co-signer on the account had withdrawn everything."

"Fuck."

"Fuck is right. My mother cleaned out my account after she left Izzy with the neighbor. Lucky for us, I kept an emergency credit card and used it to cover the rent, saving my sister and me from being thrown out on the street. I didn't even have time to lick my wounds when the next blow came. I didn't know when I could book my next job, so my agent and management firm dropped me because they didn't like not getting their 15%. Thus ending my modeling career."

"You didn't deserve any of that."

"No, I didn't."

"What did you do?"

Kari tried to burrow into West's side even more, wanting to hide her shame over her lack of education. "Well, there aren't many options for a nineteen-year-old with a GED. Either I waited on tables fifty hours a week, which left little hands-on caregiving for Izzy, or I found a job that paid well enough for me to work part-time. So…I got a job dancing burlesque three nights a week at a club called the Garden of Eden."

"They hired you underage?"

Kari shrugged. "I look my age, yet I don't. It's the height, you know? They didn't look at my ID, and I may have exaggerated my date of birth by a couple of years on the paperwork. The place didn't always play by the rules and regulations."

West grumbled. "If you weren't getting over being sick, I'd take you over my knee and turn your perfect ass a lusty shade of red for putting yourself in harm's way."

"You can't punish me when I didn't have a choice. In a way, it'd be like punishing yourself for not being there to fix it."

West sucked in a sharp breath. "You're right."

"Oh, I like it when you tell me I'm right. Mm...tell me again." Kari draped her leg over him and straddled his thighs. Their heavy conversation shifted into something more playful.

"You're right, baby girl." He gave her a wicked look and leaned in, nipping at her bottom lip. "I'll punish you for transgressions that have happened since we met."

"What transgressions?"

West pressed his forehead to hers. "I'll tell you later."

Kari pouted and let out a sigh. "Damn, we dredged some heavy shit out for each other tonight."

"You have a colorful way of describing meaningful conversation."

Kari tilted her head back and met West's amused gaze. "I'm anything but dull."

"It's something I've discovered." West leaned in and kissed her. He didn't make demands, melding their mouths until she hummed against his lips and pulled away.

"How about we lighten the mood with a fresh line of questioning? Tell me about your first time?"

West snorted with laughter. "This is how you lighten the mood?" He scratched his stubbled chin. "You know it was a long time ago."

"Ugh, stop it. You're not that old. Do you not remember?"

West stared at her, seeming to weigh what or what not to say. Then he expelled a deep breath along with his confession.

"Billy Kent. We fucked after the championship game. While the rest of the team headed out to celebrate, we stayed behind, having our own celebration in the locker room showers."

Silence fell between them. *Oh, wow.*

"Are you shocked my first time was with another man?"

"Nope," she said, popping the P.

"Why?"

Kari didn't mean to let the giggle bubble forth, trying to disguise it by clearing her throat.

Time for another truth bomb.

"My first time happened after a runway show with an older model named Indigo. She made the experience sensual for me, opening my eyes to being okay with wanting to explore my attraction to both men and women."

More silence fell between them when Kari asked, "Did we just come out to one another?"

"Aye, lass. I think we did."

"Cool," she said, kissing him.

"Cool?" he asked.

"Well...yeah...we came out to each other like it's no big deal. You know how it's supposed to be?"

"Mm...I like the sound of that, how it's supposed to be."

Chapter Eighteen

Kari

"You know about the Princess Laya kink?" West asked, staring at her with his mouth hanging open.

At Jasper's insistence, Kari took the rest of the week off even though she felt fine. West came by every day to check on her and Izzy. He didn't stay over, not wanting her to tell Izzy about them until she's ready. Yet, she missed falling asleep in his arms. The nights he stayed were some of the best sleep she's had.

West asked her to dinner tonight for her birthday. And a couple of hours ago, she dropped Izzy off at childcare and got ready for their date, dressing in a red silk blouse, dark denim, and black ankle boots.

He cupped her face and kissed her lips the moment she opened the door. "Fuck, red looks good on you. Happy birthday, baby girl." He presented her with a gorgeous bouquet of lilies, now displayed on her coffee table. With time to kill until they needed to leave for their reservation, they had a drink, talking and laughing about anything and everything...like how Kari knew about the Princess Laya kink.

"Oh, I know. I almost caused a riot when guests got a look at me in my gold bikini and the braided hair earmuffs during our May the 4th Be With You-themed masquerade party last year. Gray doubled security for the night when he saw me come out of my dressing room. He assigned Tony to stick by my side in a T-shirt with Jabba the Hutt on it." The memory made her giggle.

"It turned into a pretty epic night." When she peered up at West, she found him with a far-off look on his face. "Hey, Daddy? Want me to break out the gold bikini for you?"

West tugged her closer. "Uh, fuck yeah. I'd love to see you in the infamous gold two-piece. I always thought Laya was hot, but she wasn't my favorite."

"Who's your favorite?"

"The chick from Flashdance."

"Flashdance?"

West sighed and rubbed a hand over his face. "Fuck, I'm old. Don't tell me you've never heard of the movie Flashdance?"

"Give me one sec." Kari pulled out her phone, nibbling her lip while she tapped away on the screen. "This movie?" She tilted her screen, showing West the image of Jennifer Beals wearing the infamous off-the-shoulder sweatshirt.

"That poster hung in my room."

"It came out in 1983," she said, scrolling through the info on the movie. "You can't expect me to be familiar with every '80s film."

"It's a dance movie classic, and you're a dancer."

"The dancer thing is debatable, and I'm one to talk when my favorite musical is Singing in the Rain."

"Mm…Gene Kelly is a legend," he said.

"Right? He'd deliver a panty-melting look, then execute a flawless dance routine while singing a song. Hugh Jackman reminds me of him."

Kari clicked on the clip of one of the dance scenes. West tucked his head beside hers. "Hell, yeah. The wet chair scene."

"Damn, dude. Spoiler alert."

"I spoiled nothing." He leaned closer and said, "Watch."

The petite woman in the bit of red lace arching off the chair mesmerized Kari. When she bowed in half and reached for a cord above her, water splashed over her body, making the little red teddy transparent and even soaking the men who leaned in for a closer look. "Wow."

"Mm-hm. That scene made good spank-bank material in a young man's limited repertoire. However, it's not my favorite. May I?" he asked, gesturing to her phone. Kari handed it over.

West scrolled until he came across the clip he wanted, then handed it back. "Play the restaurant scene."

"Dang, she's a bratty little thing," Kari said with a smirk. "It seems you discovered a love for brats long before you knew what it meant."

"Yeah, I guess I did. The character's fucking sassy. I always believed the guy wanted to take her over his knee and redden her ass, then fuck her right there in the middle of the restaurant."

"Teenage you possessed a vivid imagination." Kari set her phone on the coffee table when the video finished. "How much time do we have before our reservation?"

"It's in an hour. Why?"

Kari patted his leg and stood up. "Occupy yourself for twenty minutes while I get ready."

West looked her up and down. "Aren't you already ready?"

"Mm, not quite. I want to freshen up. Give me twenty minutes. Please, Daddy?"

West smacked her ass, making her squeal. "Go do what you need to do, baby girl. I'm fine here."

"Thank you, Daddy."

Kari disappeared into her bedroom and the walk-in closet beyond, grabbing the garment bag with the outfit she wanted to change into. She stopped in front of her locked toy chest, adding a last-minute accessory to what she's going to wear.

Fifteen minutes later, she strolled back into the living room, shaking out the curls of the dark brown wig she now wore, and she tucked her other hand into her pants pocket, striking the perfect pose. "Though I'm way taller than Jennifer Beals, I figured you'd appreciate the nod to her character."

"Are you serious right now? Name the fantasy, baby girl, and it's yours. I can't believe you have a satin tuxedo in your closet."

When he reached her, West tipped her chin with his forefinger, his crystal blue eyes zeroing in on her glossy lips. "Fuck, you're beautiful." His warm breath fanned her lips, teasing them apart. Then he sealed his mouth to hers in a searing kiss, making her toes curl and her knees weak.

"I mean it. Name it, and it's yours." West offered when their lips parted.

"Um...." *Did she dare?* Kari bit her bottom lip. "Okay. Please understand I am not trying to fetishize you or your bisexuality."

"Can a bisexual fetishize a fellow bisexual?"

Kari shook her head. "Um, I'm not sure. I want you to know I am not trying to fetishize you."

"Noted," he said with a smirk.

Kari sighed. "It's... I've always wanted to peg a man, and I haven't dated one yet who will let me. I wondered if you might like to...or might be open to it."

West didn't even hesitate. "Name the time and the place, and my ass is yours for the pegging."

"For real?"

"Yup, and now that we've settled that, please tell me what you've got beneath this sexy jacket?"

Kari offered him a sultry smile and said, "Take me to dinner and find out."

"I am going to be the envy of everyone in the restaurant tonight. Let's go, sweetheart."

"I'll have the shelled lobster," Kari said with a smile for their server. She glanced at West from beneath her lashes, catching his smirk when he asked for the shrimp linguini, then gave their server the menus.

When they left, Kari pouted and said, "You know you're ruining the playing footsie part of this fantasy, what with you sitting at my side and not across from me."

West turned in his seat and said, "No need to play footsie with my cock, baby. Not when I've been hard for you all fucking night. Besides, sitting across from you is too far away." He spread his thighs wider and pulled her chair between them. "That's better."

Kari fiddled with the collar of West's shirt, still blown away by his willingness, dare she say eagerness, to let her peg him. "You're really going to let me fuck you?"

"Yes, baby. I really am. Let me be clear, though; your sweet ass is mine the moment you're done with me. Now, are you ever gonna take off this jacket and show me what you've got on beneath it?"

He pulled her chair closer and placed his lips against her ear. "I'm gonna be so fucking deep inside you, baby, you'll taste me for days."

"Oh...does tonight work for you?"

"Yes."

"Well, happy birthday to me. I can't believe we're gonna fuck each other's asses when you haven't even fucked my pussy yet."

"Oh, I'm fucking your pussy. After we've showered and you've swallowed my cum, I'm gonna fall asleep with my cock inside your tight little cunt."

"Oh, sweet fuck. Where have you been all my life?"

"Waiting for you to find me, baby girl."

Kari stood between his spread thighs. "You know...it'd be a terrible shame to get a butter stain on this jacket." She shivered as his hand trailed up and down the back of her thigh. Kari moved to undo the two buttons holding her jacket together when West covered her hands with his, stopping her.

"Let me." His soft command caused heat to pool in her belly. He slipped his finger between the lapels and popped the buttons open with a flick. He leaned back, keeping his other hand wrapped around the back of her thigh. "Now...take it off."

Kari met his gaze and rolled her shoulders, slipping the material off. Then she turned within the space of West's spread thighs and let the jacket slide off, revealing her bare back and arms, and the set of shirt cuffs, complete with cufflinks, fastened around her wrists.

"Fuck." She heard West mutter.

Kari glanced around and caught admiring looks from several of the restaurant's patrons, but only one person's desire for her mattered.

She hung her jacket over the back of her chair and then returned to her seat. Kari clasped her hands beneath her chin with her elbows on the table and gave West her best sultry pout. "How'd I do, Daddy?"

"Fuuuck," West growled. "You're lucky we aren't in front of a discerning audience. Otherwise, I'd spread you across this table and eat your pussy for fucking dinner instead."

"I'm soaked for you." She revealed a breath away from his lips.

West trailed his fingers over her shoulder and down her spine, making her shiver. "I bet you are. Daddy's going to edge you throughout dinner. Gonna get you wild and make sure you fuck me hard enough; I'll feel it for days."

"Let's go now. To hell with dinner," she said just as their server arrived.

"No, baby. We're staying for dinner. You're going to need your strength." Unfazed, the server set their plates in front of them. "Thank you," West said. Their server gave a slight bow, then left.

West draped his arm across the back of her chair, his heat keeping her warm despite her minimal clothing. "Want to try some of mine?" he asked, twirling the creamy linguini around the tines of his fork. He speared a shrimp, then offered her the succulent bite.

"Please," she said, parting her lips, her tongue peeking out, waiting for her taste. Kari relished his groan when she wrapped her lips around the fork. "Mm...delicious," she said after she swallowed. She licked her lips, catching the creamy sauce. "Yummy."

"Oh, you sweet, bratty girl. I hope you're ready to fuck all night long."

Kari picked up a meaty piece of lobster, dunked it in the warm butter, soaking the meat and her fingers. She raised it from the dish, letting the excess drip from her fingertips.

She tipped her head to the right, keeping her gaze connected with his, and slipped the lobster past her lips, sucking her fingers clean after swallowing the tender morsel.

"Want some?" Kari asked around her fingertip.

"Are you gonna feed me from your fingertips?" She nodded, too breathless to form the words. "Then yes, please."

Kari kept her gaze locked with his and sucked the butter from her thumb. She dunked another piece of lobster with her other hand when West wrapped his fingers around her wrist, stilling her movements.

"No, baby girl. Feed me with the fingers you had in your mouth. I want to be fed from them."

Kari dropped the piece of meat back into its buttery bath, sucked those fingers into her mouth, then picked it up again and held it to his lips. The dripping butter trailed over her palm.

West never let go of her wrist and pulled her hand to his mouth. "You're putting Alex Owen's brattiness to shame, baby." He bypassed the piece of lobster and licked the butter trailing down her palm, saving her cuff from being stained in one of the most sensual ways ever.

Is seductive eating a thing? Is this a new kink unlocked?

With her palm licked clean, West held her captive with his hooded gaze, wrapping his tongue around the lobster. He sucked the meat and her fingers into his mouth. Letting go when he'd gotten everything.

"Want some more linguini, baby?" West asked her like he didn't lick her hand the way he licked her pussy and twirled another bite around his fork.

"You haven't even tried it yet." Her protest was feeble as she took the offered bite.

West leaned in. "Let me rectify that right now." He licked the sauce from the corner of her mouth, then sucked her bottom lip past his teeth, driving his tongue into her mouth to capture a taste and swallow her moan.

"Fucking delicious," he said when their lips parted.

Kari mentally thanked the hostess for seating them at a corner table, allowing her to wiggle in her seat unnoticed. She licked her lips, squirming in her seat again. "Take me home, Daddy. I need to fuck you, then get fucked by you."

"Aye, lass. I need it too. Let's go." West stood and helped Kari to her feet. His heated breath fanned the curls covering her neck when he reached around her to lift her jacket from the back of the chair and pressed his hard length against her hip. "Can't have you catching a chill, baby girl," he said, drawing the jacket over her shoulders.

He buttoned it closed, grabbed his wallet from his back pocket, and threw several hundred-dollar bills on the table. Kari's eyes widened.

"What?" West asked. "Our server earned it for knowing to leave us the fuck alone." Then he placed a possessive hand at the small of her back, walking them out of the restaurant. He stayed close, and with each sway of her hips, Kari brushed the steel length of his erection.

CHAPTER NINETEEN

West

"Are you ready for me?" Kari asked from the other side of her closet door.

"He was, in fact, so fucking ready," said the voice of Morgan Freeman in his head.

On the ride back to Kari's building, West's erection never abated, not with her pressed to his side in the backseat.

The driver kept glancing at them, waiting for...well, West knew damn well what the man waited for. While playing with Kari in front of a consenting audience might tempt him, he didn't want to include anyone else tonight.

It was a rush to the elevator, and then it was a rush to her door. West pressed her against it the moment it closed. He wedged his thigh between hers. He placed his hands on either side of her head when he brushed his lips against hers, giving her the lightest kiss and the softest tease.

"Mm...." Kari lifted her chin and sought more of his mouth. The tip of her tongue licked the seam of his lips, pleading for them to part. West pulled back, denying her, and she whimpered, glaring at him. He didn't want to risk getting lost in her kiss, not with a night of wicked debauchery ahead.

On the verge of saying fuck it, West smacked her ass and sent Kari off to her room while he used the bathroom down the hall. They can shower together later. This time around required a bit of prep work. He planned to beg Kari to fuck him hard, making the prep necessary.

He stretched out on Kari's bed, ready and waiting while he listened to her get ready. Each little noise she made caused his cock to pulse against his stomach. He linked his fingers behind his head to keep from touching himself. The sound of leather being cinched and buckled is a unique brand of foreplay.

He raised his voice to make sure Kari heard him. "Oh aye, lass. I'm ready for everything you've got planned for me."

West leaned on his elbows when Kari stepped into view and almost swallowed his tongue. She'd slicked back her hair, still wet from her shower. She'd smoked up her eyes and reddened her lips. It's not what made his cock ready to explode...oh, no...sleek, black latex gloves covered her hands to her elbows. Leather straps crisscrossed her chest, framing her gorgeous breasts.

"Fuck me." West's gaze followed the leather straps across her stomach, where more encircled her waist and thighs, securing a seven-inch purple cock against her mound. The phallus bounced with each step she took toward the bed on her sky-high black stilettos.

West raised his knees and spread his thighs, putting himself on display, no longer able to deny touching himself. How could he not? He wanted to preen for her. He gripped the base of his cock, directing the glistening crown toward her, displaying everything he wanted Kari to use. Everything he planned to give her. He stroked himself from root to tip. His fingers dragged over each rung of his Jacob's ladder.

He met Kari's heated gaze. "Well, lass, are you going to introduce me to your friend?" He tipped his chin toward the rubber beast between her legs, never stopping the slow guide of his hand up and down his cock, waiting for what she'd do or say next.

The corner of Kari's luscious mouth quirked, gifting him with a sexy smirk. She popped the cap off the bottle of lube she held, squeezing a generous amount into her palm. When she snapped the lid shut, she tossed the bottle beside his hip.

"You mean this?" Kari wrapped her slick fingers around the purple phallus, putting on her own show, stroking the strap-on in a rhythm to match his. She moaned with each tug on her rubber dick, and he realized it turned her on to have that beast between her legs.

"Mm...." The movement of her hand remained slow and methodical. "This is my purple people-pleaser."

"*Damn*, baby girl. It sure looks like it's pleasing you."

"Well...I can fuck with it while also getting fucked by it." Kari turned and bent at the waist, and West almost came then and there. She spread her legs, showing him the other half of a double-headed dildo buried in her juicy pink pussy.

"Oh, sweet fucking Christ."

Not only did his girl have her pussy filled...nestled between the firm cheeks of her ass sat the red, heart-shaped jeweled end of a butt plug. The sight hit him like a sucker punch filled with desire.

It seems Kari prepped for him, too.

She smirked at the way he zeroed in on the jewel between her cheeks and moaned when she tapped it with her fingertip. "I worked this inside me when I changed for dinner. I've fantasized all night about you filling me everywhere."

West groaned, the rumble coming from deep in his chest, and he pumped his cock a little faster. "Fuck, baby. You're gonna take my ass, and fuck yourself at the same time? Such a greedy girl." He squeezed the base of his cock to stop himself from coming. No, not until Kari fucks him with her purple people-pleaser.

West scooted back until a pillow supported his head. Then he shoved another beneath his hips. "Come here. I want you to give Daddy that big, purple dick. Give it to me fucking hard, baby girl, I want to feel you for days."

Kari's gloved hands flexed against her hips. She licked her lips, adding a sheen to them. "Not...yet. Hands off my property, Daddy. No touching without my permission."

"So that's the way of it, eh, lass? Am I dealing with a bratty little Domme right now?" He's going to spank her ass until she screams, then he'll fuck her so good the moment she finishes dicking him down.

"Aye," she said, doing her best impersonation of him.

West dragged his fingertips along his cock one last time and let go, swiping the precum beading on his tip. He wanted to suck his fingers clean while Kari looked on. His hand didn't even make it halfway to his mouth when she snatched his wrist and landed a stinging slap against his thigh.

He forgot about the sting when the heat of Kari's mouth closed around his fingers. "Mm...." She licked and sucked them clean.

"You're playing a dangerous game, lass." His chuckle turned wicked. "Remember, I'm going to give you everything you do to me and then some. You'll pay for this later."

Kari's grin grew wicked when she pulled his fingers from her mouth and held them to her lips. "It's what I'm counting on, Daddy."

CHAPTER TWENTY

Kari

"Um...." Kari stared at the sexy-as-fuck man spread out on her bed. Hard and ready for her to fuck him.

For her to fuck him!

A sudden case of nerves fluttered in her stomach. She told West not to touch and smacked his thigh; the evidence of a blooming red handprint marred his tattooed skin.

Kari sat back on her heels, her purple dildo protruding garishly from between her thighs. West's expression shifted from desire to concern in the blink of an eye. He sat up and scooted toward her, his legs framing hers when he reached a hand out to cup her face. "What's wrong, lass?"

Kari dipped her gaze to avoid his inquisitive one, focusing on his tattoos and piercings. West tipped his head to the side, seeking their connection.

"Remember, we can stop. At any time. Your comfort and consent are vital to me, Kari, always."

She shook her head. "I don't want to stop, but I gave you a smack and told you not to touch. I'm sorry we didn't talk about those kinds of boundaries."

She never considered herself a switch. Is she one? Is West?

"Are you sure you want me to fuck you? Our dynamics so far have leaned toward me being submissive and you being dominant...I mean, do you like both? I think I might like both." Kari bit her lower lip, stopping her word vomit, worried West might change his mind.

He caressed her cheek. "No, it's not weird for me." His touch moved from her cheek to her throat, and she whimpered when West's hold on her throat tightened.

"I'm going to praise how hard you fuck me and tell you how good you are at rearranging my guts. I'm doing this with you because I want to share this experience with you, and I know you're going to make it fucking amazing for me."

With West, Kari wanted to submit. Craved the way he nurtured her. He's the Dom, yet he's giving her this gift of fulfilling a fantasy no one else gave to her, and she loved how enthusiastic he seemed — *wait, loved?*

Kari pushed against the hand around her throat and found no resistance. She rose over him, and West lay back on the bed. He bent his legs and placed his feet on the mattress, cradling her hips while she hovered above him. She stared into his eyes and leaned in to kiss him.

West squeezed her throat without putting pressure on her windpipe, sending a rush of endorphins through her body. He used the leverage of his grip to take control of their kiss, his tongue battling hers for dominance.

She moaned against his lips. The more passionate their kiss became, the harder they rocked against one another. The lube she'd coated her dildo with created a slick glide, making it easy to rub against his dick. She clenched around the devices inside her, just needing a little more friction on her clit, then she'd explode. "You're going to make me come."

West licked and sucked on her bottom lip, biting down on it until the sweet sting made her whimper. He held her captive between his teeth, countering the slight pain with the gentle sweep of his tongue. Her eyes rolled back in ecstasy.

"Look at me."

Kari snapped her gaze back to his.

"I want your eyes on me when you come." He pulled her tighter against him. "Fuck, you're beautiful, baby girl." He reached between them, wrapping his hand around them both, stroking them both, making her strap rub against her clit in the perfect way.

"Oh, fuck yes, right there."

"I want you to come for me. Come for Daddy and get your sweet little fuck-holes nice and juicy to take my big, pierced cock."

The heat of arousal spread from Kari's chest to her cheeks. "Fuck, I love your dirty words." *There's that pesky love word again.*

West gave her a wicked look and rocked with her. "I aim to please, lass."

The way they moved intensified. Kari's muscles tensed, and her body shook with her orgasm. She writhed against West, riding the waves of her release. She cried out his name, more like screamed it. For once, she didn't care what her neighbors heard.

"Fuck yes, baby girl." West gripped her ass with his other hand, pulling her tight to him, absorbing the last shudders of her release, his fingers digging into her flesh with enough bite to mark her.

"Mm...there's one, and I'm going to make sure you come all fucking night long." West pulled her in for another kiss, and Kari melted against his lips.

Kari pushed up with her palms against his chest. Then she slid down West's body, letting her nipples drag against his skin, making them both groan.

"What are you doing, baby girl?" West shifted onto his elbows, his gaze glued to where her open mouth hovered over his heavy sac, her warm breath making his balls tighten.

"It's your turn to keep your eyes on me, Daddy."

"There's nowhere else they're gonna be."

Kari winked, then slid her tongue over the taut skin. His dick jumped against his abdomen, desperate to reach the warmth of her mouth. She dragged her tongue up his length, swirling it around each piercing along the underside of his cock.

West whimpered when she retreated, her lips hovering over his glistening crown. "You're killin' me, lass. I'll come before you even get inside me."

Kari pursed her lips and hummed, pressing them to the tip of his cock. West shuddered, coating her lips with his precum. She licked them clean, savoring his salty flavor, then pulled away. "No, you won't, not until I say."

West made a desperate sound when she tugged on his balls, then slipped a slick finger inside him. "Fuck." He arched his hips off the bed, searching for more. "Add another. Get me ready to take you."

She popped the cap on the lube and drizzled more onto her fingers, working two back inside him, and on the next thrust, she added a third. Kari scissored her fingers, stretching him, and grazing his prostate with each deep stroke.

She dropped the lube onto the mattress beside them and pulled her fingers free. Then Kari gripped the base of her rubber phallus and lined it up with his hole, pressing the head inside.

"Easy, baby girl. Let me get used to you."

Kari tipped her chin, staring at where they joined. She bit her lip in concentration, sliding another couple of inches in.

"Fuck. Yes. More." West spread his legs wider and arched his hips until she pressed against his ass, and he'd taken all seven inches.

Braced on her palm, Kari dropped to her elbow, joining their bodies from chest to hip. Their breaths intermingled, and she tangled a hand in his hair while she stared into his stormy, desire-filled eyes, guiding his mouth to hers.

West parted his lips, welcoming her, taking her tongue and sucking it deep, like the way he took her strap. "Yes...." His groan vibrated against her lips while his hips rocked beneath her. "The way you're pressed against my prostate, you're going to make me come without even touching my dick."

Kari quirked her brow. "Hm...sounds like a challenge to me." She lifted his left leg over her shoulder and shifted her hips, making West's eyes roll back.

"I need you to fuck me, baby girl. Fuck me hard and make me come for you." He reached up and captured her lips in another searing kiss. She wanted to come when he did.

"I'm going to make you scream my name." Kari wrapped her arm around his thigh, using his leg to leverage a powerful thrust. When she pulled back until only the tip of her rubber cock remained inside him. She punched her hips forward, fucking her man deep while also pleasuring herself with the other half of the dildo inside her.

Kari pushed his right leg wider, getting deeper with each stroke. He palmed her breast and ran his thumb over her nipple while tugging hard on the ring through his. "Please," she gasped, and he gave the same treatment to her nipple, pulling and twisting her flesh until her thrusts became erratic.

"Don't stop. Keep going, baby girl. I'm close."

"Me too."

"Come with me," he commanded.

A rush of desire flooded Kari's system. West's control over her body in this moment became absolute. Her pussy clenched around the dildo and the plug in her ass.

She called his name, and he shouted hers.

West's cock pulsed. Ropes of cum shot from his tip, landing across his stomach and chest, all without laying a finger on his dick. Kari bit her lip and stared at the mess she'd helped him make. He dropped his legs to the bed and looked blissed out with his eyes closed and a sappy grin on his kiss-swollen lips.

A wicked, satisfied laugh bubbled up, and her bratty side struck again. "Mm...you're such a good boy for me."

Beneath her, West stilled. Not even taking a breath.

Uh, oh.

The hand he'd tangled in her hair tightened around the strands, gathering them in his fist. He tugged her head back and gave her a pointed stare, nipping at her chin. He trailed hot, open-mouth kisses along her jaw until his lips pressed against her ear and he said, "Understand that I'll only ever be a good boy for you."

Kari nodded.

West's cock twitched, shooting another spurt of cum onto his navel. The mini-orgasm added to the load splattered across his stomach and chest. It also reminded Kari that he's still impaled on her purple people pleaser.

She tried to pull away, but West wrapped his legs around her hips, trapping her. "You're not going anywhere, lass."

"Don't you want me to...?" Her words trailed off as she gestured at their joined bodies.

"I'm not in any rush." West's expression turned wicked. "Besides...it's your turn to be a good girl and lick Daddy clean."

CHAPTER TWENTY-ONE

West

Kari licked her lips, making no further move to follow his direction. The look in her desire-filled eyes grew more devious by the second. Her mouth parted, and her warm breath teased his chest where his splattered cum cooled.

"I know you heard me loud and clear, baby girl. You don't want your treat getting cold."

"Mm...make me eat it, Daddy."

Fuck, she really is perfect for him. "Does my baby girl want to play dirty?"

Kari nodded.

"Use your words."

"Yes," she said, and West used the grip he had on her hair to guide Kari to a splash of cum coating his nipple.

Her little pink tongue peeked out from between her kiss-swollen lips, and she swirled it around his pebbled nipple, sucking the cum from the ring pierced through it. She held it between her teeth and tugged. West groaned, and his cock twitched back to life, eager for another round.

With a bratty wink, Kari arched her back, dragging her breasts back and forth through the cum splattered across his stomach. Surprised, West let go of her hair, and when she moved back, her strap slipped from his ass, and he adjusted to her no longer being inside him.

She swirled her fingertips around her cum-coated nipples, gathering his release, then she held them to her lips and asked, "Does this work?" Kari covered her lips with his essence, as if she were applying lip gloss. Then she licked her lips clean.

"Brat, everything you do drives me wild."

Kari dropped her head down, keeping her gaze fixed on his, and lapped at the cum pooled in his belly button, like a kitten enjoying her cream.

She squealed when he turned the tables and flipped her over, laying her across his thighs. He trapped Kari's rubber cock between them. "If your goal's getting me to turn your ass an enticing shade of red before I fuck it, you've succeeded."

West unbuckled the thin leather strap that ran between her legs. "How did you manage this all by yourself?"

"Practice," she said, and West landed a smack to the meatiest part of her right cheek because the idea of her strutting around her bedroom after getting the harness cinched in place turned him the fuck on.

"So damn sassy," he growled, exposing the heart-shaped jeweled end of her butt plug. West pulled her cheeks apart, and Kari arched her back, presenting her perfectly plugged little ass.

"Is this what had you shifting in your seat at the restaurant?" West asked, tracing the heart-shaped jewel with his fingertip.

"Well...no, that was all you. The plug in my ass was a bonus."

"You're such a fucking brat. I'm going to fuck you so good, baby girl. The moment I finish spanking you."

West pressed his thumb against the center of the red heart, enjoying the way the jewel sparkled while the other end of the double-dildo filled her dripping pussy. "Stuffed so fucking full and ready to take my cock."

Fuck, he wanted to breed her. Not get her pregnant, at least...not now. He wanted to mark her and fill every one of her holes with his cum. Before he asked when Kari wanted to expand their family, he redirected his thoughts to what they're doing right now. "What's our safeword, baby girl?"

"Chickenpox."

"And if we can't talk?"

"We give a double-tap or peace sign. West...I'm enjoying everything we're doing, and if there ever comes a point I don't, I promise to let you know. Same goes for you, right?"

"Aye, the same goes for me." He liked how she checked in with him, too. He'd always been the giver, the provider in his relationships, no matter how serious or casual. From the moment they met, everything felt different with Kari. More balanced.

West massaged her ass, squeezing and rubbing her flesh, warming it up for the sting of his palm. "I know we've exchanged test results, but are you on birth control?"

"Yes, I have an IUD."

"Will you let me take you bare?" *The idea of filling her... breeding her...*

"Please...I want to feel you come inside me."

"Oh, my perfect girl. Let's get you ready to take Daddy's cock." He landed a second sharp smack on her ass. "Going to give you ten. You deserve ten spanks, don't you, baby girl?"

Kari squirmed and tried to cover her ass with her hands. West grabbed both her wrists, trapping them at the base of her spine. Then he spanked her, alternating smacks against each fleshy mound. "We don't count until you've told Daddy you deserve ten. If this is your way of getting more, you've succeeded."

Kari bounced against his thighs and squealed, "I deserve ten, Daddy."

West peppered her bottom with ten more, five landing on each cheek. He made her count and thank him after each one. When he finished, he palmed her flesh. The heat from her reddened ass radiated against his hands. "What do you say?"

Kari wriggled on his lap, teasing him before she said, "Thank you, Daddy."

West reached beneath her, putting pressure on her clit, rubbing the base of her dildo against her mound. "Are you gonna come for me stuffed full and with a red ass?"

Kari rocked her hips faster, and West gave her needy clit even more attention. "Yes. I-I'm coming, I...." Her words faded into a low, keening moan, and she shattered in his arms.

"Yes, baby. Juice all over your rubber cock. Show Daddy what you're going to do." Kari spread her legs wider, and West watched as her pussy pulsed around the end of the dildo stuffed inside her. "Such a pretty pussy. Daddy can't wait to fuck and fill you there." West traced a finger over her stretched labia, spreading her arousal.

"Please...."

"Soon, baby girl. Gotta fuck your sweet ass first." West brushed his fingers against the base of the plug. "The moment I finish filling your tight little hole, I'm going to plug you back up and leave you filled with my cum. You want that, don't you?"

For a moment, West believed he might've taken the filthy things he wanted to do to his sweet girl too far, then Kari let out a moan. "Please."

"Do you like the idea of being full of Daddy's cum when you go to sleep?"

"Yes," she cried out. "I want to be filled with you. I need it. Please fill me with everything you've got, Daddy."

"You're such a perfect girl for me. Take a deep breath, then let it out nice and slow."

West kept his eyes on Kari, ensuring she followed his directions, then he pulled on the end of the plug, opening her tight ring of muscle. He grabbed the bottle of lube and popped the cap, drizzling the cool liquid down the crack of her ass.

There's never too much lube when it comes to anal play.

"Need to get you nice and slick." West worked the toy in and out of her ass while Kari mewled and squirmed in his lap. He gave her lush, reddened cheeks a couple more hearty slaps. "Be still, baby."

West pulled the plug free, drizzling more lube inside her, then he guided the plug back in, fucking her with it until Kari said, "I-I'm close. I'm going to come again, West. Please...."

He shoved the plug all the way back inside her and gripped her tender ass cheeks hard, making Kari moan. "Baby girl, I answer to Daddy or Sir in times like this. If you want another half-dozen spanks, call me West. If you're ready for me to fuck you, you better call me Daddy."

Kari rocked in his lap, grinding her stuffed pussy and ass in the air. Then, she used her words. "Please, Daddy...I need you to fuck me."

"Such a good little slut for me. Get in the center of the bed on your hands and knees. I want your ass in the air." West smacked her ass one more time. "Press your face to the mattress. And baby? You'd better brace yourself."

He pulled the plug out of her ass and set it on the nightstand. He lubed his cock and notched the head against her winking hole. Kari tried to pull him inside, and West gripped her hips, stilling her movements, with the head of his cock pressing deeper inside her slick heat. The thick piercing beneath his crown slipped past her stretched muscle. She clenched around him, and with the dildo still stuffed inside her pussy, she gripped him like a fist.

"Fuck, you're tight."

"Please, Daddy." Kari pressed her face to the mattress; her hands braced on either side of her head when she peered at him over her shoulder. "I need you inside me. Don't make me wait any longer, please."

"The way you beg me is like music to my ears." West pushed his cock in further. "Fuck, you feel good, baby girl. Daddy is going to fill your ass with all his cum."

"No, Daddy. Not all of it. Please save some for my tummy and pussy."

West stilled, then he ran his hand up Kari's spine and squeezed the back of her neck. He leaned back and grasped her hips in his hands, pulling her onto his cock, allowing him to sink the rest of the way inside her. She shivered and clenched around him. "Fuck. You've got a stranglehold on my cock."

"I'm so full."

"Mm...I love how stuffed you are. The dildo in your pussy is rubbing the underside of my cock. You feel every one of my piercings, don't you, baby?"

"Yes. The sensation is like nothing I've ever felt. You've wrecked me for anyone else."

"I'm telling you right now, if I have my way, there will be no one else." West increased his pace, leaving Kari no time to consider such a declaration.

He slid in and out of her ass while his balls slapped against her stuffed pussy. "I'll never share you with anyone, baby girl. This is the closest you'll get to another person filling you while I fuck you like this."

"Oh...oh God...I'm gonna come."

"Fucking right you are. Now, choke my dick and milk every drop from me."

"Yes, yes, yes," Kari chanted. West let her fuck herself onto his cock, his grip tight on her hips, holding her close while she rocked against him. Her orgasm pulsed around him, drawing him deeper into her clenching grip while his raced down his spine.

"Fuuuck," he groaned. His release flooded her back passage. "Fuck yes, Kari."

West leaned over, careful to keep the bulk of his weight off her. He trailed heated kisses along her neck and cheek until he reached her lips. Kari returned his kiss with sated passion. He swallowed her moan and licked into her mouth.

"Baby, are you okay?"

"Mm-hm...so good."

"Daddy's going to put your plug back in. Keep my seed deep inside you." He didn't even try to hide the possessiveness in his voice.

He looked for signs that this might be too much; instead, she gave him a loopy smile. "Please...I want it...to be plugged full of you."

"Keep talking to me like that, and I'm never letting you go." He didn't give her a chance to respond, pulling free of her ass, his cum creaming at her opening. He had a primal urge to scoop it up with his fingers and shove it back inside her.

"Keep your ass in the air for me; I'll be right back." West took her plug to the washroom to clean it. When he came back, he stopped and stared. Kari lay on her stomach with her back arched and her ass up, waiting for him. "Fucking beautiful."

West climbed onto the bed and kneeled beside her. "Such a good girl."

He added more lube to the plug, then swirled it around her opening to work his cum in with the lube. "Gotta keep it all in, baby." He pushed the plug in, sealing his release inside her.

West traced the heart-shaped jewel. "Are you ready for more?" Not even close to being done with her tonight. He may never get enough of her.

"Yes. I need more. Please, Daddy...."

"Funny, I was thinking the same thing. Not sure I'll ever get enough of you." He worked on the harness, unbuckling the leather straps surrounding her breasts, admiring the impressions they left.

He undid the straps at her waist and pulled the dildo from her pussy. Kari moaned when he gathered her into his arms. "Let's get cleaned up. The shower's on, and it should be nice and steamy by now." West stood with her in his arms and carried her into the bathroom.

He didn't put Kari down until they stood beneath the hot spray, holding her close, tucked against his chest. West ran his hands up and down her back, pressing kisses to her temple. "Tell me if this is too much for you. Am I too much for you?" Still afraid he'd pushed things too far and too fast when she tipped her head back and met his gaze.

"No, it's not too much. I wanted someone to explore my desires and kinks with. Someone...who'd take care of me in all the ways I need." Kari's hands moved from his chest. She looped her arms around his neck and kissed him.

"I want to spend every day worshipping you," West said against her lips. He kept kissing her, stopping long enough to shampoo her hair, then massaged the conditioner over the ends.

Kari's arms slipped from his shoulders to his waist. She tucked her face in the crook of his neck and hummed. "You're great at this."

West pressed another kiss to the top of her head. "When it comes to you, I strive for perfection."

She tipped her head back and met his gaze. "I don't need perfection, Daddy. I just need you."

"Oh, baby girl. You make me want to try even harder." He left the conditioner to condition and reached for Kari's body wash. Flicking the cap open, he brought the bottle to his nose, getting a concentrated dose of the scent clinging to her skin, and he realized borrowing her soap meant he'd smell like her, too. He fucking liked that. A lot.

West lathered the soap over Kari's back and arms until he needed to put some space between them to reach her front. He set the sponge aside and used his soapy hands to clean her breasts. When the water rinsed the suds away, he dipped his head, sucking her right nipple, then the left, alternating between them until they became swollen, stiff peaks, and Kari writhed in his arms.

West absorbed her moans into their kiss, swatting her hand away when she attempted to stroke his cock. "Not yet," he growled, dropping to his knees at her feet. He reached for the sponge again, soaping her toes, then her feet, working his way up her legs.

Kari parted her thighs, giving him access, and West used his hands to wash her pussy, the suds mixing with her arousal, giving him a slippery surface for the pad of his middle finger to slide over her clit. He made sure all the soap was gone, then he slid his two middle fingers inside her and used his thumb to work her clit.

West leaned in and pressed his lips to her navel, lapping at the trail of water flowing over her skin. Kari tipped her head forward, the water rinsing the conditioner from her hair. When she met his gaze, she let out a whimper of desire. Her cry intensified when he curled his fingers and rubbed the front wall of her vagina.

She dug her fingers into his hair, holding him against her, using him to keep her balance while he pleasured her. "I can't believe you're going to make me come again."

West grinned against her belly, then nipped at her skin. He circled her clit, enjoying the way it swelled against the pad of his thumb. "Believe it, baby girl. We're nowhere near done."

Kari's pussy tightened around his fingers.

"Yes...show me what you'll do to my cock. Strangle my fingers and soak my hand with your release."

West relished the shot of pain when she pulled on his hair and screamed his name. Like he demanded, her pussy spasmed and clenched around his fingers. "I got you. You can let go. I won't let you fall." He gripped her hip with his other hand, helping her stay upright while she rode out her orgasm. The moment she calmed, West lurched to his feet and captured her mouth with his in a searing kiss.

He held Kari's face between his hands, licking past the seam of her lips to swirl his tongue against hers. He walked her back until she sat on the built-in bench, and they stared at one another while he took care of washing himself.

Kari squirmed in her seat while he soaped his chest, tweaking his nipples, tugging on the rings, then trailing a soap-covered hand over his tattooed abs toward his cock already straining for her. "See something you like, baby girl?" he asked, rinsing the suds away.

Instead of answering, Kari's hand dove between her thighs, parting her folds to strum her clit. She whimpered and rocked on her palm, fingering herself while she stared at the slow, deliberate movement of his hand up and down his cock.

West moved until he stood between Kari's spread legs, and his cock pointed at her lips. "You hungry, baby?"

Kari's lips parted, and her hot breath blew across his sensitive tip. West's balls drew tight, and he knew all bets were off once she got her mouth on him.

"I'm starving, Daddy." Kari licked her lips; the tip of her tongue grazed the head of his cock, swiping the precum pooled at his slit. She hummed, swallowing it down.

West gripped the base of his cock to stave off his impending orgasm. The urge to cover Kari's face in his release is something he'll save for another time. Right now, he needed to feed her. "Give me your mouth, baby girl. Show me how hungry you are for me."

CHAPTER TWENTY-TWO

Kari

West's salty, musky flavor flooded her taste buds. She kept her eyes locked with his and wrapped her lips over her teeth, sucking the head of his cock into her mouth, hollowing her cheeks, increasing the pressure of her suction.

"Fuck baby, you're going to suck my soul through the head of my dick."

Kari hummed, knowing the vibrations would add to the intensity. She lowered her head, taking more of him into her mouth, tonguing the first two piercings beneath his crown.

When she reached the third piercing, Kari moved her hands to West's thighs and waited, continuing to swirl her tongue around the head of his cock.

He understood what she wanted. For him to take over, to take control, and he did not disappoint.

West punched his hips forward, and the head of his cock slipped into her throat. Her eyes watered when she swallowed around him, fighting the urge to gag.

Kari wanted West to use her. Wanted him to fuck her face and make her cry. He moved his hands to the sides of her head, his long fingers tangled in her hair, pressing against her scalp. "You want something, baby girl?"

She nodded.

"You're going to have to get off my dick and use your words like a good girl." Instead, Kari gave him another thorough suck. "Fuck, baby. I won't give you what you want unless you say it."

Kari leaned back, and his dick slid from her mouth with a resounding pop. She gave him a sheepish grin, knowing exactly what she did to him.

"Well?" His cock bobbed in her face, eager to give her what she wanted. All she needs to do is say it.

"Fuck my face, Daddy. Use me like a toy and feed me your pleasure." In giving him the words he wanted, he gave her what she craved.

"Open." West let out a feral growl and used the grip he kept on her to propel her onto his cock, giving her seconds to part her lips and take a deep breath. He angled her head, and she stuck her tongue out, opening her throat to take him until her nose pressed against his groin.

He held her there until her eyes watered and tears tracked down her cheeks. "Yes, baby girl. Give me your tears while you choke on my dick." The moment her fingers clenched his thighs, West pulled out, and she gasped for air.

"What's your safeword?"

"Chickenpox." The roughness of her voice surprised her. Will she even have one when he finishes with her?

"And if your mouth's occupied like it's about to be?"

Kari tapped his thigh twice with her left hand.

"Good girl. Keep your left hand on my thigh and shove your right between your legs. From here on out, until I come down your throat, you're mine to use."

"Yes, Daddy." Kari held onto his thigh and slipped two fingers between her folds, shoving them inside her fluttering channel. She opened her mouth wide and stuck her tongue out.

West rested the head of his cock on the tip of her tongue, and aimed a wad of spit onto his crown, and it trickled into her mouth. Kari moaned, and West used his cock to smear his spit over her tongue.

"Wrap your lips around me, take a deep breath, then breathe through your nose. Daddy needs to use his toy."

The moment Kari took a deep breath, West angled her head and shoved his cock to the back of her throat over and over, dipping further with each thrust. Drool dripped from her chin onto her breasts, and tears tracked down her cheeks. All the while, he stared at her with such reverence.

Kari worked her fingers against her pussy, relaxing into the way West used her for his pleasure, giving herself over to him.

"I'm close, baby girl. I need you to come. Please tell me you're right there with me." Kari did her best to nod while taking his cock, humming around him, hoping he understood how she teetered on the edge of release herself. "Yeah, baby? You ready for me?"

"Mm-hm," she hummed around his girth, her tongue teasing his piercings each time he pushed his cock to the back of her mouth. Kari circled her clit faster, her muscles tightened, and she careened over the edge into her orgasm, and a moment later, West filled her mouth with his cum.

Kari swallowed, and West's hand moved to the back of her head, holding her to him. He moaned her name and spilled the rest of his release down her throat.

Overwhelmed by her own release, Kari forgot to breathe, and when he pulled free of her mouth, she coughed and gasped for air.

West immediately dropped to the shower floor, cupping her face. He wiped beneath her tear-filled eyes and said, "Breathe, baby girl. I got you." Then he scowled at her. "Why didn't you use your safeword? It's what you do if things are too much?"

Kari gasped. "It's not too much." Her voice was raspy from such a thorough throat fucking. She cleared it and worked to slow her breathing. "I forgot to breathe and came again."

West growled and pulled her against his chest. "Fuck, baby girl. I worried I'd hurt you."

"You didn't hurt me, I swear. I came even harder."

He cupped her face and tipped her head back until she met his scrutinizing gaze, and he checked her over. "We'll explore your breath-play kink further under stringent rules, which we'll discuss at length."

"Yes, Sir. Thank you, Daddy." Kari didn't even try to hide her satisfied expression. There is something in getting precisely what she wanted.

"Brat."

Kari let out a startled squeak when he grabbed her and pulled her onto his lap. "Wrap your legs around me." She hooked her legs around his lower back, holding his shoulders when he stood with her in his arms. He palmed her ass, and his fingertips pressed against the jeweled base of her butt plug, making her moan.

West used one hand to turn off the water, then carried her from the shower. He set her on the counter and pulled a towel from the rack, drying her first, then himself, tossing the towel into the nearby hamper. He scooped her back into his arms, kissing her while he walked them to her bed.

West placed her in the center of the mattress and caged her in, humming against her mouth. "You taste like me."

"I love the way you taste."

West stared into her eyes, the word love hanging between them. "I love the way we taste together."

"Me too."

West trailed kisses down her throat, over her collarbone, until he reached her breasts. He cupped them and squeezed them, making her moan, then cry out when he pinched her nipples. He sucked and bit her hard buds, then moved further down her body, trailing kisses over her stomach until he reached the juncture of her thighs.

His hands gripped her hips, pushing her up the bed until her head rested on a pillow. His hands then glided over her ass to the backs of her thighs, spreading them wide to make room for his shoulders to settle between them. "Grab the headboard, baby girl, and hold on. Daddy's nowhere near done with you."

Kari did what West commanded, gripping the headboard tight when his head dipped between her spread thighs. He dragged his nose along her slick folds and inhaled. "Fuck, you smell sweet, baby. I've got to have a taste."

Kari let go of the headboard with one of her hands and tangled it in his hair, ready to guide him to her sweet spot. West froze with his tongue poised above her clit, glaring at her, and denying her his touch.

"Did I tell you to take your hand off the headboard?"

"No, Sir." Yet her fingers remained tangled in his hair.

"Are you testing me, baby girl?"

"Am I?" She was, and she loved every fucking second of it. He spat on her clit; his warm saliva sliding between her pussy lips.

"What's it going to be, baby girl? Are you going to do what I say, or am I going to edge you until you scream for mercy?"

Kari let go of his hair and returned her hand to the top of the headboard. "Good girl." He praised, then his mouth enveloped her pussy, and his tongue snaked through her folds, lapping up his spit and her arousal.

"Oh, fuck, I don't know if I can come again."

West circled her clit with his index finger. "I know you've got a couple more in you."

"I've already come four times," she said, arching her hips off the mattress, seeking more of his touch.

"Only Four? Baby, that's not nearly enough."

Kari screamed when he wrapped his lips around her clit and sucked, doing a mighty fine version of what she'd done to him in the shower. "Oh, fuck," she cried when he plunged two fingers into her tight channel, pumping them in and out of her, his fingertips stroking her G-spot with each thrust.

An intense pressure centered low in her belly, and Kari knew she's gonna come. "Wes...I...." Consumed by the mounting urge to explode, Kari didn't string more than two words together.

West knew, though. "You gonna squirt for me, baby?"

"I...." *Is she going to squirt?* West pressed his palm against her lower abdomen, intensifying the sensation. "Yes," she shouted.

"Fuck, yes. Soak my face. I'm going to lap up everything you give me."

He resumed his intense sucking of her clit while his fingers curled inside her and his palm pressed down on her stomach. Pressure mounted, her muscles tensed, and her toes curled. She screamed and exploded. A flood of wetness hit West's chin, and he opened his mouth to catch what she offered. Kari rode out the waves of her release, rubbing her pussy against his face.

She may have lost consciousness for a moment. She became boneless and languid, having experienced one of the best orgasms of her life. When she came to her senses, West hovered over her, the head of his cock waiting at her opening.

"There you are, baby girl." He leaned over and kissed her, letting her taste herself on his lips. "Are you ready for me?"

"Make love to me. Please?"

"Yes, baby." He kissed her again, his tongue demanding entry into her mouth, which Kari granted, parting her lips and tangling her tongue with his. Then, in the next second, West flipped her onto her belly, his hands at her hips, arching her ass in the air. The tip of his cock kissed her pussy. Then he stopped. Waited.

Waited for what?

"Beg me."

Ah....

Kari wiggled her hips, getting the head of his cock to nudge further inside her. She hissed when his palm landed on her tender ass, his other hand going to the back of her neck. West leaned over until his lips touched her ear. "Use your words, baby girl," he said with a growl.

"Fuck me, Daddy. I need your big, pierced cock to fill me. I want you to breed me. Please...."

"Fuck, you're such a good little slut for me."

She wiggled her hips again, and this time West impaled her on his cock with one hard thrust. Kari screamed, and she clenched around his thick invasion, gasping for breath while West held himself deep inside her, letting her get used to every thick, pierced inch of his cock.

"Fuck, you've got a stranglehold on my dick. Knowing you've got my cum plugged inside your bowels makes me want to fill this pussy with another load. Give me another orgasm, baby. I need to fill you up."

"Please...I swear I'll come if you move. Please fuck me, Daddy."

West pinned Kari to the mattress with a hand at the back of her neck. His other hand gripped her hip, holding her in place. Then he shifted his hips, pulling out of her halfway. Each piercing dragged across her G-spot, making her shudder beneath him.

"Please...."

He pumped his cock in and out of her, setting a lethal pace. Kari's mouth opened in a silent scream as she came. Air left her in a rush, and spots danced across her vision.

"Oh, fuck," West said, pulling free of her pussy. He didn't give her time to protest. Flipping her over again, he plunged his cock back into her. West dropped to his elbows and slowed his pace, filling her deep and making her breath catch. Making love to her.

He smoothed her hair back from her face, where it stuck to her sweat-dampened skin. West didn't take his eyes off hers, keeping up a steady rocking motion, grinding his groin against her clit. Her nails dug into his back, and her feet hooked behind his knees.

"Kari," he whispered. His thrusts quickened, and Kari's pussy tightened around him.

"No," she said, shaking her head in disbelief, not ready to accept what her body demanded.

"Yes."

She couldn't believe she was on the verge of coming again. The moment the heat of West's release flooded her insides, she clenched around him, this orgasm catching her off guard with its unexpected intensity.

West rolled, taking her with him while he remained buried deep inside her. Kari sprawled across his chest with his heart thudding steadily against her ear. Her eyelids grew heavy, and her breathing slowed.

She relaxed into his touch.

His hand rubbed up and down her back, and he kissed the top of her head. "Rest, baby. I got you."

"Mm...," Kari released a sleepy moan, burrowing her face into the crook of his neck. "I'll keep your cock warm if you promise to fuck me awake in the morning."

The sound of his groan rumbled against her ear. "Promise, baby girl." The last thing Kari remembered when she drifted off was being full of him.

Thank goodness West knew better than to let her sleep all night. She rested for maybe half an hour, and then he fucked her awake, making her ride him until he added to the load of cum already inside her, and she orgasmed all over his cock.

Kari couldn't move another inch, so West scooped her into his arms and carried her into the bathroom, where he removed the plug from her ass and made her sit on the toilet to take care of business while he turned the shower back on.

"I don't want another shower," she said with a pout. "I want to pee, brush my teeth, and go to sleep."

West met her gaze in the mirror. "You're going to do all those things. You're also having a quick wash and change into your pajamas between the teeth brushing and the sleeping."

Kari huffed. "Fine." She flushed the toilet, and West helped her to stand. Her cheeks heated when he kissed the tip of her nose, then tugged her beneath the spray, careful to keep her hair dry this time.

Kari let him support her body while he soaped and rinsed them both clean. He didn't waste any time drying them off. He closed the toilet lid and sat Kari on it. "Stay here. I'll be right back."

A minute later, West returned, dressed in his grey sweats and carrying her black silk pajama set. "How did you know...?"

"Hush, baby. Let me get you dressed and into bed." West pulled the bottoms over her feet and up her legs, getting her to stand so he could settle them over her hips. Then he tugged the top over her shoulders, doing up each button, and lifted her into his arms.

"I can walk, you know."

"I know," he said, carrying her into her bedroom anyway.

Kari crawled to her side of the mattress, and West pulled her into his arms. "Sleep well, baby girl," he said, kissing her cheek. She snuggled against him and slept the sleep of a satisfied woman.

Kari woke with a groan. Every muscle ached in the best possible way, and she stretched beneath the covers. She'd woken up alone because, a little while ago, West had given her a gentle kiss, then slipped from the bed, promising to be back soon with everything needed for her birthday brunch.

"Go back to sleep, baby," he'd said. "I'll be back soon with all the sustenance you need." She hummed and snuggled deeper beneath her blankets.

She's awake now, though, and the reason pounded on her door again.

Kari yawned and stretched. "Did he forget to take the apartment keys?" Her stomach growled. "Maybe his arms are full of delicious brunch goodies, and he can't open the door." She stumbled out of bed, groaning at the pleasurable ache radiating from every part of her body. "Coming".

She skipped toward her door, eager to enjoy quality time with her man. *Her man?* Yeah, her man and Izzy. "Did you forget-" The rest of her words died between her and the woman standing on the other side of the door.

Oh, no.

"Damn, girl. I thought your new stud would never leave. Gotta say he's better than the last one, though a little old for you."

The last one? She hadn't seen her mother in years, yet she knew about Spencer?

"Hello, Leslie. How did you find out where I lived?" Kari widened her stance and crossed her arms over her chest, trying to block the doorway.

"Last time I saw you, you called me Mom."

"Last time I saw you, I still had one."

"Nonsense. I remembered your birthday. Aren't you gonna let me in?"

"Fuck no."

"Don't be a bitch, Katherine. After all the time to track you down, I've earned this visit."

Damn, for a neglectful, absentee mother, she sure knew how to scold.

"We have nothing to say to one another."

"You know we do. I never signed the papers granting you guardianship of your sister." Her mother tried to look around Kari into the sanctuary of her apartment. Kari moved, blocking her.

"The statute of limitations hasn't run out on your thievery, Leslie." Kari put her face right in her mother's. "In every way that matters, I'm her mother. You abandoned us years ago. Izzy doesn't even remember you."

Her mother frowned or tried to. She'd filled her face with Botox and fillers, her expression frozen when she sniffed. "Looks like you're doing well for yourself." Leslie tried looking around her again.

She knew if her mother figured out a way, she'd take this from her and Izzy, too. "No thanks to you."

Kari heard the elevator arrive and the doors open, and she hoped like hell it was West. When he rounded the corner with a bag in one hand and a tray of drinks in the other, Kari breathed a sigh of relief.

A smile spread across his face when he looked up and saw her. However, his smile faltered when he caught sight of the woman with her, and he took in Kari's stricken expression.

His long strides brought him to her, and he stepped between her and what he deemed a threat. His assessing gaze connected with Kari's. "Everything okay?" West asked when he set the food and drinks on the entryway table. He then looked closer at the woman. "Didn't we run into each other in the elevator last week?"

Kari spun around to face her mother. "You came here last week? Are you stalking me now, Mother?"

"This is your mother?" West looked between them, clocking their similarities. Then he pulled Kari to his side and forced her mother to take a measured step back.

The way he stepped in and protected her made Kari fall even more in love with him. She sucked in a sharp breath.

Oh, my God. She's in love with West.

He sensed her sudden tension and misconstrued it as being uncomfortable in her mother's presence, which isn't untrue. It's just not the real reason.

"Is there anything else you want to say to this woman right now, baby?"

"No."

He kissed her temple. "Why don't you go inside, and I'll escort...your mother out. I'll be back in a few minutes."

"Okay. Thank you."

Kari squeezed West's hand, not looking at Leslie again despite her shouting, "This isn't over."

More than afraid of what her mother might do next, Kari stepped into her apartment and locked the door.

CHAPTER TWENTY-THREE

West

He waited until the door shut and locked behind him. Only then did he turn his gaze to the woman, who stood in a pose similar to one Kari used. He gave himself a mental shake and gestured for her to move.

"Aren't you even going to ask my name?"

"Nope. If Kari wants me to know, she'll tell me."

"It's Leslie," the woman offered anyway.

He didn't like that Leslie hadn't moved yet. "Ma'am. I believe you know where the elevator is."

Leslie scoffed, then did her version of a strut down the hall. If this were an attempt to entice him, she failed. West's gaze never moved from the back of her head until they reached the bank of elevators, and he pushed the call button.

"You know I have a right to see my child."

The doors to the elevator slid open, and he once again gestured for Leslie to precede him. When they closed behind them, West leaned against the corner opposite her, keeping the length of the elevator between them. "Are you referring to Kari or Izzy?"

Leslie crossed her arms in a huff. "Kari is a grown woman. Izzy needs me. She's a child."

"The same child you abandoned over three years ago?" West's rage simmered beneath the surface while he kept a calm façade.

"Fuck you."

West didn't concern himself with the elevator's security system, not when Jasper owned the building. It didn't look like Leslie had a camera, so he took a decisive step toward the woman who'd abandoned the two people he loved.

His heart beat faster. *He's in love with Kari Davidson.* With this knowledge, he said what he said next with icy precision.

"How about under the pretense of getting to know the man Kari's dating, I tell you a bit about myself?" West moved until he stood right in front of her. "I belonged to an elite military force for a decade. I am a trained sharpshooter with one-hundred percent accuracy at two miles out."

Leslie's eyes widened in fear and understanding, yet West still drove his point home. He leaned in close and spoke in a quiet voice. "I'm also 100 percent accurate in making someone disappear." West looked her over, and

Leslie trembled beneath his gaze. "I will go to my grave protecting those I care about."

She won't hear West's declaration of love before Kari does. The elevator dinged, and the doors slid open. "This is your stop. Let's go."

West escorted her to the front desk, where he told the shocked desk clerk, "Ms. Davidson did not authorize this woman to be in this building. She is trespassing."

"I'll be on my way then." Leslie turned toward the door.

The clerk kept their voice low. "Sir, she has a guest pass."

"Stay where you are, Leslie." The woman froze. Her wide grey eyes, much like Izzy's, focused on him. West will never understand how someone could want nothing to do with their child except for nefarious reasons. He kept his eyes on Leslie and asked the desk clerk to repeat himself.

"The woman showed me her ID and said she was staying with Kari - I mean Ms. Davidson. She's Ms. Davidson's mother...I gave her a pass."

West growled. He didn't have time to discipline Jasper's gullible staff. He stomped over to Leslie and held out his hand. "Give me the pass. Now."

Leslie dug around in her purse, then slapped the badge against his palm.

"Now, get out." West kept his eyes on Leslie until the door's security lock kicked in behind her. He sighed and turned back to the quivering man behind the front desk.

West tossed the badge toward him, and the man fumbled to catch it. "What's your name?"

"Kevin, sir."

"Kevin, I'll be speaking to Mr. Jones about this incident, but I'm telling you right now, don't let it happen again."

"No, sir. I mean, yes, sir. I-"

"Shut it, Kevin." West punched the elevator call button. Done with this shit, needing to get back to his girl.

"Yes, sir."

West hit the button for the second floor to get Izzy from childcare, and when they reached the apartment, he opened the door to let them inside. Not missing Kari wiping beneath her eyes. Unfortunately, Izzy saw her tears, too. "Why are you crying, Kari? It's your birthday."

West kneeled in front of the little girl while Kari grabbed a tissue to wipe the remaining tears. "Sometimes grownups get sad on their birthdays. It doesn't mean they aren't happy about being born. Sometimes, they get emotional about being born, too."

"Ugh, grownups are weird. I'll never be sad on my birthday."

"Yeah, we are a little weird, though being a little weird is okay. I also hope you're never sad about your birthday. Either way, you have people around you who love you no matter what. How about I talk to Kari...." West lowered his voice even though he knew Kari still heard him. "You go dig out Kari's surprise and wait for me to come get you, then we'll give it to her together." He held up a hand for Izzy to high-five.

She did it with all the enthusiasm of a five-year-old.

"Yes," Izzy said, running from the room and shouting, "Happy birthday, Kari. You won't be sad when we give you your present in a minute." Seconds later, Izzy's door slammed shut.

"Hi," West said, pulling Kari into a hug. He cupped her face and tipped her head back to meet his gaze, studying her red-rimmed eyes and wanting more than anything to make her worries go away. He'd do everything to help Kari keep Izzy safe.

"Is your sister the reason you never reported your mother to the police when she drained your bank accounts?"

"Yes." Kari stiffened in his arms. "I couldn't afford to fight my mother in court and convinced myself a judge would take Izzy from me anyway if they found out I was nineteen, broke, and dancing at a questionable burlesque club to feed us and put a roof over our heads."

She let out a sigh and relaxed against him. "My finances are stable these days. I mean, I'm not making modeling contract money, but we live in a secure place, and she goes to an excellent school, yet I still worry I'll lose custody."

West wanted to do whatever he could for her. "I have some ideas about what we can do to ensure that never happens."

Kari sniffled and blinked away a fresh bout of tears. "Can we...not discuss this right now? It's my birthday. I don't want or need Leslie to darken what's becoming the best birthday I've ever had. Do you mind if we put aside talk of my mother for now?"

"Of course. We'll have to talk about the situation soon, though."

"I know, just...not right now, okay?"

"Okay, baby." He kissed the tip of her nose, making her smile. "What do you want to do today?"

"Can we do what we planned? Brunch with Izzy, then I hang out with the girls while you hang out with the guys?"

"Yes, we can." West leaned closer and tucked some wayward strands behind her ear. He kissed her forehead. "Izzy is excited to give you the present we picked out together."

"What? When? You didn't have to get me anything."

"No...I wanted to. There's this thing called the internet where you can shop for whatever you want and have it delivered to your doorstep, sometimes in a matter of hours."

Kari smacked his chest and snorted. "Don't be an ass."

He'd be an ass anytime if it made her laugh. West kissed her lips this time, pulling away when he heard Izzy's bedroom door open and shut. "Let me get Izz, and we'll give you your gift."

CHAPTER TWENTY-FOUR

Kari

I zzy and West gave her a new e-reader with a waterproof case after her sister mentioned that her current reader had fallen into the tub more than once. It still worked...well, not really. Which meant they got her the perfect gift. She hugged and thanked them both.

The three of them dug into the stack of pancakes, bacon, sausage, and scrambled eggs. Laughing and talking about anything and everything. It almost made her forget about her mother and all the trouble she'll bring now that she's found them.

Almost.

When they arrived at Jasper and Jessica's, West disappeared into the basement apartment to grab a change of clothes. Joanna arrived a few minutes after they did, without her infant daughter, much to Izzy's dismay. She demanded to go to Joanna and Jonathan's, where the guys planned to hang out and play a few rounds of cards, declaring Sara-Jane can't be the only girl there.

Jasper and West said they didn't mind, and when Jasper swept Jess into a possessive kiss and palmed her baby bump, West tugged Kari into the hallway.

"Not sure where you stood on PDA in front of our friends, and I really needed to kiss you, birthday girl."

"I'm okay with some...PDA. I'm an affectionate person, and I don't want to hide who we are to each other. Do you?"

"Fuck no." West cupped her face between his palms, pressing her against the wall, kissing her like a man who needed her lips like oxygen. "You say the word, and I'll march you back in there, and kiss you like we just said I do."

Kari snorted, and the hum of conversation in the living room stopped. "Be serious," she said in a stage whisper.

"I am being serious." West kissed her again, and Kari forgot about everyone in the other room until a throat cleared at her side.

Her cheeks burned when she turned her head to find Jasper with a smug look on his face. "We...uh...were saying goodbye."

"Mm-hm. I believe I shared a similar farewell with my wife." Jasper eyed us while we remained frozen in our version of a romance clinch cover. West let go of her, giving her a chance to catch her breath, and Jasper asked, "You ready to head out? Gray has already texted me three times."

"Yup. Give me a second, and I'll meet you by the door."

"Alright. Take care, Kari. Happy birthday." Jasper strolled away whistling a very smug-sounding tune.

"Thanks. Okay, *byeee*." The second Jasper turned the corner, West pressed Kari against the wall and kissed her again, licking past her lips, seeking to taste every part of her mouth.

"Mm...you better go. The girls are going to send out a search party looking for me at any moment."

"Fine. Give me one more kiss to sustain me. I can't wait to get you alone later." He pressed his lips to hers, and she moaned against them, melting into his arms.

"Alright, spill it."

Kari's ass hovered above the couch. Not even getting the chance to sit down, let alone get some alcohol into her system, before the inquisition started. She's going to need all the liquid courage for this conversation.

"Don't say 'spill' when I'm carrying a tray of drinks," Addie said, setting the tray with a pitcher of margaritas and some fruity, fizzy, alcohol-free cocktail for Jessica in the center of the table.

"Besides, I can't take notes on the juicy details if my hands are full." With her hands now free, sort of, one now held a salted-rim glass. Addie took a hearty sip, then licked the salt from her lips. "Damn, I make a mean margarita." She filled a glass for everyone, then sat back and gave Kari a pointed look. "Now, you can spill."

"Inspiration for your next bestseller?" Kari asked, stalling. The ladies gathered at Jess's for their monthly gossip and games. This month, it coincided with Kari's birthday. Though it's more about gossip and drinks than games. Like now.

Fun fact, it's never as much fun to be the subject of the gossip as it is to hear it.

"Stop deflecting," Joanna said between sips of her marg. "You're sporting enough beard burn to put Jess to shame."

A snort came from the phone screen set up on the corner of the table. West introduced Kari to his friend Xander, who introduced his partners Lex and Penny. The three of them are moving back to the city after they take care of some family business, and Kari thought it'd be great for Penny to get to know everyone else, but now she feels slightly ganged up on.

"Hey, I take offense at such blasphemy," Jess said, showing off the pink flush along her jawline.

"Pfft, you know I'm right." Joanna raised her glass. "To the details."

"The details," Jess, Penny, and Addie said in unison.

"Yeah, the details," Kari followed a second later.

Addie leaned over and put a hand on her knee. "Honey, you know you don't have to tell us anything you don't want to. While we love some salacious details, we never expect you to share more than you're comfortable with."

"Yes, like how Jess limits her sharing about my brother to times when I'm not here. I'm good with hearing about people I'm not related to."

"Yes," Jess gave Joanna a nudge. "Lord knows we've divulged all kinds of kinky fuckery to you. We want you to know you can always fly your freak flag with pride here." Jess raised her fruity concoction. "To all kinds of kinky fuckery!"

"To kinky fuckery," they said, toasting together this time.

Kari savored a mouthful of her margarita, thankful for Addie's generous pour. "Hm...well, I don't have an issue with giving details – well, some details – a girl needs her secrets. I'm just trying to figure out how to break it to you. I'm having the best sex of my life."

Kari's ears rang with screeches, whoops, and whistles. Jess even rolled off the couch, as her pregnancy dictated, to give her a high-five. Being the youngest among these ladies is intimidating sometimes, yet the way they embraced her...she's never experienced friendships like these.

"You look happy," Joanna said when their rowdy group settled. It was probably a good thing Izzy went with the guys. Kari needed some girly grown-up talk.

"I am happy. Fabulous sex aside, I've reached a good place in my life where I'm no longer afraid of my shadow, and I don't need or want to run anymore."

"I get that," Jessica said, laying a protective hand on her rounded tummy where her twin babies were preparing to greet the world. Kari met Jasper after Jessica left. Since they reconciled, she and Jess have become close.

Kari looked around the room.

Joanna welcomed her and Izzy with open arms when Jasper first invited them for Sunday brunch. She and Jonathan experienced some profound losses, and Joanna leaned on Kari in the absence of her best friend.

Kari wanted to be that pillar for her after the way Joanna accepted her and Izzy into her family.

When Addie met Gray, Kari and Joanna fell in love with the witty, spicy romance author who relished telling them about her latest book research and how it worked out when she and Gray tried it themselves.

"Ugh, enough. Don't leave us hanging. Spill it, girl. He's covered in tattoos...everywhere, right?" Addie sipped her drink and waited for Kari to answer.

Kari knew West wouldn't mind if she divulged this little secret. "He has a lot of tattoos...but, have y'all heard of a Jacob's Ladder?" She looked at her friends. Jess smirked and took a sip of her drink, but Addie, Penny, and Joanna gave her inquisitive looks, waiting for her to tell them.

"A Jacob's Ladder is a series of horizontal piercings along the underside of a man's penis. At least that's the way his are done."

Addie had already pulled out her phone and started searching for images. Her jaw dropped. "Oh my fucking god, my next MC is going to have one." She set her empty glass aside and pulled out the leather-bound journal she carried with her for whenever inspiration struck.

"He's pierced," Jessica's voice dropped to a stage whisper, "down there? I mean, I knew about the nipples; we all did, because West has a propensity for going without a shirt to show off all that delicious black and grey ink. Hell, he pierced mine. I really miss them," she said, ending her rant with a pout.

Something unfamiliar rippled through Kari's stomach. *Is that...jealousy?*

Jess studied Kari for a second and then burst out laughing. "Oh, honey...you've met my husband. Enough said."

Kari's cheeks heated with embarrassment. "I'm so sorry; I don't know what came over me. I think I'm jealous?"

"Meh, it's what happens when you get superb dick. Don't worry about it," Addie said, finishing her second margarita. Then they all burst out laughing.

CHAPTER TWENTY-FIVE

West

W est unwrapped a tray of sandwiches that Joanna had left for them to take to the table when Jasper came into the kitchen. "Gray and Jon want refills." His eyes widened when he spied the sandwich tray.

"Damn, my sister is the best. Is there any dessert?"

West jerked his thumb over his shoulder. "Addie sent Gray with plenty of baked goods."

"Fuck yes." Jasper opened a container and devoured one of Addie's famous chocolate chip cookies in two bites.

It's no secret that both Gray and Jasper had a notorious weakness for sweets. When Addie needed to bake to shake off her writer's block, it wasn't just the people at Lavender House who benefited.

"You haven't stayed in the apartment much in the past couple of weeks," Jasper said, reaching into the cupboard beside him for a glass.

"Kari and I are spending time together. You know this." West kept his wording careful, knowing Jasper considered Kari a part of his family and he'd be looking out for her.

Jasper shrugged and poured himself a shot of whisky, making no move to get Jon or Gray their beers. "Are you serious about her?" he asked. The tone of his voice indicated West wouldn't leave this kitchen until he received a satisfactory response.

He considered giving Jasper a long-winded answer filled with platitudes about how he's never felt this way or how he believes Kari's the love of his life. Again, he's not saying those words to anyone when he's yet to tell her.

Fuck, he really needed to tell her.

Well, Jasper liked things to be direct and to the point, and that's what West gave him. "Yes."

Again, Jasper grunted in response.

"Have you forgotten how to speak or something? You're not having a stroke, are you?" He ignored West's dig, of course. Jasper's feathers are tough to ruffle unless your name is Jessica. She can ruffle his feathers like no one else.

"What about your place in Glasgow?" he asked. "The shop? Are you selling your business? Are you moving back for good? Kari is important to all of us, and we need to know you're serious about her."

West's eyes widened. *Shit*. He never got around to telling Jasper about the second location he planned to open. With everything going on, he hadn't told Kari either. Which didn't sit well with him.

"I'm not selling the Glasgow shop, at least not yet. I found a location for a second shop, not too far from Kari's apartment. My lawyer and I are going over the paperwork. If everything's on the up and up, I'll have the deal signed by the end of the week."

Jasper leaned against the counter, eyeing West over the edge of his glass when he took a sip. It's like being scrutinized by the parent of the person he wanted to date, and he's too old for this shit. *Right?*

"Remember our conversation the night we rescued Sara-Jane?"

"You mean when you slept, and I drove?"

Jasper looked amused. "Hey, those precious few hours of shuteye kept me from falling on my ass and losing my shit when I found Jessica holding my niece after not laying eyes on her for over three years."

West tipped his bottle of beer in the air in a silent salute. "Touché." Those years apart caused them both unnecessary pain. West will always be grateful that Jess and Jasper worked through what tore them apart.

"That's the night when I knew I wanted to introduce you to Kari."

"Fuck." West ran his fingers through his hair. "Months ago?"

"I knew then, but I didn't say that it's when you needed to meet. Both you and Kari needed to sort some shit out."

"There's still shit to sort out."

"What?"

"Nothing."

Jasper gave him a scrutinizing look but let it go. "Anyway, you're here now, and like all my successful matches, I'm glad I got it right. Listen, about the basement apartment...I don't want to rush you into another decision, but I believe the twins are going to come earlier than their due date, and the nanny we hired will need to move in sooner than September."

"Say no more, brother. I've got plans to look for a place once the shop's location's all set."

"What incredible timing. I have something to help narrow your search." Jasper reached into his back pocket, pulled out a small envelope, and placed it on the counter between them.

"What's this?"

"The key and alarm code for the penthouse in Kari's building. It's available, and I believe the spacious layout is something you'll need. If you like it, let me know, and we can work something out."

"To rent or own." West liked the idea of owning a place.

"The building contains both. The penthouse is for sale. Kari also owns her apartment."

West pinned Jasper with a look. "Does Kari know she owns the apartment?" He recalled her mentioning rent several times.

Jasper shifted. For once, he looked...uncomfortable. "Kari may be under the impression she's paying rent when, in actuality, she's paying the balance of a mortgage."

"Shit, Jasper...."

"Well, it's better than throwing away money on rent. Kari's mother stole everything from her, and I wanted to ensure she had something belonging to her, something her mother could never touch." Jasper ran his hand through his hair. "Look, I didn't know when or if you'd come back here, and I wanted to give someone I consider family some stability."

"You're a good man, Jasper, and I know you mean well, but you can't keep this from Kari. She deserves to know."

"You're right. I promise I'll tell her." Jasper pushed the envelope a little closer. "So, do you want to look at the penthouse or not?"

West picked up the envelope. "Yeah, I do. Then Kari can do whatever the hell she wants with the apartment she owns because she and Izzy will live with me."

For good measure, Jasper gave him another grunt. However, West understood the approval behind it. "I know you know better than to hurt her." The warning also came crystal clear.

"Never." West put the envelope with the key to his future in his jacket pocket.

Gray's head appeared in the kitchen doorway, followed by the rest of him. "For fuck's sake, Jas. Jon and I are dying of thirst, and here I find you two gabbing like you're standing around the water cooler. How long does it take to grab a couple of beers?"

Jasper opened the fridge and grabbed two beers, giving them to Gray. "Sorry, we got talking about things."

"Yeah, well, let's chat about things together over food and cards."

West lifted the tray of sandwiches on his way out of the kitchen. "I agree. Let's eat. I'm more than ready to win some money from you lot."

CHAPTER TWENTY-SIX

West

For two weeks, Kari did everything possible to avoid discussing what to do about the situation with Leslie. West might've benefited from her sexy avoidance techniques, and for a while, he went along with the fact that Kari didn't want to talk about it.

Until yesterday, and now, avoiding the topic was no longer an option. Not when Kari caught her mother lurking outside of Izzy's school.

Today, he's going with Kari to pick up Izzy. She also agreed it's time they talked about what to do, and to tell Jasper about what's going on.

Kari squeezed his hand. They still had a couple of blocks until they reached Izzy's school, but he could feel her anxiety rise the closer they got. He tugged Kari out of the flow of pedestrians and wrapped her in his arms, kissing her forehead when she hugged him back.

"Thanks. I didn't realize how much I needed a hug."

With his sunglasses in place, he didn't stop scanning the throngs of people walking by, keeping an eye out for one in particular. "We talked about this, baby girl."

Kari nodded, her cheek grazing his throat.

"I'm here, and you're safe. Leslie won't come anywhere near you or Izzy. You took action to prevent her from doing anything foolish by talking to Izzy's teacher and principal. You are brave and resourceful. Thanks to you, they know what Leslie looks like and will keep your sister safe while she's under their supervision."

"Thank you." Her lips brushed his skin with each word she spoke. "No one has ever taken care of me like this."

"You have so many people who care about you and Izzy." West tangled his fingers in Kari's hair and tugged her head back. He lifted his sunglasses to the top of his head, wanting to connect. He stared at her while caressing her bottom lip with his thumb. "I care about you and Izzy."

While not an outright declaration of love, West knew Kari understood when she kissed the pad of his thumb and said, "We care about you, too."

West moved his thumb to caress her cheek, freeing her lips for his kiss. "Mm... we'd better go. Don't want to be late getting to the school."

"It's not like they'll give us detention, though you're right, I don't want to be a terrible parent...I mean...guardian." Her cheeks turned red, and she tried to look away.

West's hand moved to her jaw, holding her in his grasp. He refused to let her feel embarrassed by a slipup that wasn't a slipup at all.

"Uh-uh. No, baby girl. Never doubt that you are Izzy's parent in every way. With Jasper's help, we'll figure out a way to secure your guardianship once and for all."

"The way to handle my mother is with money, and while I'm in a good place right now, I don't have the funds she'll demand."

"We'll figure something out," he said, already tossing a couple of ideas around in his head. "Come on, we'd better get going." He took Kari's hand and tugged her into the flow of pedestrians. "Hey, have you talked to Jasper at all over the past couple of weeks?"

Kari scrunched her nose adorably while she considered his question. "No, he's spending more time with Jess as her pregnancy progresses and less time at Decadent. Why?"

"Damn, I thought he would've told you by now."

"Told me what?"

"Jasper did something for you, and then kind of neglected to tell you about it." He didn't think Jasper would mind when he said he'd tell her. Kari needs to know the truth. "He kind of left you with the impression that you're paying rent when you're not."

They reached the pickup and drop-off zone of Izzy's school. The bell hadn't rung yet, leaving them precious minutes for this conversation.

Kari pulled him out of listening range of the group of blonde ladies eyeing them from across the yard. "What do you mean I'm not paying rent? I give Jasper rent on the first of every month," she said, crossing her arms with a huff.

Fuck, she's adorable when she's mad.

He scanned their surroundings, and besides the nosy group of *Karens*, there was no sign of Leslie. "Look, Jasper promised to tell you. I didn't want to be the one, but you deserve to know the truth."

"What truth?"

"You don't rent your apartment. You own it."

Kari scoffed. "You're fucking with me."

"No, lass, I'm not. Jasper wanted you to have something your mother couldn't touch. He took care of the down payment, and you've paid the mortgage ever since. You have equity, though I know Jasper will fight you on using it."

"I-"

Whatever Kari wanted to say got drowned out by the ringing bell. Seconds later, the doors flew open, and children ran outside.

West spotted Izzy's halo of blonde curls bouncing down the steps. When she spied him and Kari, she grinned, showing off the two missing baby teeth when she ran up to them. "Kari. Wes," she said, jumping up and down after hugging Kari. "You both came to pick me up?"

West bent down to chat with Izzy on her level. "We sure did. I heard you're going to be making cookies with Auntie Jess, and since I live there, I asked Kari if I could walk you over, but I forgot to ask you. Is it okay if I walk with you to Jess and Jasper's?"

"Yes. We are going to make the best cookies. What's your favorite?" Izzy asked when they left her school.

"Hm... there are so many. What's your favorite?"

"Chocolate chip."

"You know what? Chocolate chip is my favorite, too."

"No way."

"Way."

He heard Kari's laughter here and there, but she let him and Izzy lead the conversation. He didn't want her to be upset and hoped she realized Jasper loved to help those he cared about most.

Jessica held the door open for them when they walked up their short drive. "Auntie Jess," Izzy shouted, rushing ahead to climb the three steps to the small porch where she stood.

"Hey, Izzy-girl. Ready to do some baking?"

"Yes, we're making chocolate chip cookies, right?"

"We are. In fact, we are making Addie's recipe, so you know they're going to be awesome."

Jess met his and Kari's amused glances and said, "Listen, the babies are craving Addie's chocolate chip cookies, and she won't be back in the city until next weekend. The babies won't wait until next weekend."

"The babies, huh?" Kari asked, hugging Jess hello when she followed Izzy inside.

"Uh, yeah." Jess palmed the sides of her belly like she was trying to cover both her baby's ears. She even lowered her voice when she said, "I'm worried they might revolt unless I meet their demands for melt-in-your-mouth chocolate chip cookies."

Jasper rounded the corner and smirked. "Are the girls making demands again, sweetheart?"

"Always. Come on, Izzy, let's get baking." Jess pecked Jasper on the lips on her way by.

"Are the babies going to come out of your tummy if they don't get a cookie?"

Jess glanced back at them, looking for help. "Don't look to us for an answer," West said. "You dug this hole."

She stuck her tongue out at him, then blanched when she heard her husband's growl.

"Uh...I don't want to find out."

Jasper shook his head. "I swear our children have unlocked my wife's inner brat. Come on, we can talk in my office."

West leaned against the wall beside the door while Kari took a seat on the small leather sofa across from him. Her foot was tapping against the hardwood floor. He wanted to comfort her, yet when he took a step toward her, Kari shook her head. Against his better judgment, he surrendered and leaned back against the wall. A moment later, he understood why.

"West told me about the apartment, Jasper. Why didn't you tell me? There's no way what I pay in rent is enough to cover a mortgage payment."

Jasper glanced his way, and West shrugged. "I asked Kari if you'd talked to her. After two weeks, I figured you would've told her by now."

"I meant to. Jess has kept me...occupied." Jasper opened a desk drawer and put a set of papers in front of Kari. "I assure you, what you pay me in rent covers the mortgage for your apartment."

"How?"

"I own the fucking building, Kari. Someone died in the apartment, and no one wanted to take it off my hands because of the bad vibes," he said, complete with air quotes.

"No fucking way."

Jasper held it for all of five seconds before he burst out laughing. "Of course not. It is, however, what I told my accountant when he questioned the price I set for the sale. The apartment is yours, Kari," he said, tapping the papers in front of her — the deed to her apartment, from the looks of it.

"I am sorry for not telling you sooner. Can you forgive me?"

Kari's eyes shimmered with unshed tears. "I don't know what to say except...thank you."

"That's all I need." Jasper rounded his desk and rested against the edge and asked, "What's going on? I know you didn't come here to talk about the apartment."

"My mother's back."

Jasper glanced his way again, then focused on Kari. "What does Leslie want?"

"What else? Money. She says she'll sign away her parental rights for a reasonable fee. My mother is anything but reasonable."

West listened while Kari told Jasper about her mother showing up at her door, and he shared how he'd run into her in the elevator a few days prior.

When she got to the part where she found Leslie lurking outside Izzy's school, he crossed the room to sit beside her, unable to keep his distance any longer. Wrapping his arm around her, he offered his strength and support while she tearfully explained the rest.

"Let us help you, Kari," Jasper said, kneeling in front of her.

Kari tucked her arms around herself. "I don't want you to feel obligated to fix my entire life, Jasper. You've done so much for Izzy and me already." She bit her bottom lip and turned her gaze to include West. "All of you have."

"It's what proper families who love and care about each other do, lass."

"But-"

Jasper pointed at Kari. "Don't you dare say you aren't part of this fucking family."

"I'll tan your ass red if you even consider it, baby girl," West said, backing Jasper.

"Not fair." Kari dared to pout.

"One hundred percent fair, lass. Jasper's right. This is what family does."

"She'll demand an exponential amount of money, and I can't ask you to cover that. I'll sell the apartment. Izzy and I can find something else."

"No, the fuck you won't."

"You can't force me to take your money either, Jasper."

"I'm not."

"Jasper's not the only one backing you here. I'm contributing too. And I bet if we run this by everyone else, they'll want to help. You're not alone in this."

"You can't. There's no way I can ask any of you to do this."

"You don't need to ask when we're offering." West cupped her cheek and pressed a kiss to her temple. With his lips against her ear, he said, "I can and I will. I want nothing more than to protect you and Izzy and keep you safe. We all want that for you."

"Kari, it's just fucking money, and money is the tip of the iceberg. I'll have my lawyer draw up binding legal documents. We can get a restraining order, or if you want, we can arrange for her to go to rehab. If she gets help, there might be hope for a relationship. I don't know, I'll call my lawyer, Bianca Hendrix, and see what she can do to help."

"Do you believe she'll choose rehab and kick her addiction?"

"If she wants to be part of yours and Izzy's lives, she will," West said. However, he believed Kari's mother would choose differently. Why not? If it's the same amount of money without the rehab or parental responsibilities.

West knew the kind of person Leslie Davidson was. She is not a responsible parent. Kari's mother wanted money. She'll sign custody over to Kari, and after years of drama and uncertainty, she'll know it's the best thing for her and Izzy.

He kept these thoughts to himself, though.

"Can I think it over? It's a lot to wrap my head around."

"Of course. It will take Bianca some time to prepare things. Nothing happens without your approval. She will go over everything with you."

"Thanks." She stood. "I'm going to check on how Izz and Jess are doing."

West stopped her by the door, moving his hands from her shoulders to her cheeks. He tilted her head to meet his gaze. "You okay, baby girl?"

"Yeah, it's...well, like I said...it's a lot."

He kissed her lips. "Don't worry, baby. We'll be ready for whatever Leslie throws at us."

"I hope so." Kari gave him a soft, reassuring smile when she pulled away and went down the hall toward the kitchen, where West could hear Jess and Izzy's laughter.

"Did you tell Kari, or are my secrets the only ones you spill?" Jasper asked from behind him.

West spun to face his friend. He didn't need Jasper to elaborate on the what...well, maybe he did. There are too many things about their future that he hasn't shared. "I haven't gotten the chance to yet."

What a fucking ridiculous and lame excuse. Maybe West needed to kick his own ass.

Jasper's brow quirked. "I guess it's not just me who needed to come clean. So...not even the fact you love her?"

"It's too soon for me to tell her. Isn't it?"

"With the way you two are around each other? Not really. You know Jessica and my history. Despite what happened between us, from the moment I laid eyes on her, I knew there would be no one else for me."

Jasper stepped closer and slapped his palms on West's shoulders, giving him the brutal truths he needed to hear.

"Brother, you know better than anyone that we have lived experiences that have shown us how precious and short life can be. When people like us find the people we consider ours, we don't wait. We seize our chance."

West nodded. "You're right. Fuck, you're right. I think the reason I haven't said those words to her or told her about things affecting our future is that...," his voice dropped to a whisper, not wanting to dare the fates, "I'm fucking terrified of losing her. When Maggie died, it tore me up with guilt." West shook his head. "If something happened to Kari or Izzy, I'd never survive it."

"Embrace that fear, especially if it gives you the opportunity for even one minute of an all-consuming love." Jasper squeezed his shoulders and moved back, shoving his hands into his pockets. "Ask Joanna and Jonathan or Addie and Gray if it's worth it. Or...take it from me when I tell you it is."

"Thank you, brother."

Jasper shrugged as if it were no big deal, even though it was a big deal.

"Anytime. Perhaps start by telling Kari how much you love her, then discuss the penthouse purchase, your new shop, and your return to Scotland. No, wait, flip the order and tell her about returning to Glasgow, then those two."

"You're going back to Scotland?"

West turned to find Kari in the doorway, holding a plate of freshly baked cookies. Jasper coughed into his hand, which sounded an awful lot like, 'Oh shit, sorry.'

"I'm going to check on my wife," he said, grabbing a cookie from Kari on his way by. "These look delicious." He took a bite. "They are delicious. Let him explain. There's a lot more to it than what you overheard."

Kari kept her eyes on West throughout her exchange with Jasper, and when his steps faded down the hall, she shut the door, set the plate of cookies on the desk, and crossed her arms, with a defiant look that she knew full well would earn her a solid spanking. She said, "Now's your chance to explain to me what's going on."

CHAPTER TWENTY-SEVEN

West

"Nope," he said, shaking his head as he closed the distance between them. "This is not how I imagined this moment playing out." West caged her against the closed door.

"First," he said, uncrossing her arms and clasping her hands between his while he kissed each of her fingertips. "You may not scowl when I'm about to say what I'm about to say. This is my fault, and I'm going to make it go away by telling you something vital."

"I'm listening."

"Baby girl, did you roll your eyes at me?"

"Maybe."

"Well, fuck. Such brattiness will have to be dealt with."

Kari gave him a look as if he'd missed the point. "It's why I did it. Are you going to explain what I overheard or not?"

West counted to ten, not because of anger, but because her sass turned him on. Kari's testing him, and he liked it. It meant she trusted him. However, now is not the time to bend her over Jasper's desk and teach her a lesson about how much he loves everything about her. He still needs to tell her he loves her first.

"Kari, I'm returning to Glasgow." The scowl returned, this time accompanied by her lower lip quivering, and he didn't want her to hurt for even a second. "I'm going to tie up some loose ends and get a permanent manager for the shop in place. I'll have to return there often for clients, though I hope you'll want to go with me when I do."

"Are you...what do you mean?"

If Kari needed him to spell it out for her, he's more than happy to. He cupped her face and looked deep into her eyes. "What I mean is, Kari Davidson, I love you, and I'm staying here."

"You love me?"

"Yes, beautiful. I love you." West kissed her. "Now that the dam has broken, I'll never stop saying it. I'm in love with you, baby girl."

Kari flung her arms around his neck and launched herself at him. West caught her ass in his palms, and her legs wrapped around his waist. "I love you, too," she said between kisses.

West smiled against her lips. "Since we've established the fact that we love each other. I have two things to show you and something to ask you."

"What?"

"Patience, baby girl. Let's relieve Jess and Jasper of Izzy, and I'll take you both by one of my surprises on the way back to your apartment."

"Alright, Mister Mysterious, I'll play along."

West nipped at her lips. "Of course you will. How else will you get your reward?"

"Does my reward involve your cock?"

"You know it does."

"Lead the way, Daddy."

They took the train and got off at the stop where Kari shopped for groceries. She gave him a curious look but said nothing. She didn't have to when Izzy asked for her.

"This isn't our stop, Wes. Where are we going?"

"I wanted to show you and Kari something. It's a surprise."

"What kind of surprise?"

"A building."

"What kind of building?"

West looked over at Kari, and she shrugged, looking away. In fact, she kept shrugging, and West realized she shook with the effort to contain her laughter. He leaned close, keeping his voice low to avoid little ears overhearing. "Keep it up, baby girl. You've got quite a spanking coming your way."

Kari gasped, and she gave him a heated look when *Izzy the Inquisitor* tugged on his hand. "Wes, you didn't answer my question."

"It's a shop."

"We're going to a store? What are we buying?"

"Not that kind of shop."

Izzy looked to Kari for another explanation. "I don't know, Izz. It's quite a puzzle."

"Well, if you look over there, you can solve it," West said when they rounded the corner, and he pointed at the building across the street. The guys hung the new signage this morning, and it did not disappoint.

"Looks good, huh?"

"Wow. This makes it real."

"What? You didn't believe me?"

"What's it say?" Izzy asked.

West lifted her up to give her a better look. "It says, West Loves Tattoos."

"Course you do. You've got lots of them." Izzy traced the one on the side of his neck, emphasizing her point.

The comment and the ticklish sensation made him laugh. "True. It's also the name of my shop." West met Kari's gaze over the top of Izzy's head. "In about six weeks, this will be where I work."

"You're really staying?"

"I am," West said, inflecting his love and devotion for Kari into those two words.

"Can I get a tattoo?"

Kari's eyes widened at Izzy's unexpected question, while he took it in stride. "Um..."

West held out his left arm, letting Izzy trace the black and red rose he'd tattooed on the top of his hand. "I'll never lie to you, Izz. I am a supporter of anyone who expresses themselves in the way they want, but...."

"There's always a but," Izzy said with a pout.

West glanced at Kari, then Izzy. "Yeah, kiddo, that's how life rolls. You understand my tattoos are forever?" Since he didn't plan to remove his, he didn't bother to explain the painful laser removal treatment to a five-year-old.

"Forever?"

"Yup. All this ink will never come off. It's why there are rules for getting them after you've reached a certain age."

"How old do I gotta be?"

West looked at Kari, who gave him a 'you're on your own' look. "Uh, you gotta be nineteen." He didn't know how well this was going to go over when she reached eighteen and discovered the actual age of consent. "You know, make sure it's what you want." He glanced at Kari, who shrugged in agreement.

"Pinkie promise?" Izzy asked, holding up her tiny pinkie finger.

"Kari?" West needed her okay to make such a promise.

"This is an agreement between the two of you. Pinkie swears are serious business. And since I want more tattoos, and I'm dating someone who is a skilled tattoo artist, I can't oppose Izzy wanting a tattoo when she turns nineteen."

"Alright, Izz, you heard Kari." West extended his pinkie and hooked it with hers. "I pinkie swear to give you the tattoo you want when you turn nineteen. In the meantime, I have special skin-safe markers if you ever want me to draw something for you on your arm or leg."

"Cool. Can we go home now? I'm tired."

"Sure." West nudged Kari's shoulder when he set Izzy down. "I'll give you a tour of the inside another time. The shop's not going anywhere."

Izzy tugged on his hand, getting his attention. "Can I have a piggyback ride, Wes? I don't wanna walk anymore." Izzy inflected the perfect amount of whine, then dragged her feet for good measure.

"We're a block away from the apartment, Izz," Kari said, offering him an out.

"Are you doubting my stamina, lass? I've run through the desert with a hundred pounds of gear strapped to my back. I can handle this wee sprite of a gel," he said, amping up his accent and getting a smile from them both.

"Did your desert runs prepare you for all the drool?"

"I don't mind." West lowered, allowing Izzy to climb onto his back. She let out a squeal of laughter when he hoisted her up. "Come on, let's get you home."

Kari smirked and fell into step beside him. "I can't say I didn't warn you."

Izzy passed out within half a block of the apartment, and understanding dawned when drool soaked the collar of his shirt. West didn't care. Why would he, when these two ladies trusted him with their hearts?

CHAPTER TWENTY-EIGHT

Kari

West didn't care about the drool. It didn't bother him in the least. There's a serene look on his face, one that Kari was sure matched her own.

Kari didn't want to dwell on her mother or what Jasper's lawyer would come up with to resolve things with her. She wanted to bask in this moment and enjoy it for all its worth.

They passed through the lobby, and when the elevator doors closed, Kari's breath caught, looking at their reflection. West wore his hair pulled back and a white T-shirt, emphasizing every muscle of his upper body and highlighting the tattoos on his arms and neck. He paired the shirt with dark blue jeans and a well-worn pair of Doc Martens.

He is such a snack.

Izzy snored on. Oblivious to it all.

West kept his voice low when he said, "Fuck, baby girl. We look damn good together, and once we put this wee lass down for a nap, you're mine."

Kari bit her bottom lip, stopping a moan. The sticky heat of arousal between her thighs dampened her panties.

West's care for them is a fucking turn-on.

The elevator came to a stop, and the doors slid open. "Lead the way, baby." West's heated gaze traveled over her like a caress when she moved past him.

"Yes, Sir."

Kari did her best to control her heart rate and breathing, yet the tension between them escalated with each step toward her apartment door.

"Hurry, baby girl." His voice remained soft despite the growl in his words.

Her steps quickened, and her fingers trembled when she unlocked the door and pushed it open, letting West go ahead of her. Kari shut and locked them in and followed him to Izzy's room.

Kari stifled her amusement at the way West maneuvered Izzy onto her bed, letting her slide off his back. He even made sure her head landed on her pillow.

Her sister didn't even stir.

West removed Izzy's shoes and tucked her in. Then he prowled toward Kari, crowding her into the hallway until he pulled Izzy's bedroom door shut with a resounding click. He moved fast, wrapping a hand around her throat and crowding her body against the wall across from Izzy's room.

His thumb caressed her jaw, then circled her racing pulse, his smile growing wicked at the way her heart raced. "Nervous, baby girl?"

"Excited."

"Mm...," West grazed his nose along hers. His gaze locked with hers in a moment so intimate it stole her breath. "Breathe, lass. We've got hours of pleasure ahead of us."

Kari sucked in a breath, then let it out. "Yes."

"Good girl," he said, praising her when she kept her breath slow and steady. "I want you to go to your room and stand in front of your mirror, facing your bed."

He kissed her lips, sliding his hand from her throat down between her breasts to her waist. Turning her toward her room, the sting resonated a second after the smack landed against her ass. The jeans she wore muffled the sound, but not the impact.

She hissed, absorbing the sting when West said, "You've got a punishment coming, baby girl. Go, I'll be there in a moment."

"Yes, Sir." Kari rushed across the living room, reaching her bedroom in record time.

She faced the mirror, catching the flush coloring her skin from the V of her shirt to her rosy cheeks, and did her best to tame her wayward hair when she heard West's footsteps approaching her open door.

Kari spun toward the bed, mimicking a submissive pose she'd witnessed many do at the club. She clasped her hands behind her back and stood with her feet shoulder-width apart, lowering her gaze when West entered the room.

He walked toward her until his feet, now bare, came into view, circling her until he stopped in front of her. "Beautiful," he said against her neck, making her shiver. "You honor me with your submission."

Kari trembled. Her arousal soaked her underwear, and she wanted more than anything to please him. She didn't look up when he took a couple of steps back, and she heard him undo his pants. Next came a soft thump when he sat on her mattress. "Look at me," he commanded.

She lifted her gaze, taking in his spread legs and undone jeans. West's cock strained beyond the waistband of his briefs. He'd removed his shirt, and all his black and grey tattoos were everywhere she looked. The rings through his nipples shone in the lamplight, and when her gaze collided with his, Kari wanted to drop to her knees and worship him.

West gave her a cocky grin and leaned back on his palms, giving her an even better view of his tatted torso and the precum gathering at the tip of his cock. "Strip for me."

Kari licked her lips, desperate to have his taste on her tongue. She unbuttoned and unzipped her pants. "Turn and face the mirror, baby girl." She did, the angle allowing her to look at herself and catch West's reaction when she hooked her thumbs beneath the waistband of her pants and underwear, bent at the waist, and slid them over her ass and down her thighs.

"Fuck, you're dripping. The idea of being punished turns you on, doesn't it?"

"Yes, Daddy," she said, stepping out of her pants and kicking them aside.

"Turn back around and take off the rest. I want to look at all of you."

Kari turned and moaned when she caught West gripping his erection through his briefs while he circled the crown with his thumb, spreading the precum over the head. She didn't bother unbuttoning her shirt, choosing to whip it over her head. Her bra went last, sailing into the closet next to her.

West crooked his finger, and she stepped between his spread thighs. "Bend over my lap and lay your upper body on the mattress." He closed his legs, keeping hers trapped between them, and gave her a wicked chuckle. "Gotta make sure you can't wriggle away, lass. Now, bend over."

Kari lowered herself over West's thigh, lying her upper body on her bed. She pressed her cheek to the comforter and fisted the material, bracing herself for the stinging, pleasure-pain of his impending smack.

West placed his left hand in the center of her back and skimmed his right palm over her upturned ass and thighs. "Do you know why I'm punishing you?"

"Because it's fun, and we both get off on it." Kari gasped when his caress changed to a smack across both cheeks. She bucked her hips. The sting turned into pulsing pleasure and radiating heat.

West made a tsking sound, then she felt his fingers dip between her labia, grazing her clit. His touch was too light to give her the relief she craved.

Kari moaned when he plunged two fingers inside her. He dragged them over her reddened cheeks, leaving a trail of her arousal behind. Then she heard a distinct sucking sound when he licked his fingers clean. "True. Why else?"

"There's a possibility I may have sassed you and rolled my eyes. I also doubted you, and I'm sorry for that."

"You did. And I'll accept your apology right after I turn your ass a lovely shade of red. Since I don't believe you will control it, you have permission to come at any time."

"You think I'll come from being spanked?"

"I know you will." West landed another one on the fleshy part of her right cheek. She arched and rocked against his lap, gasping when the sensation coursed through her. "I'm going to give you twenty. These two don't count. Now, widen your feet and arch your ass a little higher."

Why did she need to spread her legs?

West bent over and pressed his lips to her ear. "Because all twenty are for your sweet little cunt."

Kari gasped. *He's going to spank her pussy?* Her gasp morphed into a moan when West slapped four fingers against her center. "Oh, fuck, Daddy."

"Wait until you get to twenty, baby girl. You'll be screaming for a different reason." West landed several smacks in a row. Each one sounded wetter than the last, and the steady pulse of the radiating heat spiraled Kari to the very edge.

"I...I...."

"Is my baby girl ready to come?"

"Yes...Daddy...please."

"Take the rest of your punishment and come for me." West landed ten more consecutive smacks, and Kari screamed her release by the time he landed the last one. She sobbed and moaned while her orgasm kept pulsing through her.

"Please...I need you." Kari's pussy clenched around nothing, desperate for West to fill her with his cock.

He pulled her up and onto his lap, facing the mirror, and used his thighs to spread her legs wider. With his left arm across her chest and his hand around her throat, West growled. The sound reverberated through her back.

"Look at us," he said, holding her in place. The head of his cock split her folds, poised at her entrance.

"Look how fucking perfect we are together. Your pussy is weeping for me, soaking the head of my cock in your desire."

"Yes...I want you so much. Please fuck me, Daddy. I need you to fuck me." Kari stared at where they were almost joined, transfixed.

West gripped the backs of her knees, lowering her onto his cock. Each piercing stroked her G-spot when he pressed inside her.

"I love the way you beg me," he said, settling deep enough that the tip of his cock kissed her cervix. West lowered her legs until her feet touched the floor, and his left hand moved to her throat. He rested his chin on her right shoulder, and they both stared, transfixed by how he stretched and filled her.

"Fuck, you're tight. The way your cunt is clenching around me, you're going to milk every drop of cum from me, aren't you?" he asked, groaning against her ear, which sent shivers down her spine.

His cock jerked inside her, and Kari whimpered, "Please, Daddy...."

West's grip on the sides of her throat tightened while his other hand slipped between her thighs, her swollen clit easy to find. He circled it with his thumb, sliding his fingers lower to explore where they fit like two perfect puzzle pieces. "Please...."

"Patience." He reached lower, cupping his balls, showing her how tight they'd drawn to his body. "I'm not gonna last. You've got my cock in a stranglehold, and it's the best torture I've ever experienced. Ride me and stroke your clit. I want you to come all over me." He moved his hand from between her legs and settled it on her hip, using his grip on her to guide her up and down his length.

Kari cupped her right breast and tugged at the nipple. Her left slipped between her thighs. She rubbed her clit with one finger and kept the others pressed against her opening, stroking West's cock each time she raised off him, intensifying things for them both with each stroke.

"Fuck yes, baby. Work my cock in and out of your pussy. Look at the way you're taking me." His hand moved from her throat to clasp her jaw, and he shoved two fingers into her mouth. "Suck."

Kari wrapped her lips around them, licking their calloused pads and sucking him to the back of her mouth. He pressed on her tongue, and she moaned, sucking harder, worshiping his fingers the way she loved to worship his dick.

Kari tipped her head back against his shoulder, arching her body, taking his cock deeper inside her. She worked her clit faster, circling her swollen bud when her pussy clamped around West's cock. Her orgasm was sudden, taking over her body when she heard him curse and felt the heat of his release.

Kari screamed his name, muffled by his fingers in her mouth as wave after wave shook her body until she went limp in his arms.

"I love you, baby girl. I need to worship at the altar of your pussy." West trailed open-mouthed kisses along her neck.

Kari tilted her head, giving him more access. "Isn't that what you just did with your cock?"

His hand slipped between her thighs, cupping them where they joined. He kept his hand there when he pulled his cock from inside, holding his cum from escaping.

Kari didn't have time to do more than squeak when West lifted her and turned, placing her on the edge of the bed and him on his knees between her spread thighs.

"What are you doing?"

West palmed her ass, tipping her hips in the air, offering her pussy like a cup he planned to sip from. *Oh, fuck, he planned to feast on her after coming in her.*

His face hovered an inch above her pussy when he met her gaze and asked, "Is this okay?"

Desperate to hear his filthy words, she asked, "Is what okay?"

West held her ass in the air with one hand and slapped her pussy with the other. The wet squelch sounded obscene in the quiet of her room.

"I want to tongue-fuck my cum into your pussy. I want to savor our combined flavor and make you come again with my mouth. Then, I want to kiss you and share it with you while I fuck one more load into you. Was that the details you were looking for?"

Kari's pussy fluttered, and some of his cum slipped free. West's mouth covered her opening, tonguing what spilled back inside. She sank her fingers into his hair and rubbed her pussy over the lower half of his face.

He moaned against her, and he sucked her labia into his mouth, the vibrations traveling straight to her clit. She tugged on his hair, and he moved his mouth higher, his lips surrounding her clit. He sucked hard while flicking his tongue against her swollen bundle of nerves just the way she needed to get off.

He slipped two fingers inside her, fucking them in and out of her at a brutal pace. The wet sounds when he curled his fingers to rub her G-spot filled the room, along with their heavy breaths and passionate moans.

Kari pulled his hair. She clamped her legs around his head when her orgasm overtook her. She shuddered and rocked against his mouth. "Yes. Yes. Yes. So...fucking...good."

The moment her legs fell open, West moved above her and drove his cock inside her. "Fuck, baby girl, I love you, and I already know I'll never get enough of you."

"Love you too, Daddy." She meant it from the very depths of her soul. She'll never get enough of him either.

CHAPTER TWENTY-NINE

West

When they made it to the shower, and Kari remembered there were two things he wanted to show her, she begged West to tell her his second surprise while on her knees worshiping his cock.

Despite her divine efforts, the water had cooled by the time they got out. West's balls drained of everything he could give her, and she still didn't know the surprise he had in store for her.

Edging can come in many forms.

West put on his jeans and grabbed a clean shirt, then threw his damp hair into a topknot. He dressed Kari in his hoodie and a pair of her cut-off shorts. He smiled when he caught her sniffing the collar and said, "I like you in my clothes."

Color heated Kari's cheeks, and she took another sniff of his sweater, showing him how much she liked the way he smelled.

"I like being surrounded by you." She wrapped her arms around herself, hugging his sweater to her, and West's heart fluttered for several beats.

They walked into the living room hand-in-hand, and with no sound coming from the direction of Izzy's room, West seated Kari on her couch and covered her legs with a soft blanket. "Do you want water or juice?"

He needed to take care of Kari, but he also recognized this for what it was. He needed to do something to keep his nerves in check.

"Water, please," she said, looking up at him.

He kissed the tip of her nose. "How do apple slices and dark chocolate sound?" Her tummy rumbled at the prospect, making him smile. "No worries. Your stomach tattled on you. After the way we went at it, you need to replenish your energy."

"So do you."

"Don't worry, baby. I'm making enough for both of us. Be right back." West grabbed two bottles of water, taking one to Kari for her to rehydrate while he grabbed their snack, stealing another taste of her lips on his way.

He sliced the apples and broke up the bar of dark chocolate. He set the plate on the table next to the couch, then lifted Kari into his lap. West didn't miss her gaze shifting toward Izzy's room. "Are you apprehensive about Izzy seeing us together like this?"

"No, just worried, you know?"

Did he know?

"It's alright, lass. We'll figure things out." He set the plate on her lap and raised a square of chocolate to her lips, stifling a groan when the tip of her tongue darted out to lick the melted chocolate from his fingers. Then he offered her a slice of apple. She bit off half, and he popped the other half into his mouth. "You remember telling Izz we're dating this afternoon, right?"

"I did, didn't I?"

West chuckled. "Yeah, you did, and she didn't even bat an eye."

"I like that your new shop is nearby," she said, and West pulled her closer until she snuggled against his chest.

"I do, too, baby." He kissed the top of her head.

"What's your other surprise?"

"Nice try, lass. I'll show you and Izzy when she wakes up." West fed Kari the last chocolate square when a door creaked open down the hall, and little feet carried a re-energized Izzy into the living room.

West tightened his grip on Kari's hip, keeping her nestled against him when Izzy walked into the room, rubbing the sleep from her eyes. "It's okay, baby." West kept his voice low next to her ear. He kissed the corner of her jaw when Kari relaxed against him.

"Hey, Izzy, girl. Did you have a good nap?" Kari asked, drawing her attention.

"Yes, I'm hungry. Can I have a snack? Hi, Wes," she said, coming closer.

"Hi, Izz. I put some cheese, crackers, apple slices, and grapes at your coloring table," West said, pointing to the plate he'd also prepared for her.

"Yes...," Izzy said, pumping her little fist. "How come you're sitting on Wes? Are you hurt?" she asked Kari, stuffing a piece of cheese into her mouth. Her halo of blonde curls floated around her while she chewed.

"No, I'm not hurt. Do you remember this afternoon when I said I'm dating a tattoo artist?"

"Yeah, so?"

"You know I meant West, right?"

"Duh," Izzy said, surprising them both enough to make them laugh.

"Hey, Izz? I want to ask you something," West said with a surprising amount of nerves. He wanted Izzy to want him to be part of her life.

"What?" she asked around a mouthful of apple.

"How does the idea of the three of us spending a lot more time together sound?"

She studied him; her grey eyes scrupulous, looking between him and her sister. "Like a family? With a mom and a dad and me?"

West held Kari a little tighter. "You, me, and Kari could have our own special version if you want, yes."

"Cool," Izzy said, finishing her snack. "Is it okay if I play now?"

"I have a surprise for you both. Is it okay if I show you first?"

"A surprise? For us? Like a present?" Izzy ran over and tugged on Kari's hand. "Come on, Kari, Wes can't give us the surprise if you're sitting on him."

"Okay, okay. I'm coming...wait...where is this surprise? Do I need to change?"

"You're good. We don't need to leave the building, though we will take the elevator. Grab your sandals, baby," West said, leading them out of her apartment.

"Up or down, Wes? Up or down?" Izzy asked, hovering her finger over the buttons.

"Actually, Izz, we need a special key." West inserted the key he'd pulled from his pocket and opened a panel above the buttons for the regular floors, revealing a single button labeled P. He lifted Izzy and said, "You need to press this one."

"Is this a secret place?" Izzy asked when she pressed the button, and the elevator doors closed.

"Sort of." West glanced at Kari, trying to decipher her reaction. She was staring at the panel, tugging on her bottom lip with a pensive look on her face. "The people who own this place get this key."

"But you have a key," Izzy said. Kari's gaze snapped to his.

"That's right." When the elevator came to a stop, the doors slid open, revealing a private lobby with a door across the way. "Come on, let me show you."

He opened the door and ushered them inside. Kari gasped, spinning in a slow circle, and West got a little giddy watching her take it all in. Izzy shouted, getting excited by her echo as it reverberated through the space.

Kari moved toward the wall of windows to check out the view. West stepped behind her and wrapped his arms around her, pulling her back against his chest. He pointed out features of the open floor plan while Izzy ran around, exploring.

"What do you think?" West hoped they'd soon fill the place with furniture they'd picked out together.

"It's a beautiful space."

He pointed to the hall on their left. "The primary suite is down there. It has an ensuite, walk-in closet, and two other rooms which can make a great office, library, nursery...or maybe even an adult playroom."

Kari hummed, and West nipped her earlobe. "Something to consider."

"These are quite the possibilities." Kari spun in his arms. "Why are we touring the penthouse, West?"

"I just wanted to show you the possibilities." West pointed to the hallway on Kari's right. "There are three bedrooms with a shared bathroom." He decided to shoot his shot and laid all his cards out. "There's lots of space for Izzy and lots of privacy for us. What do you think about you and Izzy moving in here with me?"

Kari's mouth dropped open as she stared at him. Her hands pressed against his chest. "What about my apartment? I just found out I own it, for crying out loud."

West shrugged, moving Kari's arms to circle his neck. "Sublet it, sell it, or let it sit empty if you need it to be there. I want to live with you, baby girl, and build a life with you and Izzy. Can you picture all the love and happiness we will fill this place with? I don't want to wait, do you?"

"No, I don't want to wait. I want to say this is crazy, but this feels so fucking right." She smiled at him. "Okay."

"Okay?" *That's it; it's that easy?*

"Yeah, let's do this."

West laughed and picked Kari up, kissing her and spinning her around. Having her and Izzy here, in what will soon be their home, made him want to march downstairs and pack up their belongings tonight.

Kari broke their kiss. "Put me down. There's someone else who needs to give you their okay. Otherwise, this is a no-go."

West set her down. "You're right. Hey, Izz?" he called.

A few seconds later, she came running from the hallway where her bedroom would be. "Oh, my gosh," Izzy said with a literal squeal. "There's a pink room down there. Did you know pink is my favorite color? I wish I had a pink room."

Kari snorted. "I don't believe you'll have any issues convincing her," she said in a stage whisper.

"Do you want the pink room to be yours, Izz? Because I want you and Kari to live here with me."

"Umm...." Izzy ran around the living room and shouted, "Yes, if we can get a puppy!"

West tugged Kari to his side. "You've got a deal, kiddo."

"YESSS...I can't wait to tell my friends. Oh, can the puppy walk to school with us? Can I name the puppy? It can sleep in my room."

"Uh...wait, what now?" Did he just get bamboozled by a five-year-old?

Kari laughed so hard, tears ran down her cheeks. "There's no getting out of this now."

He never wanted out. West leaned in, and right before he kissed her, he said, "I'm all in, baby."

CHAPTER THIRTY

Kari

She never wanted to come down from this high, but her impending face-to-face with her mother slapped her back to reality.

Kari arrived for work a few hours early to meet Bianca Hendrix, the lawyer tasked with handling the legalities of their solution with Leslie.

Kari knocked on Japer's door. Instead of his normal 'enter,' he opened it, catching her off guard, though he did his best to give her a reassuring smile.

"Hey, Kari." When Jasper didn't step aside to allow her into his office, she followed his gaze to the empty hall behind her. "Where's West?"

"He...." Kari looked away from Jasper's all-too-knowing gaze. "I didn't tell him."

"What? Why?"

"In my defense, I have a good reason. West scheduled interviews to hire staff for his new shop. I didn't tell him because I knew he'd cancel to be here with me."

"Yeah, he would have." Jasper sighed. "He won't like your deciding this for him, though."

"I know." Kari squared her shoulders and met Jasper's gaze head-on. "And as much as I like the way he takes care of me, and how you and Gray and everyone else look out for me, you all need to remember that I'm more than capable of standing up for myself."

"Of course, you're more than capable. You're strong and independent, but you're also part of our ragtag family, and no matter what, we will always look out for you."

"I don't know what I did to deserve such friendship and loyalty, but thank you."

"It's quite simple; you're you. Come on. Bianca's waiting."

Kari took a deep breath to steady her nerves and walked into the office. When she moved past Jasper, she said with just enough sass to give her a little boost, "She wouldn't be waiting if you weren't out here giving me the third degree."

"Save your sass for the man who appreciates it."

Kari's smile faltered. "He will not be happy with me, will he?"

Jasper put a comforting hand on her shoulder. "Kari, I've never seen West happier. Your heart's in the right place. It's the part where you kept this from him. That's what he might take issue with. Talk to him. I'm sure it will all be fine." With that last bit of sage advice, Jasper let her step past him into his office.

Bianca Hendrix stood to greet Kari when Jasper closed the door. "Ms. Davidson, hello. It's a pleasure to meet you in person." The stunning blonde in a tailored three-piece suit said, holding out her hand for Kari to shake.

Her grip was sure, firm, and confident. Bianca's sharp gaze assessed her and unnerved her, and Kari forgot how to respond until Jasper nudged her elbow.

"Um, hi. It's nice to meet you, too. And please call me Kari."

They'd been corresponding by email for the past week, with Kari giving Ms. Hendrix a detailed account of the events that led to her raising her younger sister. She included copies of the bank statements proving Leslie's thievery and the contact information for Mrs. Palmer, the neighbor she left Izzy with.

"Call me Bianca." Bianca undid the two buttons holding her suit jacket closed, revealing a fitted vest over a crisp white button-down shirt. Kari couldn't help admiring her style. She took a seat, all business, sliding the black frames of her glasses onto her nose. "I spoke with Mrs. Palmer, and she provided a very detailed statement in your favor."

Kari gave a little shrug. "I kept in touch with her, sending her updates about Izzy. We get together for lunch once a month."

"Mm...yes, she told me each time you come over for lunch, you show up with bags of groceries."

"Well, yeah, Estelle's on a fixed income, and what I bring helps her out. It's the least I can do when she looked after Izzy."

"Yes, she called you instead of Child Services when your mother failed to return, correct?"

"She called me instead of putting Izzy into the system, yes. I can never repay her for that kindness. Extra groceries are the least I can do."

"Well, she's a very favorable witness if needed when we go before the courts."

"We still have to go to court?" Why didn't she consider this? "Can a judge still take Izzy from me even if Leslie signs over guardianship?"

Bianca leveled her gaze on Kari, resting her chin on her clasped hands, and Kari swallowed hard, feeling more exposed than she liked.

"To make it official and legal, a judge must approve the arrangement, Kari. Your mother abandoned your sister on someone else's doorstep. I'm sure Mrs. Palmer would have spoken on your behalf back then, too. What I want to know is, why didn't you petition the court for guardianship when this first happened?"

Kari looked over at Jasper, who met her gaze with sympathetic eyes. He tipped his chin toward Bianca. "Tell her. You have nothing to be ashamed of."

"I'm not ashamed, but I was nineteen, and my mother had just made off with every dollar I earned from my modeling career. I didn't have many choices. My sister needed me, and I needed to make money. Fast. In the statement I gave you, I told you I worked at a club, but I didn't say what kind."

Bianca stopped taking notes, then met her gaze. "What kind of club was it?"

"It was a club where they looked the other way when hiring a nine-teen-year-old to dance. I danced burlesque, but the girls who worked the VIP rooms did more. I still made enough to pay rent and put food on our table, and it allowed me to be there for Izzy, but I know what it would look like to a judge. It wouldn't be difficult to learn what kind of reputation the Garden of Eden had. So I just went about life as if I'd taken care of it already."

Tears clouded her vision, and her lower lip trembled when she asked, "And what about here? This is a BDSM club."

"Kari, have you looked at your paystub?" Jasper asked, interrupting her.

Kari wiped the tears from her eyelashes and gave Jasper a questioning look. "Of course I have."

"Do you? Or do you just check the amount to ensure I haven't upped your clothing allowance again?"

"I...." Yeah, she's guilty of that. Damn the man for knowing her all too well. "Alright, you got me. Just tell me what you're hedging at already."

Jasper retrieved a paper from the file cabinet in the corner and handed it to her. Kari glanced down to find a letter. "What's this?"

"For crying out loud, just read it."

"Okay, okay."

"Jones Corp LLP

Re: Kari Davidson

Front of House Logistics Manager"

Kari's hand trembled, and the paper rattled. Yet she still read, *"From the Office of the President and Shareholders."*

"That is where you work, and that is your official title. It's what's written on every one of your paystubs, employee forms, and tax forms. No one will question what you do or where you work. All our employees have this privacy."

"And this letter?"

"I wanted you to read it before Bianca presented it to the judge. No one is going to take Izzy away from you. You're her guardian, and we're going to make sure everyone recognizes that."

Jasper squeezed her shoulder. "You're going to get through this meeting with Leslie. Then, when you go before a judge to make it all legal, it will just be a formality."

God, she hoped Jasper was right.

CHAPTER THIRTY-ONE

West

West found some great people during the first round of interviews, hiring two artists and a shop manager. With that out of the way, he can focus on Kari. If he has his way, she won't ever have to worry about Izzy being a pawn in her mother's cruelty again.

He sent Jasper a text to let him know he was coming to the club tonight, when something else occurred to him.

> **West: Hey, when's the lawyer supposed to meet with Kari?**

He watched those dots appear and disappear until three damning words popped up on his screen.

> **Jasper: Talk to Kari.**

He dialed Kari's number, and it went to voicemail. He called Jasper next.

"I told you to talk to Kari," Jasper said when he connected the call.

"She didn't answer her phone, so I called you."

Jasper's sigh was audible over the line. "She's in her dressing room getting ready for her shift. The reception is shit there. I need to get the IT guy to fix it."

"Are you going to fill me in or what?"

"Kari met with Bianca this afternoon."

"They met today?" *Why didn't Kari tell him*?

"She didn't tell you because she didn't want you to cancel the interviews you scheduled. She knew you'd cancel them if you did."

West opened his mouth to protest, then shut it. It's kind of impossible to argue with the truth.

Jasper sounded amused. "She got pretty bratty about it, though."

Now, this caught his attention. "What time does Kari's shift start?"

"Seven."

West glanced at his watch. It's almost five. There's time. "I'll be at the club tonight."

"You already told me."

"I'm letting you know I'm on my way."

"Whatever you have in mind, she'd better still be able to do her job."

"She will."

"She'd better."

"I've gotta go. See you tonight."

West knocked on Kari's dressing room door, and when she opened it, she smiled with pleasant surprise. "Hey, what are you doing here?"

His gaze swept over her. Kari did her makeup in soft pinks with glossy lips. She braided in hair extensions, turning her shoulder-length hair into two French braids, the ends curling around her breasts covered by her black silk robe.

Fuck, she's beautiful.

He leaned in and kissed her cheek. "Mm...good you're not dressed yet. May I come in?"

"Yeah, of course." She tugged him inside and shut the door. "So...why does it matter if I'm dressed? You got plans for me, Daddy?"

He breathed in her soothing lavender scent. West wanted to drown in it...drown in her. "I spoke to Jasper a little while ago because I couldn't get ahold of you."

Her brow creased with worry. "Is everything alright? The service in this part of the building is awful. I'll tell Jasper to get the IT guy to fix it."

The comment made him laugh. "Jasper said the same thing. He's already working on it."

"That's why he's the boss." Her fingers twisted in the tie at her waist.

"Jasper mentioned your meeting with the lawyer and why you didn't tell me."

Kari turned pleading eyes to him. "I planned to tell you everything when I got home. I needed a bit of time to process, and I didn't want you to miss the interviews you'd scheduled."

"Did everything go okay?"

"Yeah. Bianca was thorough and laid out an ironclad agreement. After petitioning a judge, I will have full custody of Izzy, and if Leslie wants to be in Izzy's life at all, she'll go to rehab and therapy, or she can simply sign over her rights and walk out the door. Either way, Izzy will be safe, and Leslie can never hurt her again."

West backed Kari against the counter where her cosmetics lay scattered across the surface. He raised her chin with his index finger, making sure she read the honesty in his eyes when he said, "She will never hurt you again, either."

"How did the interviews go?" The question was her not-so-subtle way of changing the subject. He'd humor her for the moment.

"I hired two new artists along with a shop manager."

"Worth it, then."

"Do you think I'm going to punish you?"

"Aren't you?"

"Fuck, no," he said, kissing her glossy lips. He kept the touch light, not wanting to ruin her makeup... at least not yet.

"I may want to stand by your side and be your protector in all things, but I know you're strong, brave, and more than capable of taking care of yourself. This growing partnership of ours is equal, and I appreciate you looking out for my best interests the way I want to look out for yours."

West swept the braid on her right behind her shoulder, his lips finding her pulse point, pressing hot, open-mouth kisses against the rapid beat. "I am, however, going to drive you wild all night until you are a whimpering mess, and search for me after your shift, and beg me to fuck you."

He spun Kari around to face the mirror and placed the black drawstring bag he'd brought with him beside her hand on the counter. Her eyes drifted to the bag, then she met his gaze in the mirror. "Did you bring me a present, Daddy?"

"Yes, I'll show you in a minute." West undid the tie of her robe. The silk parted, and he pulled it from her arms and hung it on a hook beside the mirror, exposing endless amounts of creamy skin, pert dusky nipples, and her pussy already weeping for him.

His lusty swallow was audible. "What outfit are you wearing tonight?"

Kari pointed to the chair behind them.

"Fuck me," West growled when he turned to find black leather combat-style boots in front of the chair for Kari to lace to the middle of her shin. Black rubber bikini-cut bottoms lay on the seat, waiting to be slid over her lubricated skin, then rubbed with oil to a glossy shine. Draped over the back of the chair lay a black lace bra, fishnet stockings, a utility belt, and a ribbed white tank.

"Lara Croft?"

Kari gave him a sexy smirk. "Yup."

"Holy shit. You're going to be the sexiest tomb raider anyone's ever seen." He tapped the inside of her bare foot with his booted one. "Spread your legs wider for me, Daddy wants to give you your gift."

Kari broadened her stance, bending at the waist, and sticking her pert ass in the air. West crowded around her, grinding his trapped cock between her cheeks. "Fuck, this is going to be a long night for both of us. More fulfilling for you, though," he said, pressing kisses along her neck.

West picked up the drawstring bag and opened it. "Hold out your hand." When she did, he tipped the bag upside down. "It's called the Creamsicle. I believe it's named for the way it makes the wearer...cream."

"You...want me to wear this while I work? Orgasm while I welcome our guests tonight?" Kari shivered, her nipples puckering at the prospect.

West cupped her breasts, teasing her tight buds with his thumbs, circling them with light strokes as she pressed them into his palms, searching for more.

"Remember, you can say no, though I don't believe you want to. Tell me I'm right. Tell me how my girl wants to orgasm in public. Wants the challenge of keeping her pleasure a secret. Say it," he said against her ear, their gazes connecting in the mirror.

"Yes, I want it. Please, Daddy...." Kari arched her hips, rocking against his straining cock, bringing him closer to his own release until he gripped her hips, stilling her movements.

"Easy, baby girl. You're the one who gets to come repeatedly. Not me." He took the orange-colored vibrator from her hand and slipped it between her legs, coating the device in her arousal. He parted her folds and teased her swollen clit. Then he held it to her entrance and pushed it inside until the flat base pressed against her mound.

Kari moaned. "Turn it on, Daddy. Make sure it works."

West gave her a wicked chuckle. "Such a brat for me. I love it...I love you."

"I love you, too."

He snatched the remote from her hand. "Close your legs. You need to hold it in place since you're not dressed yet, and I want to see what this little gadget will do to you."

Kari clenched her thighs together, and West pressed the remote's button. He increased the intensity a little at a time until she whimpered, rocking her hips while the toy amped up her desire.

"How does it feel, baby?"

"Amazing."

"Come for me, then I'll turn it off and help you dress." West upped the intensity one more time and set the remote on the counter, freeing his hands to cup her breasts. He twisted and plucked her nipples while pressing open-mouth kisses to her throat, sending Kari toward a shuddering release.

She snagged her bottom lip between her teeth and didn't make a fucking sound.

West nipped her earlobe. "You think you can stay silent all night? I believe you'll scream my name no matter who's around."

"I'll keep quiet, Daddy," Kari said with a little moan and a lot of determination. The last of the aftershocks trembled through her body when he turned off the vibrator and pocketed the remote.

"What if I don't want you to be?" His expression turned serious when he turned Kari to face him. "Who's working the inner door tonight?"

"Tony. Why?"

"If at any time you need me to stop, say your safeword. I'll make sure Tony knows that if he hears you say chickenpox, he will tell me, and I will come and make sure you're alright. Okay?"

"Okay. Thank you," Kari said, giving him a shy smile.

West cupped her face and kissed her lips. "Making sure you're safe and happy is a top priority for me."

"You make me feel safe, visible, and loved. No one's ever done that for me."

"You're with me now, and I promise I'll always take care of you."

"I promise to take care of you, too."

"I know you will, baby girl." He kissed the tops of her shoulders. "Let me help you get dressed."

West picked up the bottle of lavender-scented massage oil and poured some into his palms, then he massaged the length of Kari's legs, to the globes of her ass, making her skin slick and soft.

"Lean back against the counter, baby."

"Mm...you have magic hands."

"I always aim to please, lass." He picked up her bottoms, helping her step into them, sliding them over her hips until the rubber cupped her cheeks, keeping the vibrator pressed inside her. Then he added more oil to his palms and rubbed her shorts until they shone.

Next, he gathered her large-mesh fishnets and picked up her left foot, resting it on his thigh. He got the stocking over her foot, sliding it up her leg until the thick band wrapped around her upper thigh.

West kissed the curve of her knee, then set her foot down, giving her right leg the same treatment until those sexy fishnets emphasized her endless legs. He reached for her boots and carefully laced them up. "Not too tight?"

"No, it's perfect," she said, her voice a little breathy, making him smile. He loved dressing her. The act of service allowed him to worship every part of her.

West stood, kissing the tips of her breasts before covering them with her black lace bra. He pulled her ribbed tank over her head and buckled the utility belt into place. He took a step back to get the full effect as he raked his gaze over her from head to toe and back again. "Fuck, you're beautiful, baby."

"Thank you, Daddy."

"Let me walk you to the front. I'll talk to Tony, then settle in at the bar. What do you do if you need things to stop?"

"I say my safeword, and Tony will come get you."

"That's right, baby." West held the door open for her, then made sure it locked behind them.

"Why is my best employee checking in guests looking like a blissed-out, satisfied sex-kitten?" Jasper asked, taking the seat beside West.

"Hey, I take offense at that comment," Gray said, taking the stool on West's other side. "I'm your best employee/co-owner."

"Whatever you say, Gray."

West rubbed his thumb over the remote he kept tucked in his palm, letting his friends banter while he let his thoughts wander. He wanted to go back to the door, where Tony obliged him, opening it enough for West to watch his baby girl try to keep her moans and body shaking orgasms to herself.

He'd wait until the guests moved away to make her come. The moment she stood alone, he amped up the vibrator until she gripped the edges of the counter in orgasmic bliss. He wanted to give Kari another to cap off her shift. "It's just a bit of funishment. I wanted to take her mind off the meeting with her mother."

"Well, that's nice of you," Gray said with utter sincerity.

Jasper snorted, and the three of them clinked their glasses in a fucked-up cheers before taking a drink.

West checked his watch. Kari's shift was minutes away from being done. His smile shifted into something wicked. Time to amp things up one more time. He went to the highest setting on the remote, then moved off his stool, intent on catching the moment she came in person.

He didn't make it more than a few steps when he heard it. Tony must have propped the door open.

"Oh...fuck...I'm coming, Daddy. Fuck...yes...West. I need you."

He was on the move. Kari was faster, meeting him just past the bar. She looked unhinged.

Was that last orgasm too much?

Kari jumped into his arms, and he gripped the backs of her thighs when she wrapped her legs around his waist.

Her hands tangled in his hair, pulling his topknot free. Kari's lips pressed to his, frantic with need, and her words tumbled into his mouth. "I've booked the Red Room. Take me there right now. I need you."

"Yes, ma'am." West tipped his chin toward his friends, who stared back at him with amusement. "Later, boys. My baby girl needs her Daddy."

CHAPTER THIRTY-TWO

Kari

West didn't put her down, carrying her past security and across to the private rooms. Though Kari doubted she could walk at the moment, anyway. Her legs still trembled from the multiple orgasms he'd given her.

With a quick consent check-in at the desk and directions to the third door on the right, West had her up against the closed door within minutes. Kari sucked his tongue into her mouth, the way she was desperate to suck his cock.

Her hands tangled in his hair, bringing him closer, and his grip on her ass tightened when suddenly, the vibrations in her pussy started up again.

"Oh...no...I can't, please...I want to make you come. Please, Daddy."

His lips dragged along her jaw until his mouth was at her ear. "One more, baby. Rub your pussy over my trapped cock. Drive me wild. Take me right to the edge, then I'll let you swallow my cum."

Kari whimpered, and the vibrations grew bolder. West urged her to rock her hips faster. She craved the taste of him, to get down on her knees for him. The power she held from such a position of submission fueled her race to completion.

"That's it, baby girl. Come all over my cock. Show Daddy how much you need me."

She pulled him closer; his face tucked against her throat as she arched her back and her pussy clenched around the toy that had driven her to distraction all night. "Yes...oh, God...yes, Daddy."

When the last flutters of her orgasm abated. Kari begged West to turn off the vibe. He did, even handing her the remote for good measure. She unhooked her legs from around his waist, and he let her slide down the length of his body...all the way to the floor.

Kari tore open the button and zipper of his pants, freeing his length. She pressed her face against his groin, breathing him in. *Gawd, he smelled so fucking good.* His scent made her feral, and she guided her tongue over each piercing along the underside of his cock until she kissed his tip.

Her gaze locked with his as she licked the precum from her lips. "Don't make me wait, Daddy."

"Baby girl, you can beg for it better than that."

West's right. She can offer him more and fulfill every single one of her desires. All she needed was to be vulnerable. To submit. To ask for it all. Beg for it.

"Please, Daddy. Fuck my mouth and feed me your cum. I'm hungry for you. I want you to fill my belly with your seed."

"Fuuuck, your dirty little mouth is about to get all my cum."

"I need it. Don't make me wait anymore." She opened her mouth, and West held his cock to her parted lips.

"Are you ready, Kari?" Her brow furrowed. *What happened to calling her baby girl?*

..."Kari?"

"Hm?"

"Kari, are you ready for this?"

"What?" She blinked, bringing the dark wood of the conference table into focus. *Did she really zone out and get lost in the memory of what West did to her last night?* The heat scorching her cheeks and West's concerned look told her she did.

"Oh, shit, um, yeah. Yeah, I'm ready."

West leaned in close, his words just for her. "You get through this, and I promise we'll recreate what distracted you for the past ten minutes."

Kari bit her bottom lip, relishing the sting from her kiss-ravaged lips. "I'm not sure if I'm ready for a repeat of last night. Not when I'm plugged full of your cum."

"Baby girl, the moment I get you out of here...."

A throat cleared at the end of the table, and Bianca garnered their attention. "The lobby receptionist has informed me that Ms. Davidson is on her way up. It won't be long now."

Kari's stomach twisted. Well, there's one way to throw a bucket of ice water on her libido. Her mother's almost here. She took a deep breath to calm her nerves, and West squeezed her hand beneath the table. "Everything will be okay."

She gave him a look that asked, *Will it?* The boardroom door opened, and Elite Security's receptionist ushered Leslie in.

When Jonathan suggested using the boardroom at his office as a neutral third-party location to meet with Leslie, Kari thought it was a great idea. Now she felt exposed and judged by the woman who had given birth to her.

Leslie whistled long and low, looking around. She took stock of what a place like this cost, perhaps calculating what she might get out of all this. Thank God they were ready for her.

"Ms. Davidson," Bianca said, taking charge. "If you'll take a seat, we can get started." She gestured to the chair across from Kari, and Leslie slid into it.

"Was I supposed to come with a lawyer or something? This seems very official. Maybe I should leave and come back another time." Leslie stood from the chair.

A fire lit in Kari's stomach. Her mother is not controlling this narrative. She'd already taken enough from her and Izzy. No, this is ending today.

"Sit down, Mother. This office is just a neutral place for us to meet. Don't bother reading into it any more than that. Ms. Hendrix is here to answer questions you may have about the document you will sign today."

Leslie dropped into the chair. Kari didn't believe her mother expected this kind of pushback. Hell, it surprised her, but Kari embraced her growing strength and confidence. She had people in her corner and wasn't alone anymore.

West squeezed her hand, and Kari glanced his way. He gave her a smile filled with love and reassurance. When she turned her attention back to her mother, Kari met her calculating stare head-on.

Leslie tipped her chin in their direction. "What's this?" Her index finger with its manicured nail flicked in a circle, encompassing her and West. "Is it serious?"

This time, Kari squeezed his hand, then let go, setting his hand on her thigh. She leaned forward and said, "My personal life isn't part of this discussion. We are here in Izzy's best interests."

"Oh? Is this man in my daughter's best interest?"

Without hesitation, Kari said, "Yes." Speaking for both her and Izzy, she knew beyond any doubt, he'd be part of their lives for the rest of his.

Bianca took that opportune moment to set two sets of papers and their duplicates in front of Leslie. Kari swallowed. The desire to hold her breath until her mother said something almost overwhelmed her. West squeezed her thigh, and she breathed deep. In through her nose and out through her mouth.

"What's all this?"

Bianca returned to her seat. "If you'd like to read them over, they're-"

"Nah. Give me the cliff notes version, sweetheart. I don't have time to read all this."

"I did not graduate at the top of my class from the Columbia School of Law for you to call me sweetheart, Ms. Davidson. You will address me as Ms. Hendrix or not at all. Are we clear?"

Damn, Kari sat up a little straighter at Bianca's steel-like tone and watched as her mother immediately backed down.

"Crystal clear, Ms. Hendrix." Leslie picked up the pen that Bianca had provided. Tapping it impatiently against the table, she picked up the first set of papers. "Well, are you going to give me the rundown or not?"

Bianca sighed, and Kari didn't blame her for the momentary show of frustration. "I strongly recommend that you read each document."

"Yeah, yeah," Leslie said, dismissing her with a flick of her finger, and Kari clenched her hands together, stifling her irritation.

"You abandoned your youngest child with the neighbor when she was two, correct?" Leslie sputtered; otherwise, she didn't respond, and Bianca asked again. "Yes or no, Ms. Davidson?"

"Yes," she hissed. "Listen, I can explain."

Kari cut in. "There is no excuse you can offer that will ever make amends for abandoning Izzy with Mrs. Palmer. She could have handed her over to child protective services. Thank God she called me. I have more than enough evidence to support this. More than enough to expose everything."

In the silence following such a statement, Kari heard her mother swallow. She cleared her throat and shifted her gaze back to Bianca. "There are lots of pages here."

"The package you're holding contains an agreement to surrender your parental rights to Isabella Rose Davidson. Ms. Kari Davidson will petition the court to obtain guardianship. There is a restraining order; you are to stay away from their residence and Isabella's school. However, there's a caveat."

"Oh, and what's that?"

"Rehab. A treatment center paid for in full, if you choose to go, Ms. Kari Davidson will look at future visitations for you and Isabella, so you may rebuild your relationship."

Leslie shifted in her seat, her grey eyes similar to Izzy's, yet not. While Izzy's shone with light and joy, Leslie's almost seemed cold and lifeless. Kari shivered.

"Is there anything else in it...for me?"

And that's what all this boiled down to. How much money can Leslie get from this?

"Haven't you taken enough?" It hurt to ask, but she needed to know.

Leslie leaned over, and Kari leaned back ever so slightly before she caught herself. She won't back down, not from this.

"I had you when I was sixteen. You owed me."

"I owed you? Every dollar I earned for being born? Despite the precariousness of my existence, you still had options. I didn't owe you anything. You left us with nothing, not even a roof over our heads."

"Looks like you landed on your feet to me."

A low rumble sounded beside her. West had remained a silent wall of support, but a glance at his hardened expression told Kari he'd reached his limit. "It's okay," she said, squeezing the hand he still had planted on her thigh.

West turned his head and looked at Kari. His silent stare, relaying how much he believed it wasn't. "I'm okay." His gaze flickered over her face. Then his eyes closed, and he nodded. Kari turned back to her mother.

"Is it all gone? I mean, it must be, since you're sniffing around Izzy and me again. How much do you owe?"

"I resent that," Leslie said, yet Kari could see her weighing her options.

"How much?"

Having children never stopped Leslie's desire to party and gamble. "A hundred grand. Alright?" Leslie's gaze shifted to the papers on the table.

West pulled out his phone and sent a message. It buzzed with a response thirty seconds later, and he leaned in close. "You have what you need." He didn't need to say anything else because she knew there was now a hundred thousand dollars sitting in her account.

Kari retrieved the blank certified check from her bank, filled it out, and placed it above the papers Leslie had yet to sign. "There."

Leslie reached for the check, and Kari put her hand over it, stopping her. "You don't get this until you've signed."

"Anything else I need to know about this one?" Leslie asked, acknowledging Bianca again.

"Any monetary contribution undertaken today will be a onetime offer."

Leslie's face tinged with rage. No doubt bitter, she didn't ask for more. "Alright. Forfeiting my parental rights, a onetime payment, and rehab. What's option two?"

She didn't mention the chance of still being in their lives.

Kari's stomach became leaden.

"It's the same minus the rehab and the chance for future visitation," Bianca said.

Leslie didn't even hesitate. She flipped over the copy of the first option and signed both copies of the second. Kari's hand fell away from the check, and Leslie snatched it up. "Does it matter which copy is mine?"

"No, they're both the same," Kari said before Bianca could.

Leslie shoved her copy and the check into her purse and stood, heading toward the door. Kari pushed back her chair, rounding the table to follow. "Wait."

Leslie froze with her hand on the door.

"Don't you care at all?" Kari hated the pain in her voice, but she wasn't backing down.

Leslie wouldn't look at her when she said, "I'm no one's mother." Then, she walked out the door.

Kari stood in the open doorway, staring at the back of Leslie while someone who suspiciously looked like Mistress Eve in a perfectly fitted charcoal suit, escorted her from the building.

Kari felt...relieved.

She took a deep breath or tried to and sniffled. She raised a hand to her cheek, and her fingertips came away wet. *Is she...crying?*

West stepped in front of her, filling her blurry vision. The warmth from his calloused palms broke through the numbness encasing her. "Hey, baby girl," he said, catching her tears with his thumbs. "I got you. It's over, and I got you."

He tugged her from the doorway and into his arms. Kari wrapped her arms around his waist and pressed her face into the crook of his neck and sobbed. West's arms wove around her shoulders and back, encompassing her in a blanket of security as she let go.

"I guess there was this part of me that believed she'd sign the one to get help. Despite everything, she wanted to be a part of our lives. My mom really didn't want us."

West shifted his hand, moving it beneath her chin to tip her head back and meet his gaze. "Despite how it looks, the choice Leslie made today was the best thing for you and your sister. I know it hurts, and I'm sure there will come a point where Izzy has questions or lashes out, but as hard as it is to accept right now, your mother did right by you today."

Kari knew West was right. She and Izzy would be better off in the long run. It's just...*why did it have to hurt so fucking much?*

"I know, baby." West handed her a tissue from the box left beside them. Kari looked around. "It's just us," he said, reassuring her. "Bianca stepped out a minute ago. We'll talk to her when we leave and find out how quickly we can get before the judge. Izzy's safe. She's going to stay with you...with us."

Us.

They'd picked out some furniture for their impending move to the penthouse already. "We're a family." The words for herself, Kari didn't even realize she'd said them aloud in the quietest whisper. West heard her anyway.

"Yes, baby girl. We're a family." And his lips pressed against hers in the tenderest of kisses.

CHAPTER THIRTY-THREE

Kari

Two Months Later.

Kari peeked around the edge of the curtain. Jasper stood at the corner of the stage by the stairs, waiting to help Kari down those steps when the time came. Gray stood on the other side. Same deal, except he'd help her up the steps. They both wore black-on-black suits, blending into the shadows cast by the stage spotlights.

She could just make out Addie and Jess in the front row on either side of West, ready to play their part because he's the one in the dark tonight.

After returning from Glasgow late last night, Kari let him sleep most of the day. Under the guise of working this evening, she convinced West to come to the club, promising to join him once her shift finished, and asked him to keep Addie and Jess company since Gray and Jasper were working tonight's event.

The moment she'd checked West in and he'd gone through the main doors of the club, Kari high-tailed it to her dressing room to change for tonight's...entertainment.

Rumors spread when she disappeared from her post, or more likely, her replacement spilled the beans, and the seats in front of the stage filled, spilling to standing room on the dance floor when members crowded around to catch their favorite hostess take center stage.

She's the opening act for what she hoped was the first of many burlesque nights at the club, and Kari had a feeling West might lose his mind tonight.

The official move into the penthouse occurred the week after Kari went before the judge to seek legal guardianship of Izzy. She picked Izzy up from school after volunteering at Lavender House all day, only to come home to an empty apartment. Empty except for the man waiting for them to escort them to their new home on the top floor.

The week after that, West flew to Glasgow to tie up loose ends. And while he was gone for those endless four weeks, Kari rehearsed and put together a lineup of acts. The way tonight has evolved into this burlesque variety show with a mix of drag, burlesque, and BDSM demonstrations has made the long hours and effort worth it.

Fuck, she'd missed him, though.

"Ready, Kari?" Zane asked, coming up behind her dressed as his version of the Emcee in Cabaret. He volunteered for the role, and it's time to announce her performance.

Kari breathed deep, centering herself, as she glanced at West from her hiding place. He must have felt her eyes on him, because he looked toward the darkened corner where she hid.

West's stare intensified, and he quirked a brow, asking his own silent question. She might reply to Zane, but it's her Daddy she spoke to. "Yes, I am."

She took another deep breath, and Zane gave her a reassuring smile, squeezing her hand. "You've got this. I saw your dress rehearsal. West is going to love *all* of it. Now go take your mark. It's my turn to announce you."

"Thanks."

"You're gonna knock that man off his feet."

Kari knew what her co-worker was doing. "He's already sitting, Zane," she said, rolling her eyes for good measure.

"Lucky for him, isn't it?" Zane stepped in front of the curtain to a round of applause.

This is it.

"Good evening, everyone, and welcome to Decadent's first – of what I hope is many – burlesque variety nights." Zane's sultry, deep voice echoed through the speakers while Kari took her mark at the back of the stage.

"Tonight, we shall entertain you. Titillate...even discombobulate you into a frenzy of heightened desire. Perhaps some of you may even find these performances nostalgic. A fulfillment of a fantasy you never expected to come true...our first performer is someone familiar to many of you. Infamous for her many outfits...everyone please welcome our host with the most...Kari."

The curtain parted, and she schooled her features while the opening to Sweet Dreams by the Eurythmics played. Kari strutted from the back of the stage and stepped into the spotlight.

West was visible beyond the shadows. He sat forward in his chair. His hands clasped between his spread thighs, and his elbows balanced on his knees.

The way he stared...everything he wanted to do to her the moment she left this stage poured from his gaze. And all of it would lead to multiple orgasms for her.

When Kari reached the front of the stage, she paused and bit her gloved index finger between her glossy red lips. She rolled her shoulders and turned, giving the audience her back while she untied the belt at her waist. She held the gown closed by its lapels and spun back around, shimmying in place.

Kari teased her dress open and closed twice, tempting the audience with a view beneath while she rolled her right shoulder. The material slipped, pooling at the crook of her elbow, and she moved across the stage toward the steps where Jasper waited while the audience hooted and hollered.

When she reached the stairs, Kari let the gown slip from her left shoulder. She straightened her arms, and the material pooled around her feet. Jasper stepped forward and held out his hand, helping her manage the steps in her six-inch heels before returning to the shadows.

Kari spun and twirled, sashaying in her revealed silver corset and shimmering fringed skirt. With each twirl, she drew closer to her friends and the man she loved, giving the audience a glimpse of the red lace beneath.

West leaned back in his chair when Kari approached. She raised her left leg, placing the toe of her stiletto between his spread thighs. He cupped the back of her ankle and said, "Hey, baby girl. This is quite a surprise."

Kari leaned in, grazing her satin-gloved hand along West's jaw until she cupped his cheek, and he leaned into her touch. "The best surprises are just for you, Daddy."

She shimmied her hips to the beat and lifted her hand from his cheek, taking the tip of the middle finger between her teeth. She tugged it loose. Then she leaned across West, offering her hand to Addie to remove it. Kari took the glove from Addie's hand and draped it over West's shoulder.

She then leaned to his right and offered her other hand to Jessica, who tugged each fingertip of Kari's glove loose, drawing out the anticipation before she pulled it off.

Kari blew Jess a kiss, then draped that glove over West's other shoulder. Straightening, she gave him a sultry smirk and nodded at his grip on her ankle.

She might want West to keep touching her, but there's a show to finish first.

He gave her a wicked look, pressing her foot against his hard length. She winked and mouthed the word, 'Later,' then spun away, dancing and teasing the audience, making her way to the other side of the stage where Gray stepped from the shadows, taking her hand to help her up the steps.

When Kari reached the top, she unhooked the fringe skirting, revealing her red lacy bottoms, and The Eurythmics' Sweet Dreams morphed into He's a Dream by Shandi in a wicked mix she and the club's DJ put together.

That's when Kari heard West utter, "Oh, Fuuuck."

Kari strutted back to her original mark while undoing the eyelet hooks of her corset. She did a spin, stopping with her feet spread, facing the audience. She ripped the corset open and flung it aside, revealing the red lace teddy underneath.

The curtain dropped closed. Kari teased the audience with a show of leg from behind the curtain, allowing a staff member to bring out the chair and place it on the markers below the chain now visible above. What's not visible is the bucket of water the chain's attached to. The curtain opened again, and the cheers grew louder while Kari gave West and the entire audience her version of the water scene from Flashdance.

When she spun and dropped into the chair, Kari extended one of her legs, bracing her foot on the floor. She arched out of the seat and reached for the chain. The water plunged down, soaking her and a bit of the audience.

The crowd went wild.

She dropped out of the seat and slid onto her knees, pounding the leather with her fists. Then she launched into a spin, flinging the water droplets from her hair and body with the biggest grin on her face.

Toward the end of her performance, West moved to the front of the stage, gripping the edge, not taking his eyes off her as everyone around them applauded and cheered.

"Fuck, baby girl, I don't have the words to describe how hot that was."

"I'm glad you liked your surprise." Kari gave him a relieved smile when he draped the robe she'd left at the side of the stage over her shoulders. The water she'd rained down on herself was lukewarm at best, making her shiver as her adrenaline ebbed.

"Liked it?" West asked with awe, which made her cheeks flush. He tied her robe and pulled her close, grinding his hips against hers. "No, baby, I fucking loved it, and I love you." He pressed his lips to hers, and Kari melted against him. West swallowed her moan the moment her lips parted, stroking her tongue with his.

"Love you too, Daddy," Kari said against his mouth.

"Mm...how about *Doctor* Daddy takes you to the medical theme room? I can give you a thorough exam...make sure you didn't suffer any undue strains during your show," he said, nipping at the spot below her ear.

"Dr. Daddy, now, is it?" Kari bit her bottom lip and gazed at West from beneath her lashes. She trailed a hand over her collarbone to her breasts, teasing her nipples through the material of her robe.

"It's hard here, and...." Her words trailed off, and West's intense gaze followed the path her hand took until it slipped between her thighs through the split in her robe. "Mm...and it's wet here. Can you help me?"

"I've got nine inches of cure right here, baby girl." West rocked against her. His thick shaft pressed into the juncture of her thighs. Kari swore she might come until a startled shout made them turn and search the lingering crowd at the front of the stage.

Kari's heart dropped when she saw Jess clutching her stomach with Addie on one side of her and Jasper on the other. "Oh my god, Jess." In an instant, both she and West moved down the stairs and to their friends.

Kari saw Jess's wet pants, soaked from her lap to her ankles, and jumped to a different conclusion. "Oh, no. You got caught in the splash zone? I've got pants you can change into in my dressing room. I'm sorry, Jess."

"Not...that...kind...of...splash...zone," Jess said between panting breaths. She gripped her belly and spoke to it. "Why now, girls? We had a plan. You're not supposed to be here yet." Jess whimpered, her eyes flooding with tears. "My water broke, Jasper...."

"It's okay, sweetheart. I got you. You're safe. The girls are okay. They're coming a little earlier than planned. They're eager to say hello to their mom and dad, and we're going to head to the hospital right now." Jasper kissed her cheek, his excitement growing when he said to Jess, "We're gonna meet our girls. I love you so fucking much, sweetheart."

"Love you too, Jas." Jess winced with pain when another contraction seized her. "I can't believe our girls are coming."

Jasper led Jess away when West said, "Here, take this," and handed Jasper the towel he'd dried her hair with. "Do you need anything? I know you didn't expect this. Kari and I can go grab your hospital bag and meet you there."

"Thanks, brother, already taken care of. The bags have been in the trunk since the day I saw two little ones on the ultrasound."

"We'll make sure everything here is good, then we'll be in the waiting room for you guys, excited to meet your girls," Gray said, holding Addie in his arms.

"You've got this," West said, pulling Kari close. "Love you guys."

"Love you guys, too. But we gotta go." Jasper put a hand on Jess's lower back, and his other hand cupped her elbow, supporting her as they headed to the hospital to meet their twins.

The next morning, Jasper ushered them into Jess's hospital room, where she sat with both babies cradled in her arms, positively glowing.

"Hi," Kari said, tiptoeing closer. Two sleeping cherubs peeked out from their swaddling blankets. "Oh, you guys, they're beautiful. Did you decide on names?"

Jasper leaned against his wife's side, a look of utter adoration on his tired face. "We did. May I introduce Jade and Julia Jones?"

"Oh, em gee. I love them."

Jess looked up at Kari. "They are perfect, aren't they? Would you like to hold one of them?"

"Yes," Kari said, scooping the baby closest to her into her arms with the utmost care. She stared at the baby's sleeping, angelic face. "Which one are you?" Kari cooed.

"You've got Jade there. West, how'd you like to hold Julia?"

West swallowed and cleared his throat. "I'm honored." Jasper transferred Julia from her mother's arms to West's.

"Goddamn, brother. You're blessed. Hi Jules. I'm your uncle Wes, your favorite uncle."

"Uh, Jon might beg to differ."

"Shhh...don't listen to your dad. Uncle Jon's not here."

Kari stared at the man she loved, transfixed by how tiny and perfect Julia looked in his arms, and how perfect Jade looked in hers. She wanted this...with West. The moment the thought materialized, he looked up and met her gaze, understanding everything running through her mind.

"Someday?" He mouthed the word, keeping the conversation between them. Kari bit her bottom lip and nodded.

Yeah, someday.

Epilogue Kari

"When do you want to host the club's next burlesque night?"

Jasper returned after some much-deserved personal time spent with Jess, Jade, and Julia.

He'd asked Kari to come to Decadent an hour early to meet with him. She was excited to discuss adding more burlesque nights to the club's lineup. She had other ideas, too. His abrupt answer halted those thoughts.

"I don't."

Kari sat up straighter in her seat. Did she misread the message he sent her last week? "I don't understand. You said you wanted to discuss going further with burlesque."

"I did, but hosting another night at Decadent wasn't what I had in mind."

Well, that's not at all cryptic. Kari rolled her eyes, confident that at some point her boss would tell her boyfriend she did. He narrowed his. *Bingo.* "What do you have in mind, then?"

Jasper leaned forward, linking his fingers together on his desk. Kari almost rolled her eyes again at all his dramatics. "There's something I haven't told you...another confession, if you will."

Kari fell back against her chair and crossed her arms. "Is there a chance I'm going to be pissed about this latest confession?" To be fair, none of his confessions angered her. Overwhelmed her, yes. Pissed her off? No.

"No. At least I don't think it will."

"Okay then, boss man. Lay it on me, and once again confess your sins. Does this mean I get to ask another personal question?"

"You've asked at least a dozen questions since you got here, and there's nothing sinful about this, not anymore. I righted a wrong for you by creating a new investment opportunity for me."

"Huh?"

"It never sat right with me that the piece of shit who owned the Garden of Eden took advantage of a nineteen-year-old girl. So, I made use of some of my connections and had the bastard's club shut down, and him slapped with numerous fines and penalties, some of which led to jail time."

"You didn't."

"I did. Then I bought the building. An excellent investment for an excellent price."

Kari's mouth parted in shock over the lengths Jasper had gone to on her behalf. "I can't believe you did that."

"You are family, Kari. Believe it. Also, I want you to run it."

"Uh, you mind saying that again, boss man?"

"I want to open a burlesque club, speakeasy-type lounge that also has a studio with burlesque lessons, and I want you to run it."

The renovations to the new club took five months, and Club Divine has now been open for a year.

Except for these ten days.

Decadent and Divine are closed because everyone who worked there is currently in New Zealand with friends and family at a private resort, all on Jasper's dime for his and Jessica's vow-renewal celebration.

After their twins were born, Jasper asked Jess if she wanted him to take over planning their ceremony, and it turned out to be one of those best decision-ever sort of situations.

Jess believed they were getting married on a beach in the Hamptons until she got on the plane.

Now here they were, along with Joanna, Addie, and Penny, fussing over Jessica as she got ready, and Kari had a secret.

She wasn't hiding it...exactly; she just wasn't saying anything. *This is Jessica's special day. Kari will tell the girls after they return home.* Then her hands got yanked toward the two people standing in front of her.

"Why's your engagement ring on your right hand?" Addie asked.

"And why is there a fresh tattoo on the ring finger of your left hand?" Jess asked, examining the intricate design West had given her...on their wedding night.

"I...."

"It's stunning," Penny said, sticking her head between Jess and Addie to get a closer look.

"When did you get married?"

Kari felt a substantial twinge of guilt for keeping it to herself, but she wouldn't change what had happened for the world.

"It happened on our second night here." The room erupted in chaos.

"What?"

"Oh, em gee. Details. We need details."

The distinct sound of a cork popping from a bottle of champagne almost drowned out Jessica's question and the tinge of hurt behind it. "You guys got married without us?"

Addie shoved a glass of champagne into each of their hands, and Kari took a grateful drink and said, "We were going to have a party at the penthouse next month. I mean, it's no secret we planned to get married; I'm not flashing this princess-cut diamond around for nothing, but West planned this intimate, private moment for me and Izzy and...." Her words trailed off, unsure of what else to say.

Penny took a sip from her glass. "Hey, I get it. Xander, Lex, and I had an officiant and a witness."

"Girl, give us the deets and make them swoon-worthy."

Kari blushed. "I don't have to make them swoon-worthy. They are."

"Yes, cheers." Addie clinked each of their glasses, and they all took another sip.

"Well, it started with the spa day." The girls nodded. "That was all West's doing. He booked the massages, mani-pedis, hair, and makeup."

"But I thought, Jas...."

"I did too. All part of West's plan. When Izzy and I got back to the suite, West was waiting for us. He bought Izzy and me outfits and arranged for dinner to be set up on our balcony while we got changed."

"And you had no suspicions at this point?"

"Nope, none."

"Damn, he's good."

"You're making mental notes for your next book, aren't you?"

Addie shrugged. "I mean, I'm not-not making mental notes." They all looked at her. "What? Stop having such inspirational love lives, then. Now, please continue."

"Don't jump right to dinner. What did West choose for you to wear? Oh, wait. What did he wear?" Penny asked.

"Mm...a white linen button-down with the sleeves rolled up to his elbows."

"Forearm porn, nice."

"Oh my God, Addie."

"What?"

"Anyway, he tied his hair back in a topknot and wore a pair of black fitted trousers. He looked...."

"Really fucking good?"

"Yeah, really fucking good."

"Izzy's favorite color is pink, and West got her a princess dress with a gauzy skirt and puffy sleeves." Kari laughed at the memory. "She lost her mind when he gave her pink sparkling wings and a fairy wand."

"Aw...."

Joanna tipped her glass in Addie's direction, asking for a refill, which she obliged. "And your dress?" She smirked. "Was your dress pink, too?"

"No...definitely not pink. It was an ice white, silk sheath with spaghetti straps and a low back. It slipped over my body like water and felt like I was wearing nothing while being completely covered."

The room fell silent. "Please tell me you took pictures," Addie said.

"West snapped a couple when I came down the hall from the bedroom." Kari opened her phone and showed them what her...husband had captured. They gathered around her as she scrolled through the pics.

"Aw...Izzy is adorable. With her halo of curls, she embodies a little sprite," Joanna said.

West had taken pictures of Izzy before she joined them, and when she got to the ones he'd taken of her, they stared in stunned silence.

"Oh, Kari, you are breathtaking," Jess said.

A second later, Addie smacked her shoulder. "How did you not know? You're carrying a bouquet."

"I might've had an inkling at this point."

West left the four white lilies tied together with a ribbon beside the dress, and she'd taken them with her when she left the bedroom to join him and Izzy for dinner.

The photos he'd captured made it look as though she walked down an aisle, and, given where the night went, she supposed she had.

"I don't know. We were here for you and Jasper, and it wasn't something I was thinking about."

"Did he tell you how beautiful you were, because my *Gawd* woman," Penny said, zooming in on her dress.

"All night."

"Tick tock, girl. The time of my wedding approaches."

"Right, sorry. Staff served us fresh seafood and roasted vegetables, and pizza for Izz. Then West asked us if we'd like to go for a walk. Izzy handed me the bouquet and told me to bring it because the flowers went with my dress."

"Dang, the little devil was in on it, too, huh?"

"Yup, though it turns out we had a surprise for her, too."

"Oh my God, you're pregnant?"

It was Kari's turn to smack Addie on the shoulder. "No. Not yet, anyway. I'm getting to the surprise. We walked along the beach for a bit, and Izzy ran a few steps ahead, waving the wand West gave her. These little fairy lights started appearing as Izzy skipped past, then we rounded the corner to a secluded beach; Izzy spun around, and the entire area lit up."

The surreal moment played out like a movie when she closed her eyes. "I didn't even notice the officiant standing in the middle of it all, waiting for us to walk up the little aisle and join him. West took my hands and said, You know how I told you the papers we've been working on with Bianca won't be ready until we get back?"

"Of course, I knew what he meant. And then he told me he'd lied. The officiant has them, and they're ready for us to sign. Then he knelt when

344

Izzy came over." Kari's eyes teared up at the memory, and she blinked them away.

"He asked her if she wanted to become a Sharpe and make the three of us an official family. He looked up at me from where he balanced on one knee and asked me if I'd marry him then and there. And I said, Yes."

Epilogue West

West caught a pair of grey eyes surrounded by a halo of curls peeking around his open office door. He didn't hide his smile, overflowing with love for the girl he considered his daughter.

Izzy captured his heart from the moment he met her, and over the past year and a half, the three of them had become this unique little unit, and he wanted to make them official.

"Hey, Izz."

"Can I ask you something?" Izzy asked, coming into the room and climbing onto the sofa in the corner, looking very serious.

"You just did."

Izzy gave him a look that he expected to be etched on her features throughout her teen years. He and Kari braced themselves for those tumultuous years, planning to weather those storms together.

"This is serious," she said, planting her hands on her knees and leaning forward. Her face scrunched into its most serious expression.

West lifted his hands in surrender. "Okay, okay. No more teasing. What did you want to ask me?"

Her words tumbled out in a rush. "Do you want to be a dad?" He didn't get the chance to answer this loaded question when Izzy hit him with another, and he blinked at the tears filling his eyes. "Do you want to be my dad?"

West sniffled and cleared his throat, trying to get the words past the emotions. "Is that what you want, Izz?" He put his hand to his heart. "Because I'd love to be your dad."

It's something he and Kari talked about. The words they shared late at night after they'd fucked each other senseless became more and more about their future.

Marriage, more children, and their adopting Izzy. He and Kari spoke with Bianca Hendrix a couple of weeks ago to start the process, and every day since, West has dreamed of their little unit being known as the Sharpes.

"Really?"

"Yes, really. Can we hug?" West always asked, wanting to instill the importance of consent and boundaries, like Kari did. Speaking of... West caught sight of more movement outside his office door, where she listened.

"Yes!" Izzy jumped off the couch and launched herself into his arms. West caught her and squeezed her tight. Over her shoulder, he met Kari's tear-filled gaze. She blew him a kiss, and he mouthed, "I love you." Then Izzy snagged his attention.

"Will you and Mom – I mean, will you and Kari adopt me? I know she's my sister, but she's like my mom, and if you're going to marry her and be my dad, then she should be my mom. Right?"

Well, there goes the romantic dinner proposal he planned, but somehow this seemed a hell of a lot better. West looked back at Kari, finding tears running unchecked down her cheeks. Damn, he wanted to hold her, too. Kari shook her head, remaining the silent observer a little longer.

"You're right, I am going to marry Kari," he said, staring right at her. Her eyes widened, and more tears spilled over her lashes. She moved her hand away from her mouth and nodded, giving him a nonverbal yes. He'll give her the ring tonight, right after he makes her scream yes over and over.

Later.

"And Kari is your mom in every way that matters. She loves you, and I love you. Our little unit can be whatever we want it to be. How about we go find Kari and talk about this together?"

"Like a family?"

"Yeah, bug. Like a family."

Kari blew him a teary kiss and escaped down the hall to compose herself, though West believed there'd be more tears before the night was over.

"Come on, Izz. Let's go find your Ma."

"Hey. Where did you disappear to?" Kari asked, pulling him from his memories.

West squeezed her thigh, rubbing his thumb in soft circles against her skin as he leaned in close. "Mm...the day Izzy asked us to be a family, and I asked you to marry me."

Kari leaned over and rested her head on his shoulder, looping her arm around his and nestling her hand in the crook of his elbow. "Yes, that was a good day."

"Just a good day?"

She tipped her chin and kissed his cheek. "Alright, it was...a very good day."

"Bratting when I can't do anything about it for the next two weeks? Do you think I'm going to forget between now and then?"

"I'm hoping that when the time comes, you'll have an entire list. Maybe...you'll have to call me down to the principal's office, bend me over your desk and pull my white ruffled panties down while you flip my little plaid skirt up, and spank me for each indiscretion."

And he's fucking hard at his best friend's wedding.

West remembered the night they'd met with Kari in the outfit she described. "Fuck, baby girl. You're so fucking perfect for me." He cupped her chin and kissed her lips in the fiercest kiss he could muster. "I love you."

Kari sighed against his lips. "I love you, too." She settled against him. "I told the girls about our wedding."

He pressed his lips to her ear. "Did you tell them everything?" Her blush heated his skin, and he kissed her temple.

"No. The girls know about this one." Kari held up her left hand between them and West, clasped her fingertips, examining the tattoo he'd designed for her.

"It's healing well. I can't wait to see your engagement ring surrounded by it." He kissed the top of her knuckles, careful to avoid the fresh ink. "And the rest?"

Kari rolled her eyes, adding another infraction to her growing list. "The same as when you examined me so thoroughly this morning."

"You're not feeling any discomfort?" Any minute, Jess and Jasper will walk down the aisle to renew their vows, but he needed to make sure Kari was okay.

Her lips quirked. "I'm not in any pain." Her voice dropped to a whisper. "My nipples are so sensitive. Each time I move, the material of my dress brushes against them, making me want to moan. And the VCH piercing has made me orgasm twice just from walking. Christ, I want you to fuck me."

"You know we can't, not until your piercings and tattoos heal. The sensation will calm, I promise."

Kari patted his arm and pressed a finger to his lips. "Shhh, Daddy," she said with a soft giggle. "We need to put a pin in this; the wedding's about to start."

Everyone collectively turned in their chairs to watch Jess and Jasper make their way down the aisle hand-in-hand.

Bonus Epilogue West

E leven years later.

"Hey, Dad," Izzy called when she entered his shop.

He, Kari, their son Cam, and their daughter Ella still lived in the penthouse, but Izzy moved into the dorms at NYU last month, and they missed their eldest something fierce.

West stepped out of the back room with a ready smile, his arms outstretched for the hug Izzy reached to give him. "Izz, this is unexpected. Don't you have class until four?"

Isabella Rose Sharpe grew into a smart, talented, and beautiful young woman. West's still in shock; she's turning nineteen today. *Where did the time go?*

Oblivious to his inner spiral, Izzy said, "Yeah, my friend is recording the lecture. It's my birthday, and I have a long-standing appointment."

"You do? At the hair salon across the street? Here," he said, pulling out his wallet and removing a few bills. "My treat."

Izzy rolled her eyes. "Ugh. How long are you going to tease me? Though I'd like to get my hair done next week," she said, taking the money he offered and slipping it into her back pocket. "Thanks, Dad, you know I appreciate it. Now back to me and my actual birthday present."

"Five hundred bucks isn't real enough for you?" West asked, still playing along. He stopped pretending he didn't spoil Izzy ages ago. Hell, he spoiled his entire family with no plans of ever stopping.

"Dad...you pinky swore."

"I did, didn't I?" West smiled, remembering the day he told Kari he loved her for the first time, asking her and Izzy to move into the penthouse with him. Amid it all, he'd made a pinky promise with a five-year-old about giving her a tattoo when she turned nineteen, making her wait a whole extra year after being legally able, making sure it's what she wanted.

"And you can't renege on a pinky swear."

"Didn't have any plans to do something so outrageous." West ushered Izzy into his room. He put on a pair of gloves to sanitize his station, something he did in front of every client.

"What is it you want done?" He had a pretty good idea. Lord knows she's hinted since she was little and flat-out asked for from the time she turned thirteen. Those years held a challenge he and Kari expected and also hoped wouldn't happen when Izzy rebelled when she asked about her birth mother and Leslie's subsequent rejection.

Therapy is a blessing.

Kari often joked about how lucky they got when Izzy found no one to give her a tattoo. To which he told her, "You think I didn't warn every artist on the East Coast that if they dared ink her, they'd be dead?"

Then West dragged Kari somewhere private to punish and ravage his wife for *daring* to doubt him. After all these years together, he's one hundred percent certain she does it on purpose.

Once a brat, always a brat.

"I want a rose like yours," Izzy said, bringing West back to the present. He finished wiping down his station. Removed the gloves, washed his hands, and grabbed a fresh pair. He didn't mess around with keeping things sterile.

"Oh yeah? Where do you want it?" West knew this too. Every birthday, he drew it in the same spot.

"The inside of my wrist," Izz said, holding her left arm out. "I want to get a second one on the top, creating a cuff. Can I have the one on the inside of my wrist first?"

"Of course. Take a seat on the chair and put your arm on the armrest. You want it like mine with the black and grey shading surrounding the red rose?"

"Yes, just like yours."

West didn't hide his smile, elated to have this amazing young woman in his life. "I'm going to freestyle it, okay?" He sat on his stool and grabbed a marker, pulled off the cap, and drew out the rose with its surrounding leaves when, right on cue, Izzy let out a peel of laughter, which he joined in. "Never fails. You've gotta be still, Izz. I don't want to fuck up your first bit of ink."

"Pretty sure the tattoo gun won't tickle. I'll be still. I don't want a fucked-up tattoo either."

"Does Kari know you're here?" If not, he may need to do some major groveling.

"Duh. She says hi, by the way."

West zoned out, sketching the outline of Izzy's rose.

"She got the same sappy, love-sick look on her face when I mentioned you, too. You know, in classic rom-com style, it's supposed to ick me out, but I've grown to find your love adorable. It's goals to be honest."

"Thanks, kiddo."

Izzy rolled her eyes. "Still?" she asked, referring to the nickname he called her from time to time.

"Always, kiddo. You're the daughter of my heart."

"I know, but-"

"No buts. You're mine and Kari's, like Cam is our son, Ella is our daughter, and the one on the way who hasn't let us know yet."

Izz gaped at him. "I'm going to be a big sister? Again? You and Mom are insatiable."

"Don't hate."

"I'm not, I swear. You guys have set the bar high, and it's going to take quite an exceptional person to snag me."

"Oh? Are you dating anyone?"

"No one of consequence. I'll let you know when there is."

West kept his opinion to himself about how she ought to concentrate on school and have fun with her friends. He sat back and looked at what he'd sketched out on her wrist. "Do you like it? I can change it up if you don't."

Izzy examined the drawing. "No, it's perfect. It looks like yours."

"I can add a few vines to the sides of your wrist and along the edge of your palm to give it something unique while keeping the flower like mine."

"Yeah, I'd love that."

"Let's get to it then." West lined up the ink cups. "Ready?"

"Give me my first official tattoo, Dad."

The hum of the tattoo gun filled the room, and West started the outline. "Let me know if the pressure is too much or if you need a break, okay?"

"Yup."

West dipped the needle, bent over her wrist, and pressed the foot pedal to turn on his gun. "Deep breath." Then, he put the needle against her skin.

"You doing okay?" he asked, checking in with her after outlining one leaf.

"Yeah, once the numbness set in, I kind of zoned out."

"That's normal. We don't have to talk if you don't want to. Do you need to stop for a drink?"

"No, I'm good, and I'd like to talk," Izzy said with a bit of a wince when he put the gun to her skin again.

"How are the pieces for your first art show coming?" West and Kari put it in their calendars, and Jess, Jasper, Joanna, Jonathan, Addie, and Gray all planned to attend. Bidding wars over who would buy which painting had already erupted in their group chat.

"Great. The first two pieces are done, and I'm hoping I'll have the other two done in a couple of weeks."

"I can't wait to see them. You're an incredible artist, Izz."

"I know."

"I wish I possessed the confidence you have already found at your age."

"Dude, weren't you already in the military then?"

"Doesn't mean I didn't struggle with confidence in myself."

"Wes?"

"Yeah, kiddo?"

"I know what I want to do with my art degree."

"Oh, yeah?" West dipped the needle again. "What do you want to do? Run a gallery in Paris? Teach art history at Cambridge?"

Izzy snorted. "Seriously? No, I don't want to do either of those things. I want to be a tattooist."

West took his foot off the pedal. "You want to become a tattoo artist?"

"Yup. Can I apprentice with you?"

"Well, yeah. I'd love to work with my kid. You sure you want to work with your old man, though?"

"Since when is fifty old?"

West grunted. *Since he served a decade in the military, ran his own business for over twenty years, and is about to become a father for the fourth time.*

"Ugh, you've been hanging out with Uncle Jas too much again," Izzy said with a huff.

"Maybe." West cleared his throat. "Listen, if you're serious about apprenticing with me, I'd love to teach you."

"Oh, em gee, I'm so excited. You'll tell Mom for me, right?"

He let out a sigh, like it's such a hardship for him to break the news to his wife when they made a bet years ago, and Kari is about to collect on their wager.

And West couldn't wait.

"Yeah, I'll break the news."

"Yes!"

Thank You

Thank you for reading. If you enjoyed this book, please consider leaving a review on Amazon and/or Goodreads. Reviews help Indie Authors so much, and I appreciate every one of you. Happy Reading!

Also by K.C. Ford

Club Decadent Series

One Night at Club Decadent (prequel) (MF/FF/FFM/MFM/MMF Married Couple Polysexual Romance)

Their Protective Dom Bk 1(MMF Bodyguard Sword-Crossing Age-Gap Romance)

Addie & Gray Bk 2 (MF Older Woman/Younger Man Romance)

Jess & Jasper Bk 3 (MF Second-Chance Married Couple Romance)

Their Valentine Dom (novella) (MMF Holiday Smut-filled Romance)

Kari & West Bk 4 (MF Bi4Bi Age-Gap Romance)

<u>Standalones – Wide Releases Available Everywhere</u>

<u>The Contract</u> (novella) (MMF Married Couple Cuckhold Bi-Awakening Romance)

Follow Me

Follow my Amazon Author Page to get notified of my latest release.

<u>K.C. Ford Author Page</u>

Visit my website for First Chapter Previews, Content Warnings, and Bonus Chapters.

<u>Author K.C. Ford Website</u>